Praise for *The Lost Dragon M...*

"With nods to both Dashiell Hamme ... ry's newest mystery is a perfect story to ... winter's night. Twists and turns abound as we follow Detective Henry Lau and his niece, Detective Janet Lau, as they sift through the motives and means of a potential historic art theft, one that may have led to murder. Mallory's strong writing and atmospheric Minnesota setting grabbed me from the first page!"

--Ellen Hart, Mystery Writers of America
Grandmaster and Award Winner.

"Delightful! A fun whodunit with characters I want to hang out with."
--Anne Frasier, *New York Times* Bestselling Author

"Michael Allan Mallory's talent as a storyteller shines through in *Lost Dragon*. The first paragraph captured me and I relished the story to the end. His characters seem like real people. Some you'd like to hang out with and others you'd want to avoid. I loved walking alongside protagonists Henry Lau and Janet Lau as they worked through a complex investigation to uncover a killer's identity. Mallory's impressive knowledge of martial arts is keenly woven into the plot and adds a key element in this compelling story. I hope *Lost Dragon* is the first book in a series because I'm ready for the next. Two thumbs up!"

--Christine Husom, author, the Winnebago
County Mysteries and the Snow Globe Shop Mysteries.

"Filled with great details and wonderfully crafted language, *The Lost Dragon Murder* is sure to please readers of all tastes. In Henry Lau, Michael Allan Mallory has created an exciting and welcomed new addition to the fictional detective family."

--Sue Ann Jaffarian, author of the popular Odelia Grey and Ghost of Granny Apples mysteries

"Mallory brings us an interesting...detective [in a story that] concludes with a heart-stopping contest..."

--*St. Paul Pioneer Press*

THE LOST DRAGON MURDER

Michael Allan Mallory

BookLocker
Trenton, Georgia

Dedication

To anyone who has ever chased a dream only
to find the dream is gaining ground.

CHAPTER 1

For a man who hated violence Henry Lau was awfully good at it. Well schooled in the way of the fist, he had considerable experience in its use. Not that you'd know it to look at him. Slightly under average height with an affable face and a rangy, athletic build more suitable to a tennis player than a fighter, there was nothing remotely intimidating about him.

Until he touched you.

By then it was too late. By then the pummeling had exploded on you with the heart-stopping suddenness of a high-speed car wreck in whose aftermath laid the rubble of contusions, numb joints or broken bones. Henry's niece, a perceptive young woman who appreciated both the fine arts and word play, liked to call him a virtuoso of destruction. At the moment he didn't feel like a virtuoso of anything unless it was of aches and pains. A bum knee and dodgy lower vertebrae made him feel every day of his forty-four years as he loped along the sidewalk, glad his car was parked a block away. A vigorous workout had left him looking forward to home, a hot shower, and leftovers.

A sound—faint, transitory—pinged into his awareness, a blip against the urban street noise of West Lake Street. Most people wouldn't have noticed. Henry did. Two decades of training and experience had sensitized him to things out of the ordinary. As his first kung fu teacher had said, "In nature, animals are vigilant to disturbances in the world around them, no matter how small. If they aren't, they get killed."

Henry paid attention.

Another sound. This time a muffled chuff against the pavement.

It was late evening in mid-October, a Minnesota October, one where darkness fell like a steel curtain before the first snowfall made the night world bright again. The glow of street lamps didn't quite reach into the shadows between the rear of the buildings across the street. Henry couldn't get a bead on the sound. Slowing his gait, he squinted into the dark recess between Jasmine Imported Foods and the Falafel Palace. Perhaps it was nothing, someone taking out the trash, a stray cat. His instincts said no. He crossed the street at an angle to ensure the street lights didn't backlight him, moved with caution into the alcove. As he drew near, vague outlines took on solid shapes. He could make out three figures by a dumpster, a fourth crumpled on the asphalt, clutching his belly and groaning.

It was a mugging. Or worse.

Henry noiselessly slipped off his backpack and reached inside.

No gun or badge.

Locked in the car with his smartphone. Bringing a loaded weapon to a martial arts class wasn't a good idea. For everyone's safety, he thought it better to leave his sidearm locked in his trunk, where it was useless right now. He estimated the distance to his Chevy Malibu. Too far. By the time he got there and back, it might be too late. Retrieving his gun would be the smart thing to do, so would calling for backup. Walking unarmed into a potentially dangerous situation was reckless. Even so, he was compelled to do it. Long ago he'd made a bargain with himself never to let a person come to harm due to inaction on his part. That kind of thinking might not have made Henry Lau a prudent lawman, but it went far in addressing the guilt of an old wrong.

Henry slipped on his backpack again to free his arms, sucked in a deep breath, and entered the lion's den. The thugs hadn't noticed him yet, too focused on their prey whose wire-framed glasses sat askew on their victim's battered face. Hurt and disheveled, a puppy among hyenas. His attackers enjoyed his suffering. Their leader had a hard rawboned face whose mouth twisted into a cruel grin. Long stringy hair dangled over his eyes like a ragged curtain. Legs covered in dark sweatpants with white side stripes stood over the fallen man; an arm above those legs raised a clenched fist.

Glasses raised an arm to ward off the blow. "I don't have it," he said in a desperate voice, one near the breaking point.

Stripes smacked his head. "Don't lie. You got it."

"No! It's the truth."

"Yeah, how's this truth?" A steel toe boot rammed into unprotected ribs. Glasses grimaced painfully. Stripes shook his head. "Stop wastin' my time, chump. You got one last chance."

Glasses grabbed the dumpster and struggled to his feet. "How many times do I have to tell you I don't have it anymore?"

"Even if that's true, you know where it is."

Glasses glanced anxiously between his attackers and remained silent.

One of the thugs threw up his arms in frustration. "Screw this." A beefy, thick-necked brute with a raspy voice opened and closed disturbingly large, meaty fingers. "I say we beat the crap out of him and call it a day."

"Maybe you're right," Stripes admitted, his cruel grin directed at Glasses. "After Crusher gets done with you, you'll wish you were dead. Last chance, chump."

Glasses shook his head in a useless effort to persuade the others to stop. Narrow shoulders drooped in grim acceptance of his fate.

"Hey, who's that?" said the third attacker, a twentyish, wiry Asian man with scruffy sideburns and chin whiskers.

They all turned toward Henry.

Stripes glared daggers at him. "What do you want? If you don't wanna be dead, get your sorry ass outta here."

Whiskers couldn't believe it when Henry kept advancing. "This dude must be deaf. Or stupid."

Henry moved forward in slow, measured steps, assessing the situation. *No guns. None he could see. Good, that was a relief.* "Let him go," Henry said with as much authority as he could muster. "I called the cops; they're on their way." It was a bluff. He had nothing to lose.

Stripes snorted contemptuously. "Bullshit."

So much for that. Henry didn't relent. Kept a determined face. He knew he'd inspire more apprehension if he'd been larger and uglier like the big goon with the face like sixty grit sandpaper. Even in the dim alcove light, he could see the man called Crusher was one scary-looking guy. In macho stare-downs, Henry did not fare well. His youthful good looks and manner could charm the bite out of a junkyard dog. Charm and looks were lost on men like these. Ugly sells tough. Inspired fear. *If you were smart, you'd leave.* But intelligence had nothing to do with it. The warning would go unheeded. Some things were more important than personal safety.

Henry advanced.

Stripes turned to the big man with the ham hock fists. "We don't have time for this shit. Crusher, waste this shithead."

"Glad to." Crusher flashed a malignant smirk, stepped forward, inflated his chest and brought up meaty paws—

Too late.

Henry rocketed at him with startling speed, closing the distance between them in three steps. He yanked down the other's lead arm as it extended, jerking a wide-eyed Crusher's face into Henry's fist. A volley of chain punches erupted with machine-gun speed, followed by a triple knife hand to the throat. Crusher crumpled like paper mache, gasping for air. With no time to waste, Henry grabbed handfuls of hair and wrenched Crusher's head around. The rest of him had no choice but to follow. Sensing movement in his periphery vision, Henry's head snapped to the side just in time to see Crusher's two friends charging toward him. With a hard yank of the bruiser's head, Henry spun him around and, with double palms, propelled him into the others. Stripes managed to jump out of the way. Whiskers wasn't as lucky, receiving the full impact of the big man slamming into him.

Henry's attention swung back to Stripes, who lunged at him with a razor knife in his outstretched hand. Henry barely pivoted out of the way, the blade grazing off his sweatshirt sleeve. Henry jumped back, ripped off his backpack and held it in front of him as a shield. *He didn't have time for this!* The others would be up any second. Stripes jumped forward. Henry barely parried the thrust to his stomach with the backpack, then hop-stepped forward to deliver a savage side kick to his attacker's thigh. Henry's extended foot stomped down hard on the other's ankle. After he stripped away the razor knife, Henry's palm macerated into a conveniently nearby nose. The head jerked sideways, whiplashing lank hair across his face. Stripes dropped like a sack of bricks.

Henry's eyes flicked back to the first two attackers, still down and moaning. They weren't going anywhere soon. Relaxing out of his ready stance, Henry felt his heart thudding against his chest. The rush of fear was slow to ebb, a survival fear that sensitized nerves and supercharged muscles. It wasn't over yet.

"You okay?" he said to Glasses.

"Yeah."

"Wanna press charges against these guys?"

"No. Just get me to my car." Glasses glanced anxiously toward his three attackers curled up on the ground like yesterday's trash.

Henry stepped aside to let him pass. Not wasting a second, Glasses scurried by him in labored steps, eager to get away. Henry followed, finally getting a good look at him. Fiftyish and fit, the man had the tawny, undernourished build of a long-distance runner. Clad in a denim shirt and khakis. His short, rust-colored hair crowned a high forehead. Soulful eyes looked out from behind wire-framed glasses as if they'd seen too much of the grungy underbelly of the world that evening.

"That's my car," he said after half a block. "The blue hatchback." The Honda was parked by the curb under the glow of a street light.

"Do you know those guys?"

"Never saw them before."

"What'd they want?"

"Money. Just money."

"Just money?" Henry was skeptical.

Glasses let the remark pass without comment. At the car, he fished for his keys, turning to Henry afterward, haggard, scared yet sincere. "Thanks for your help back there. I don't want to seem ungrateful, but I don't want to hang around or talk about it." With a shaky hand, he unlocked the door. Not before one nervous glance toward the alcove.

"They're gone," Henry assured. "I heard them slink off the other way."

Relief washed over the other's face. "Thanks again."

"You were lucky I came along when I did."

"I was." The words tumbled out like a confession. "You were amazing back there. I do martial arts, a beginner. I've never seen anyone move like that. Do what you did with your hands."

Henry shrugged. "It worked out. Sometimes it doesn't." He could afford to be sanguine about it now, knowing all too well things could have turned out differently and not to his favor. "You sure you're okay? Those guys worked you over pretty bad."

"I'm fine."

"Don't be macho. See a doctor. I mean it."

Glasses nodded an anemic half-smile and climbed into his car with a groan. A trembling hand fastened the seatbelt harness and started the engine.

Henry stepped back and watched the car pull away to fade into the darkness, already second-guessing himself. Glasses hadn't been totally honest. More was going on here than a simple mugging. Should he have pressed harder for answers? Henry wondered. The thing was, he was tired and off duty, and this wasn't even his jurisdiction. And he could have been wrong. A man had to choose his battles.

Crisis over, he could finally let his guard down. Sore muscles barked at him at being further abused after a hard workout. That hot shower was looking better and better—

He stopped. Looked down at his white sneakers and saw a fresh splatter of crimson. Then another. Blood. Fresh blood.

CHAPTER 2

Detective Janet Lau folded her arms across her chest and willed herself to view the body sprawled across the checkerboard floor like a broken manikin. Her slender fingers squeezed into the backs of her arms to steel her nerves. She hated this part of the job. This was only the second death call she'd handled in the five months since making detective, the first actual homicide. Not that she was squeamish. Viewing human remains didn't really bother her; it was the cruelty behind this killing. Some person or persons had taken perverse pleasure heaping abuse upon the body. The dead man wasn't just beaten to death; it was punishment.

Janet exhaled softly. *Be calm. Stay professional. Would she ever develop a thick skin to this stuff?* "What a mess," she said with more distaste than she had intended. She hoped Kowalski hadn't noticed. She stole a glance in his direction.

Officer Kowalski shifted his weight with the finesse of a Mississippi river barge. A burly man with a broad chest and a fence post for a neck, subtle movements were not his forte. The breath wheezing out of him sounded like a truck tire deflating. Did the mangled corpse bother even him? Janet wondered. If a veteran like Dan Kowalski was disturbed by the condition of the dead man, Janet didn't feel like such a rookie.

"Who is he?" she asked in a pleasant, educated voice.

"Name's Roger Beckman. He's a professor at St. Luke's."

"A teacher? He live here alone?"

"Yeah."

Beckman, in a plain gray T-shirt and pajama bottoms, lay on his back, face battered, bruised, and scratched, lifelessly staring at the ceiling. A pair of wire-framed eyeglasses lay under the kitchen table, likely knocked there from a violent blow. One of many violent blows, judging by his condition. Janet winced at the bruised and tortured arms, bent in ways that would make a contortionist wince. The tops of Beckman's bare feet were deep purple.

"So vicious." The graceful contours of Janet's face turned away from the human wreckage to address Kowalski. "Looks like multiple fractures in both arms, bruising everywhere—and that's just the stuff we can see."

He grunted back. "Yeah, bruises on top of bruises. Nasty."

"Ever seen anything like this?"

"No, and I've seen guys worked over. This is off the chart. Whoever did this enjoyed it."

"Yeah, a little too much."

"The son of a bitch just kept going and going and going. Really sick."

"You think it's one guy?"

Shoulders the size of a Mack truck shrugged. "Can't say."

Her brow creased as she remembered something. "Didn't you say Beckman was a prof at St. Luke's?"

"I did."

"What was his subject?"

"Asian Studies. Hey, that makes you perfect for this case!"

Janet Lau silently counted to five. Okay, she was half Chinese. That much was obvious from her looks. If Beckman had taught Celtic Arts, would Kowalski have made the same remark? Probably not, even though she was half Scottish. Kowalski grinned at her as if he'd made the insight of the decade. She offered a tight smile back. He was harmless. Meant well. No point in making a big deal out of his remark, even if it could be considered marginally crossing a line. He didn't understand what it was like having your race regularly pointed out to you. Perhaps she was being too sensitive. She didn't want to make waves. The police department in Gillette, Minnesota, wasn't that large, and she didn't want to start her promotion to detective by getting a reputation for being difficult.

Putting on her game face, Janet tucked back a stray lock of dark brown hair and looked at Kowalski. "Who found the body?"

"Cleaning lady. Mrs. Dorsetti."

"Anything there?"

"Not really. She comes in every other Wednesday. Has her own key. Soon as she saw Beckman, she freaked. Ran to the neighbor to call 911."

"No mobile?"

"Nope, she's old school."

Janet's eye went to the kitchen wall phone. In a world overtaken by mobile technology, Beckman had a museum piece mounted on his wall, a classic retro Princess phone like her grandmother used to have. "Does that phone work, or is it just for show?"

"It works. She just didn't want to be near the body."

"I get that. I'll want to talk to her."

"She's still at the neighbor's."

"Good," Janet replied in a faraway voice as her gaze swept the room to make sure she hadn't missed anything. The kitchen was vintage 1950s era with flat-fronted cabinets and lemonade yellow Formica countertops banded by an aluminum edge. The appliances were fairly new. An open bread bag lay on the table. Two slices of cold toasted bread sat in the toaster. The faint scent of cinnamon raisin reminded her she'd rushed out the door that morning without eating breakfast.

She felt her stomach rumble. "No stab wounds or bullet holes. Going out on a limb here and thinking Beckman died from blunt force trauma."

A grunt from Kowalski. "Probably a safe bet."

"Find any weapons?"

"No."

"I suppose the killer could have taken it with him."

Another grunt from Kowalski. Grunting seemed his preferred method of communication, perhaps because it required less effort than forming actual words. Although a moment later, he did make an effort. "Maybe a weapon wasn't left behind 'cause there was no weapon."

"Oh?"

"My first years as a cop were in Chicago. I've seen guys beat up with all kinds of things: pipes, bats, chains. This isn't like that. The M.E. will say if there are any weapon marks, but it's possible someone did this with his bare hands."

Janet felt a cold chill in her gut; such sadistic cruelty was unimaginable to her. A sudden desire for a change of scenery took her into the living room, which was like walking a minefield. Each step had to be carefully taken to avoid the litter of papers, magazines, books, sofa cushions, and knick-knacks that had been strewn on the carpet. The place looked like a tornado had hit it. Standing by a padded armchair, she surveyed the mess. Her nose scrunched thoughtfully.

"What does this tell you, Dan?"

Kowalski didn't miss a beat. "This was no smash and grab. Beckman's wallet is on the table by the front door. Full of credit cards. Eighty bucks cash."

Janet's caramel-colored eyes flicked toward the slender walnut desk then sized up the entertainment center nearby. "The flat screen TV is untouched. Neither are any of the other electronics. And that's got to be a jade figurine, worth a few hundred, if not more." The object of her attention rested on the entertainment center, a twelve-inch tall statuette of a medieval Mongol warrior astride his war pony. "The killer wanted something specific, something whose hiding place he had to beat out of Beckman."

Kowalski grunted affirmative.

"Makes you wonder," Janet continued, "if the killer found what he was looking for, or did Beckman die keeping that secret?"

"The rest of the house looks the same. Closets emptied. Every drawer ripped out, contents dumped. Valuable items left untouched. A back window was broken. That's how the killer got in."

Janet glanced at her watch, a gesture somewhat uncommon in the smartphone era as many women no longer wore wristwatches except as a fashion accessory. Not her. She liked the convenience of a handy chronometer. "It's 9:40, so rough time of death may be three hours ago, going by that cinnamon toast and the condition of the body."

"Unless he wanted toast for a bedtime snack," Kowalski suggested. "I've done that."

"Me too. In any case, the autopsy'll give us the actual TOD. Too bad there wasn't a witness," she joked.

"Funny you should say that."

She gave him a side-eye. It was the way he said it.

Smiling cryptically, Kowalski motioned for her to follow. He led her to a small sun porch on the other side of the kitchen. His mitt of a hand indicated the house beyond Beckman's backyard on the other side of the block. Janet's eyes were assaulted by a terra-cotta-colored stucco bungalow with deep purple shutters and yellow trim where a woman in her senior years watered her garden. Her outfit was a fruity fiesta of color: a neon yellow blouse, flamingo pink capri pants, green canvas deck shoes, and a violet headband. No doubt the homeowner. A scruffy little dog sniffed at the flower bed by her feet.

"The neighbor lady," Janet said. "She's your witness."

"Um, no."

Janet swung toward Officer Kowalski, her face a question. "I don't understand."

He cleared his throat. "Not her, the dog."

Janet's eyebrows arched.

"That's Mrs. Stademeyer," he said. "Barnaby is the dog. She lets him out at 5:30 every morning to do his business. He's very protective of his yard. Always barks at strangers. Normally that early in the morning, no one's around."

"Except today."

Kowalski nodded. "Except today."

She eyeballed the connecting lawns. "The killer went through her yard. That could be useful down the road. Should help us with the time of death."

They left the sunroom and returned to the kitchen where Kowalski's portable radio squawked, followed by a female voice. He pressed the button on his shoulder mic and acknowledged. "That's all I got," he said to Janet afterward. "DeMarco's outside."

"One second." Janet held out her Nitrile-gloved hand. The CSI techs could wait in the crime scene van a little longer. A thought had flashed through Janet's mind, and she jammed shut her eyes, trying to recapture the image. This was her first homicide, and she wanted to make a good impression. She broke off from Kowalski, strode to the middle of the kitchen, and knelt on the checkerboard tiles to study the purplish-blue stains on Beckman's arms.

"What is it?" Kowalski asked.

"I just thought of something. May be nothing. This bruising is likely postmortem, caused by the beating Beckman took. Check out his forearms."

Kowalski leaned in, squinting. "What am I looking for?"

"Under the fresh bruises are faint yellow patches. Old bruises. Right? You can see them in the gaps."

The big man squatted down for a better look. His duty belt creaked from the effort, as did his knees. "Yup, definitely old bruises. Quite a few of them."

"A week old, I'd say. And only on the outside edge of both forearms, along the radius bone."

"You an expert on contusions, Detective?"

"No, but I've seen bruising like that before."

And she knew just the man to help her decipher them.

CHAPTER 3

The attacks were relentless. Punches, pulls, jabs, elbows, knife hands, wrists, forearms, kicks. They flew at Henry one after the other. Each one he flicked aside or neutralized with a single hand without altering the calm, almost meditative expression on his face. *Pak sau* (slapping hand) flipped to *tan sau* (deflecting arm) into *wu sau* (praying hand) or *bong sau* (wing arm) with a slight pivot of his body, each movement utilizing different surfaces of the same arm.

As the attacks intensified, he recruited both arms, one to intercept the strike and the other to simultaneously counter-attack. Then came a flurry of multiple attacks that required more subtle, quicker countermoves, the last of which slipped by Henry's defense. Henry pivoted just in time with a covering elbow to deflect the sizzling *fak sau* (chopping hand) flying toward his windpipe.

"Nice save!" Alan Zhu said with admiration. It was a natural break in the action. The friends stepped apart, catching their breaths. "For a second, I thought I had you."

"So did I!" Henry laughed. A mistake, a rare one, had left an opening that took someone with Alan's advanced skill to exploit. While not a real fight, the intense sparring honed skills developed over several decades.

Alan, shorter, skinnier, and rounder in the shoulders than Henry, didn't seem bothered at being bested. One of the things Henry liked most about his best friend was his appreciation of other people's skills. Alan was so positive and encouraging; he just radiated good vibes. He now grinned unabashedly at his old friend. "Man, you're on fire today! You really made me work."

"You were pretty good yourself."

"Not quite quick enough. How many times did you get me? Twenty?"

"I wasn't counting."

"How many times did I get you?"

"Five."

Alan's agreeable round face beamed with triumph. "Five's good! But you had twenty."

Alan's top kung fu students, many of whom had trained with him for years, couldn't stop even one of his attacks, let alone land a blow on him.

"You're getting better," Henry said with an appreciative nod. "Your movements are tighter than ever."

"Thanks. But I'll never catch up to you!" Alan lamented behind an amiable grin. They both knew Alan was being generous, that part of the reason he'd done so well owed as much to Henry's current physical challenges as to any improvement in Alan's skill. Lower back tightness and knee joint flare-ups still dogged Henry from time to time.

Among other ailments.

But he was making progress on those and believed they'd soon be a thing of the past.

Taking a break, the two friends rested by the room's bank of windows that overlooked the rooftops of west Minneapolis and the trendy Uptown neighborhood. It was then Alan noticed something, indicating the pine bench across the room near the weathered wooden door.

"We have a visitor," he said.

Smiling at them was a lovely young woman with sleek dark hair and soft, intelligent eyes. Her looks were simple and unfussy and more appealing because they seemed natural and not overdone. It was a face that drew you in by its warmth and honesty, a face you felt you could trust, a face with vague similarities to Henry's.

Janet Lau had been quietly watching Henry and Alan for the past ten minutes, not wanting to disturb the class. Not that difficult to do, considering the size of the single room. Alan's *kwoon* was compact. *Kwoon* not *dojo*. *Dojos* were Japanese. This school taught Chinese kung fu. The training space was just under a thousand square feet, little more than a hole in the wall on the sixth floor of an old office building converted into art space and hobby center. You couldn't get any more bare-bones than this. A large row of mirrors dominated the front wall. Nine students stood in the middle of the floor, some working on two-person drills, others working independently. She was thrilled she'd arrive there in time to see her uncle and Alan working out together. After a friendly wave to her, they resumed their sparring. Witnessing two high-level practitioners applying their skills fascinated her. Wing Chun kung fu was famous for its aggressive, close-range fighting style. Janet had never seen a fighting art with such dazzling and efficient arm and hand work. Henry moved with the fluidity of a dancer as he flowed from one position to the next. Poetry in motion, as the saying goes, albeit poets trying to wreak havoc on each other.

The students wore simple workout clothes: T-shirts, shorts or sweatpants, athletic shoes. A few students glanced sideward to get a view of the two elders "going at it."

While the curriculum at Alan's *kwoon* was traditional, the school itself was not. In your typical martial arts school, the head man, the "master," is the top-skilled martial artist, the one with the highest ranking. Here that honor belonged to Henry Lau. He'd always been the more skilled fighter than Alan but had never wanted to run his own school. Besides, as Henry was quick to explain, "Alan's a better teacher than me. He's much more patient."

But there was no misunderstanding. This was Alan's *kwoon*. Henry was a sort of professor emeritus, a respected elder who always deferred to Alan when he visited class. These were Alan's students, and Henry made sure everyone understood that and treated their *sifu* (teacher) with the respect he deserved. Janet admired her uncle for that. He was never showy, didn't need to prove himself, didn't want his best friend to feel second rate—not that Alan was. She was so grateful for that friendship. Twenty years ago, when the worst tragedy of Henry's life knocked him down, it was Alan who'd picked him up and got him through the worst of it. And six months ago, Alan was there when Henry needed him again.

Janet would never forget the phone call.

It had come on a rain-soaked evening in April. Janet was off duty, staring into her fridge, trying to decide what to make for supper. Even the way her smartphone rang had seemed ominous. Her mother wasted no time.

"Janet, thank God you answered!"

"Mom? What's wrong?"

"Get to North Memorial Hospital. Your Uncle Henry was hit by a car."

Janet's stomach twisted. "Is it bad?"

"*Yes,*" Abby Lau rasped. "Very bad, honey. He may not make it. He's in a coma."

"What? No!"

"It was a hit and run. They say the car jumped the curb and went right for him. Knocked him in the air ten feet."

"Did they get the guy?"

"No. We can talk later. Get to the hospital. We're on our way."

"Wait! Don't hang up. How's dad doing?"

"He's pretty shaken up. The doctors aren't sure Henry will last the night."

Waiting at the hospital was agony. Janet never forgot the look on her father's face. For twenty-seven years, her only image of Douglas Lau had been of a caring and confident man whose hugs comforted her when she crashed her tricycle, the man who'd always encouraged her, the man who always knew what to do. Except now. Like them, he was powerless except to wait in anguish over the thought of losing his little brother.

For days Henry was touch and go. In time his vital signs strengthened. Not long afterward, his eyes fluttered open to view his family gathered round his bed staring down at him with grave expressions. His scratched and swollen face managed a quirk of a smile, one that gave them hope. The prognosis wasn't good. Eight broken bones, three in his right leg, including a compound fracture, a cracked pelvis, skull fracture, a punctured lung. Henry, in his surgeon's estimation, would never walk again without the aid of a cane or walker.

Now look at him!

Six months on he was not only back on his feet without leg braces or crutches, he was whupping Alan's skinny little butt with masterful kung fu moves. His recovery had amazed his doctors. She was glad he'd put back on the weight he'd lost during his recovery and had regained his stamina, most of it. She was also happy his hair had grown back after the surgeon had shaved it off to insert the metal plate in his skull. He'd always worn his hair long, contrary to the military cut of most cops. It suited him. His thick black shag was now etched with a few new strands of silver.

God, he looked healthy! She knew he wasn't a hundred percent recovered, still suffered a few aches and pains, but for as far as she was concerned, Henry Lau was back!

A heavy grunt from the other side of the room stole her attention. A muscular young man twenty feet away struggled with the first form. He looked barely in his twenties. Swedish American, going by the flag on his T-shirt. Well-developed shoulders and pecs filled out that shirt. Impressive biceps too. Muscle Boy could scarcely hold the *Yee Gee Kim Yeung Ma*, the Wing Chun basic training stance. Low stance with knees almost touching, butt tucked under, back straight. All the while relaxing—or attempting to—in this impossible configuration for twelve minutes. Janet was sympathetic. A new student, she could tell. You could always tell from the agony in their faces and the tremble in their legs.

"Sink lower," Henry said, by now at the struggling student's side, having finished the special workout with Alan, who was adjusting the body alignment of another student.

The young student clenched his jaw. "It's hard."

"Yes, it is hard. Try to relax. Your neck muscles are tight. Keep your butt tucked under. Watch out. Now your knees are too wide. Don't lean forward. Oh, your butt's sticking out again."

Muscle Boy grimaced while his legs trembled for ten more seconds before he gave up. "This is bogus!" He stood up in defeat, shaking out his legs.

"You'll get there. It takes months of daily practice to get comfortable," Henry explained in a nonthreatening manner. "It takes time to build up knee muscles you don't normally use. We have a saying: 'You have to first taste the bitterness of the fruit before you can enjoy its sweetness.'"

The college kid blew him off. "That's martial arts bullshit. I'm a collegiate wrestler. I've done golden gloves boxing, some karate, and Brazilian Jiu Jitsu. I think I know a little about what it takes to be a fighter. This is a waste of time. I'm not going to learn kung fu by standing."

Janet's eyes went wide. She mouthed a silent "Uh-oh" to herself. She noticed a few students stopped their practice to look at the beginner. Sure, his wrestler's physique was impressive. His attitude, however, revealed a lack of maturity and ignorance. Young and dumb. Full of himself. He showed appalling disrespect to the *kwoon,* if not to Henry. Janet held her breath, wondering what would happen next. She would not be disappointed.

A stone-faced Henry eyed the young man. "What's your name?"

"Rick."

"How long have you been training here, Rick?"

"Three weeks."

"You think beginner's training is a waste of time?"

"Sure do. It's just busywork to weed out people and to collect fees."

Henry shook his head. "People weed themselves out. At this point, you need to develop your foundation skills. Everything else depends on those. A tree is only as strong as its roots."

Rick wasn't impressed. "I already have a solid base from my other martial arts. I didn't come here to learn how to stand. I came here to learn Wing Chun."

Henry drew in a deep calming breath. After an appraising look at the moody man-child, he bent his middle-aged knees and elevated his arms to the ready stance. "Hit me," he said. Not an invitation; it was a command. He was all business. His expression focused. Alert.

Ready.

"Sorry?"

"Hit me."

"You want me to hit you?"

"You think you know all about fighting. Show me what you've got. Hit me."

"I don't want to hit you."

"Either you hit me, or in five seconds, I hit you."

The young man sized up Henry. Saw his resolve and raised his fists. He shifted his weight and launched a probing jab.

Henry didn't react. Not even a blink. But his eyes analyzed. Janet knew that look. Long ago, Alan had told her that when Henry first started, he had spent hundreds of hours watching and re-watching old boxing and other fight videos. Any fight video he could get. Any style. He studied how fighters moved. Looked for "tells." Like some poker players have a tell when they had a great hand and are trying to hide it. Henry analyzed the biomechanics of movement, watched how some fighters would make a tiny preparatory motion or tense up before a strike or kick or grabbling move. The action might be subtle—the eyes or head, the shoulder, a foot or weight shift—but it was often there. Over time, augmented by his own natural perception, he had developed skill in reading those movements.

A calm, loose, alert Henry waited like a panther ready to pounce. The muscular young student changed to a ready stance, shifted back and forth. Arms in guard position. A quick shoulder fake was followed by a blistering jab—

To a target no longer there.

Henry flew at the other, deflecting the left jab, neutralizing the right cross that followed before it got halfway to him. With impressive agility, the young man lurched to the side and circled his right cross fist into an uppercut that would have clipped Henry's jaw had he not been ready for it, shooting out his left forearm into a *jum sau* that jammed Rick's punching arm. But Rick realized he had another hand, closing the fingers into a fist. However, to load it, he had to shift his weight.

The punch was shut down before it was launched.

The instant Henry sensed the release of pressure against his *jum sau* forearm—angled conveniently toward Rick's face with fingers only inches away—he fully extended the arm. The suppressed palm thrust into the other's throat forced back Rick's head. His body teetered backward. Any power he'd applied to his left hook dissipated like smoke in the wind. In the blink of an eye, Henry circled his palm strike hand to the back of the other's neck and pulled his head into a savage punch to the nose—or would have if Henry had not stopped his fist two inches from Rick's astonished face.

Janet cracked a smile. She knew from long conversations with Henry how fine-tuned his reactions were after decades of training. Even she could read his actions here.

Rick was beaten and knew it. She could see in his face. Henry pantomimed striking him in the nose before he let go and stepped away. "You're bigger and stronger than me," he said. "You're half my age, yet I had total control of your body." He leaned in for emphasis. "You have no root. It only takes a few pounds of force to move a person. Wing Chun isn't about techniques, isn't about hitting or kicking, although they have their place. Wing Chun is about energy. First you learn how to find your center and how to redirect energy inside yourself, then you learn how to feel that energy in your opponent and put him at a disadvantage with a simple touch. How is that done? From spending thousands of hours in that stance you think is a waste of time. Without that, the punching and kicking are just waving your arms and legs. Some students never get that part. They only see the external."

The young student swallowed hard and gave a nod of understanding. Chastened, he resumed his horse stance. In a low voice intended only for him but which Janet overheard due to her proximity, Henry added, "You don't know what you don't know. If you don't like what we teach, you can leave. No one is stopping you. No one has to teach you, either." Henry paused to let the point sink in. "It doesn't matter what you've learned elsewhere; if you want to get this, you need to open your mind."

Rick nodded.

Henry said, "You were disrespectful. If you'd spoken like that to Alan, he would have shoved you into the wall. And make no mistake. He can do it."

Janet suppressed a smirk. No way would Alan have done that. Henry maybe, but never Alan, who was about the mellowest guy she'd ever known. Henry was messing with Rick, and it appeared to have had the desired effect. The know-it-all beginner glanced at Alan with new respect.

Minutes later, Alan stepped in front of the class and clapped his hands to get their attention. "Time to wrap it up. Let's do our closing exercises."

At the end of class, students gathered their belongings. Janet moved out of their way, relocating to the wall where the *mook yan jong*, the wooden dummy, was mounted. To the uninitiated, it was a bizarre-looking contraption made up of a vertical log of wood supported by two springy slats of rosewood set in a frame. Within this core were mounted three short conical arms and a bent leg of wood. The *jong* was the most famous and most copied training device in Wing Chun. On the wall above the wooden man was a line of black and white framed photographs. Two were of old masters from the mid-twentieth century, Leung Sheung and his teacher, the legendary Yip Man. A third portrait showed Eric Kwan with Leung Sheung in the late1960s. The final black and white photo showed a very young Henry Lau and Alan Zhu grinning to the camera as they posed with the *jong.*

They looked so young! Younger than she was now.

She gazed upon the photo with contentment, relishing her uncle's youthful face bursting with enthusiasm. You couldn't help liking that face.

Movement caught her eye. Henry was walking over. The same youthful face greeted her, though one tempered by hardship and experience. The photo made her realize that she'd never seen her uncle looking as jubilant or carefree as he was in that old picture. She felt a touch of sadness that life had left such an indelible stamp on him. Perhaps time hammered on everyone this way. What did she know? She wasn't even thirty.

As Henry drew near, she banished dreary thoughts and put on a cheery face. "How'd it go at the doctor? Did he give you a clean bill of health?"

"Blood work is normal. Knee and back are holding up, though my doctor thinks I'll probably need a knee replacement in a few years." Henry shrugged it off, eyeing her with curiosity. "What brings you here on a work day? Not my health."

Janet patted him on the cheek. "You need to check for messages. I called your cell hours ago. Left a message."

"The phone's in the car."

"I figured. That's why I came. Good thing I remembered there was a class this morning."

She got him quickly up to speed on the death of Roger Beckman. "Take a look at this." On her iPhone she showed photos of Beckman's bruised forearms. "What does remind you of?"

"Beginner *lap sau*."

Her thin lips curled with vindication. Around the third month of training in Alan's school, a student began the *lap sau* drill, a coordinated two-person exercise in which each partner sent out a punch that was intercepted and deflected by his partner's *bong sau* arm. Back and forth dozens if not hundreds of times. The punches were relaxed but forceful. Bruising was common in the early days until the skin toughened, at which time the bruising ceased. The exercise was also called "bone-building" in that it built up the ulna bone in the forearm, which was why Henry and Alan's forearms hit you with the impact of two by fours.

Janet seized on Henry's words. "Maybe our murder victim had recently started studying Wing Chun."

"Or another southern Chinese system that teaches bone building. Some of these are odd." Henry indicated a couple of strange patterns from a close-up of the chest and thigh, partial rectangular bruises in a three-bar pattern. "Is that from a weapon?"

"No idea. Whatever it's from, the pattern's minor compared to the rest of him."

By now Alan had joined them. He'd caught the tail end of Janet's narrative and was peering over her shoulder at the photos. "What's his name?"

"Roger Beckman. He's a professor of Asian Studies at St. Luke's University."

Alan shook his head. "Not one of my guys."

Janet searched her uncle's face. "You know most of the martial arts schools in the area, especially those that teach some form of Wing Chun or variations like Jeet Kune Do."

"There aren't many. And these days, some people are cherry-picking techniques, not wanting to learn the art, just pieces of it."

"Still a good lead," she said, hoping for his approval.

"It is," Henry agreed. "Hey, I've met this guy." He'd been thumbing through the other photos and was now looking at a close up of Beckman's battered face. "I think it's the same guy. A little hard to tell. The guy I'm thinking of wore glasses."

Janet was taken aback. "So did Beckman. They were knocked off his face. Wait. You've met him? When?"

"Last evening. I never got his name, but this looks like him. He drove off in a blue hatchback." He told her of his encounter in the alley a block away from where they were now standing. Then he lifted his left forearm to show a three-inch bandage. "I even have a souvenir. The guy with the razor knife nicked me."

Her mouth fell open. "You saw Beckman on the street a block away? And geez! You got cut? Did you need stitches?"

"No. Wasn't deep enough. Just grazed the skin."

"You're okay. That's what matters. When was this?"

"Right after class. Around ten after nine."

"And nine hours later, Beckman's murdered." Janet's face lit up. "Maybe the same guys caught up with Beckman later at his house. Do you remember what these muggers looked like?"

"A general idea. It was dark, and I was a little busy trying not to get killed. I might be able to come up with a description.

"Cool. We'll see what that turns up. By the way," Janet shot him a disapproving look, "thank you for not getting killed. I'd be really pissed off at you if you had."

"Give me a few minutes to change, and I can join you."

"Aren't you taking a PTO day?"

"Half day for my medical follow-up."

"Well, then I guess you can come with me to St. Paul. Ever been to St. Luke's University?"

CHAPTER 4

The faculty offices for the history and social science departments were tucked away in the basement of the Carl G. Noman Building, a remote outpost on the small campus of St. Luke's University. The joke on campus was that the more esoteric the subject, the farther away your office was from the Administration Building. The Noman building—aka Noman's Land—was the farthest structure from the main office. The windowless basement corridor and Linoleum floor tiles suggested an old library annex, a place where musty and forgotten books went to die.

The detectives found the door with Roger Beckman's name on it. A stream of young people flowed around them on their way to their next classes. Seconds later, the students were gone, leaving the corridor eerily quiet. Henry removed the key he'd borrowed from the secretary at the front office, inserted it in the Yale lock. It turned. He could never explain why something as mundane as turning a key in a lock made the world feel right. But it did. In a world going virtual, the simple tactile feedback of a mechanical lock moving tumblers and the sensation of a metallic bolt sliding back seemed disproportionally satisfying.

Beckman's office was small. Room for a desk, two chairs, a bookcase, and a tiny work table, and not much else. Tidy and well kept, stark as a zen garden. Few frills save for a poster of a lush green bamboo forest and a framed color photograph of a much younger Roger Beckman standing in triumph on top of the Great Wall of China. The desk was clean. An empty computer docking station, a slim LCD monitor, keyboard, and mouse. No loose papers. Papers would have disturbed the sparse aesthetics of the room.

Henry looked to Janet. "Was there a computer laptop at Beckman's house?"

"No, nothing. Not even a cell phone. The killer may have taken them. Hard to know."

"We should check with the university IT department to see if we can access Beckman's e-mail. Might be something there." Henry surveyed the tidy state of the office. A wire basket of papers rested on the file cabinet; a weekly planner sat on the desk. He pulled back the cover. "Beckman's calendar is fairly open this week. Meetings with faculty and students, an entry for an appointment this Friday with L.H. Interesting."

"Oh?"

"For everyone else, he writes in a first name, last name, or both. L.H. is the only one with initials."

"Someone he was familiar with."

"Right. And get this, he had an appointment with L.H. yesterday."

She looked over. "The day he was killed. Coincidence?"

"Maybe."

"There's another reason why Beckman might've used initials for L.H.: secrecy."

"That, too." Henry was taken by a doodle in the margin. "Check this out."

Janet moved beside him. "S...A...C...H. SACH. Is that a word? All caps. An abbreviation?" Her eyes lifted to meet his.

"Made two weeks ago, going by this notation. See how he circled the word three times? And two exclamation marks after it with a line going to a day when he had a meeting with L.H."

"Is SACH is an acronym for something? I've no idea what for."

"Me neither."

Henry scanned the office one last time in hopes of finding any reference, any crumb that might be helpful. The place was too orderly, as perfectly organized as a *Better Homes and Garden* photo layout. Which is why Henry didn't like neatniks. He preferred slobs. Slobs left things lying around, often for months, sometimes years, Easter eggs waiting to be found. There was nothing here.

Outside the office a minute later, Henry locked the office door and—because he'd once gotten in trouble as a boy for not checking the door and the dog got out—pulled the knob twice to make sure it was indeed locked.

"Did Roger finally get in?"

The inquisitive voice came from down the hall. It belonged to a middle-aged woman with untamable frizzy hair and mirthful eyes. She wore a tea-colored blouse, dark brown slacks, and black comfortable-looking sneakers. Her left arm clutched a canvas messenger bag to her chest as though it contained priceless objects. Walking beside her was a man with rugged Hispanic good looks. Wary brown eyes regarded them from behind rimless glasses. He wore a black T-shirt beneath a sports jacket with rolled-up sleeves. Contrived cool, Henry thought, and a little too 1980s.

Henry gave Janet a look, a nod to take the lead. She was in training, and he took his responsibility seriously. And though leading by example was important, so was letting her try things on her own.

"Actually, we're the police," Janet explained, displaying her badge wallet. "Perhaps you can help us. Do either of you work with Dr. Beckman?"

Polite, professional, authoritative. Henry smiled inwardly. Detective Janet Lau was a far cry from the fumbling, awkward little girl he once had to coax into speaking in front of strangers to sell her Girl Scout cookies.

The woman with unruly hair gestured to the office next to Beckman's. "We're colleagues. This is my office. Paul's is down a few doors. Did you have an appointment with Roger? I haven't seen him today."

Janet broke the news.

"Murdered? Did you hear that, Paul?"

Considering the excellent acoustics around them, Henry thought it would've been nearly impossible for Paul not to have heard, and yet his face barely registered a ripple of emotion. Total indifference to the death of a colleague? Or wasn't the death news to him?

After the initial shock, the woman collected herself. "Sorry, I'm Maureen Levy. This is Paul Rivera," she said with a heartfelt sigh, her voice almost quavering. "Yes, glad to help. But not out here." Levy motioned to her office door.

In size and layout, Maureen Levy's office was the twin sister of Beckman's. But there the similarities ended. While his was a mantra to Asian austerity, hers was a belch to ordered clutter. Leaning towers of magazines and papers. If it was loose and could be stacked on something, it was. Books, folders, three-ringed binders, paper plates stood in precarious-looking columns.

Janet took the chair opposite Levy; the men stood by the closed door.

Levy sighed. "I can't believe Roger's dead. And murdered, you say?"

"Beaten to death," Henry elaborated.

She visibly winced at the news. On the other hand, Rivera remained unmoved. Henry found that odd. He'd intentionally mentioned the beating for its brutality to see how they'd react. Rivera hadn't. Henry felt compelled to comment. "Mister Rivera—"

"*Doctor.*"

"Dr. Rivera, pardon me for saying this, but you don't seem disturbed by any of this."

A puzzled Rivera looked back. "What do you mean?"

"You just learned someone you know was brutally murdered, yet you're remarkably unfazed."

"Oh, it's not that. What you said was horrible. I was thinking about Mary Jo, Roger's ex-wife. This'll be a shock to her. Has she been told?"

"Not yet," Janet said.

"This'll hit her hard."

"I'm sure it will."

"Well, not quite as bad as you think. Mary Jo and Roger have been divorced for two years. The divorce was amicable."

"They kept in touch?"

"Somewhat."

Henry cleared his throat. "Nice of you to think about her." Though he wondered why concern about the ex-Mrs. Beckman was forefront on Rivera's radar. First impressions made Rivera seem like a bit of a cold fish. A little too detached. Or was he being protective? Henry changed the subject. "How often did you and Dr. Beckman talk?"

Rivera made a dismissive gesture. "Not often. We had different schedules. We didn't have much in common. My area is Central and South American native cultures. Sure, we'd bump into each other, talk for a minute in passing. Not much beyond that."

Henry looked to Levy. "And your subject?"

"Ancient Middle Eastern History," she answered. "Unlike Paul, I spoke with Roger at least once a week. Our fields overlap around Central Asia. We also shared an interest in art." Her wide mouth stretched into a polite smile.

Janet stirred. "Any idea—either of you—who might've wanted to hurt Dr. Beckman?"

Blank looks came back from both.

"Did he mention upcoming plans? A trip? A new project?"

Maureen Levy made a vague gesture. "Roger taught several classes on Asian culture and history; he was also an authority on Chinese art. Did freelance appraisal work. Last month I saw him in the parking lot; he was really excited about a new consulting gig."

"Excited?"

"Jazzed."

"Did he say what the gig was for?"

"No. In fact, he cut himself off. Realized he was blabbing too much. This was a confidential client, and he wasn't supposed to say anything."

"Confidential client," Henry repeated, liking the sound of it. "I suppose he didn't mention who this client was."

"No."

It was worth a shot. Henry shrugged to Janet, who lobbed the next question carefully. "Do the initials L.H. mean anything to you?"

"No idea."

"How about S.A.C.H?"

Levy shook her head.

Janet shifted her weight. "This consulting gig. Any idea what it was for? A painting? A ceramic?"

Levy's hands rose behind her head and grabbed handfuls of hair as if tugging hard enough would pluck free the memory. "Oooh, man, it's on the tip of my tongue. I want to say it was a statue or figure. Remember, Paul? Roger told us about it when he first got the gig, before the parking lot episode. The three of us were in the hall, one of the few times all of us were in our offices at the same time."

"Oh, right."

"Roger mentioned some art piece."

"A figure, a bronze figure," Rivera said, recalling. "A dragon, I think. Roger didn't think much of it at first." Well-manicured fingers came up to adjust the rimless eyeglasses. If eyebrows could shrug, Rivera's did.

Janet looked back with interest. "A bronze dragon figure. Thanks. That's helpful. Anything else?"

Rivera shook his head. "Sorry. Although, like Maureen, I do remember seeing Roger some weeks later, and he seemed pretty stoked about something."

"How stoked?"

"Like a kid in a candy store. Now that I think about it, it might've been the same day Maureen saw Roger."

"And you think his excitement was about this dragon figure?"

"Yeah. I asked him directly how the appraisal was going. After a burst of enthusiasm, he clammed up like he was saying too much. The way he was talking, it sounded like he might be onto something big."

"Big?"

"That was the word."

Janet turned to Maureen Levy. "And this was around the time you said Beckman was jazzed about the artifact?"

"Seems like it."

"I think that's all for now." Janet glanced at Henry for confirmation. He had nothing else. Handing her business cards to each of the academics, Janet said, "If you think of anything, please call."

Just as Rivera tucked the card into his jacket pocket, his cell phone chirped. "I should take this." He excused himself and exited. The sound of his retreating hard-soled shoes echoed off the empty corridor.

"Was there something else, Dr. Levy?" Henry had noticed her suggestive face trying to catch his eye.

The professor shifted uncomfortably in her chair. She seemed to wait until she was certain Rivera was too far away to catch what she was about to say. "I'm not sure I should be telling you this. It probably has nothing to do with Roger's death, but...well, Paul's been seeing Roger's ex, Mary Jo."

"Seeing as in dating?"

"Yeah."

"For how long?"

"Eight months, give or take. I'll bet that was Mary Jo on the phone."

"She calls him often?"

"All the time."

"That doesn't sound like a casual relationship."

"They're way beyond casual, let me tell you. They've got the serious hots for each other."

Janet lowered her voice so it wouldn't carry. "Did Rivera cause the Beckmans marriage breakup?"

Levy gave an emphatic shake of her head. "No. I'd never say that. Paul and Mary Jo didn't start going out until a year after she divorced Roger."

"As far as you know," Henry suggested.

"True," she admitted, "though what I can tell you is that in the past four months, Paul's been seeing a lot of Mary Jo Beckman."

Henry shot Janet a private look. He could see she also found the news about Dr. Rivera's love life interesting.

CHAPTER 5

Roger Beckman's house was a French Bulldog of a structure—squat, muscular, with a homely charm supplied by its Craftsman-style bracketed gables and exposed beams. A tidy front yard was bordered by enough flowering plants for eye appeal, though not enough to require a major effort to maintain.

The wooden steps to the porch creaked as Janet and Henry climbed them. She undid one corner of the yellow police tape that stretched across the front door and let it dangle. It fluttered in the light breeze, twisting and flapping like the paper Chinese dragons she used to see as a child at festivals. She had a fondness for paper dragons, having crafted a shoebox full of lucky dragons as a young girl.

Inside they paused to take in the sights. The living room looked different than the first time she'd set eyes on it. Gone were the scattered piles of paper, pillows, overturned sofa cushions, emptied curio cabinets and what not. Janet waited patiently for Henry's impressions as he compared the forensic photos against the live view. From the way his eyes wandered from object to object, from ceiling to carpet, window to doorway, she knew he was getting the feel of the place. He believed a crime scene gave off its own harmonic energy. With enough sensitivity, he'd once told her, a perceptive investigator could feel the pulse of that vibe and let it guide him toward the truth. Whether that was true or not didn't matter. It worked for him. She had faith in Henry. He was her mentor.

How long he'd remain her mentor was up in the air.

It was an unorthodox pairing. The Gillette police department was temporarily understaffed after the sudden death of one of its senior investigators while another investigator was wrapping up military service overseas. After months out on short-term disability, Henry had only recently returned to active duty.

Chief Bowman had not minced words about the assignment. "This is temporary, you and Henry," he had said in a voice as rich as Swiss chocolate. She knew something was up when he had her close his office door behind her. Nothing said here was to go beyond these walls. Bowman sat at his desk, a medium-framed African American man pushing fifty. Salt and pepper hair, dark mustache. He'd leveled intense but careworn eyes onto her. "Department policy is not to pair blood relations or spouses. But some rules have an exception." He cracked a subversive smile that put Janet at ease and shook his head in disbelief. "To be honest, I never thought Henry would come back. The man was a train wreck. He could barely walk a few months ago. His prospects looked grim. I figured—we all figured—if he got better, he'd play out his disability and retire. He didn't. He got better! I've never seen anyone so broken make that kind of recovery."

She nodded in agreement.

His gaze searched her out. "Be honest, did you expect him to fully recover?"

"No."

The blunt unambiguousness of her answer surprised her. Surprised her because she'd always believed Henry would make a full recovery, hoped and prayed for it, but deep in the shadows there'd always lurked a shred of uncertainty.

Chief Bowman spoke plainly. "Henry's fit and ready to return to the job. Physically he seems as good as ever. Psychologically, I'm not so sure."

"Didn't he pass his psych eval?"

"He did."

"I don't understand. What's the problem?"

Bowman hesitated. Looking ill at ease behind his desk, he searched the ceiling for the right words. "Hard to say. He seems different."

"Different how?"

"Yeah, that's vague. Sorry. It's...well, it's like there's a spark missing. Henry's always been a contradiction. Easy going yet high energy at the same time. Y'know what I mean?"

She did.

The chief went on. "The only way I can put it is he doesn't seem as spontaneous. He's more...guarded."

"Is that a bad thing? He was almost killed."

"I didn't put that well. What I mean is he seems to be second-guessing himself more often."

Janet listened carefully. Said nothing, not wanting to be disloyal to her uncle. Truth was she understood where Bowman was coming from. She too had noticed a slight change in Henry since the accident: his pervasive grin didn't flash as often; he seemed more introspective. She'd always figured it was part of the long healing process. Until now, it had never occurred to her that her uncle's old dynamic personality wouldn't bounce back.

Bowman leaned forward, his mellow voice embracing her. "Partnering you and Henry has an advantage. You know him better than any of us. You can silently evaluate him."

Janet didn't like the sound of that. "I'm not going to spy on him."

"That's not what I'm asking. Just pay attention to him. Think of it like this: you're new to the detective position. You can use a mentor. Having you work side by side with Henry for a short while benefits him as well. Training you gives him an incentive to keep mentally sharp."

"Okay."

"You also get to watch over him."

Be Henry's guardian angel. Now that she could buy into.

Bowman, noting her acceptance of this pitch, relaxed and settled back in his chair. "I may get some flak for violating policy, but I don't care. For the next ninety days, you and Henry will be partners. After that, we'll see."

"Got it. And thanks, Chief."

"I expect you to take care of him. Henry's one of my best men."

The meeting had given Janet a special purpose, and she relished it. Days afterward, she replayed what Bowman had said about Henry and wondered if his assessment was slightly off. Maybe her uncle's current introspection had nothing to do with the car attack. Maybe it was from another wound, one older and far deeper that had scabbed over but never fully healed.

Kay McAdams.

Henry's college girlfriend. Janet had never gotten the full story on Kay, only that her death—her murder—had devastated him. Healing had come over time, the way it does. Twenty years on, though, perhaps the ordeal of recovering from the car incident had pulled the scab off that old injury.

"Janet…?"

The sound of her name pulled her back into the present moment. She whirled round to see Henry's inquisitive face.

"Sorry," she said. "I drifted off. Were you asking me something?"

"Only said your description was spot on."

"Oh, thanks."

"The first thing that caught my eye was this piece." Henry walked to the media center and picked up the jade Mongol warrior figurine. He felt the heft of it and turned it around to admire the craftsmanship. "Real jade. And it was left behind."

Janet knew where he was going. Dark, intuitive eyes rested on him. "Portable and pawnable and not taken. Nor was his cash or anything else that could be easily sold."

"If the thieves knew its value. My guess is they weren't interested in it," he said, still admiring the figurine. He turned to her suddenly. "Did you know the Mongol bow could shoot nearly six hundred yards? Legend has it the Mongols wore silk shirts into battle because arrows can't penetrate silk. If a warrior was struck by an enemy arrow, the arrowhead pulled the silk cloth into the wound. The warrior then tugged on the silk to extract the arrow, which reduced getting infected by wood splinters. Pretty slick!"

She gave a lopsided smirk. "You're full of esoterica, aren't you?"

"I like resourceful people." He turned over the jade figure and looked at the base.

Janet approached, craning her neck for a better view. "Find something?"

"Just a price tag." He indicated a small white sticker on the base: SRI $299.00. Putting back the figure, he faced the nearby wall to admire three Chinese bamboo wall hangings: a crane, a tiger, and a red dragon.

Janet's curiosity got the better of her. "Anything special going on with those wall hangings?"

"No, just enjoying them."

"I see. How are the vibes working for you today?"

"What vibes?"

"You know that thing you do to soak in the energy from a crime scene."

"Sorry, I got nothing."

"This way, then." She directed him to the kitchen. "Beckman's body was here." Janet gestured toward the checkerboard tiles by the dishwasher. "Unlike the other rooms, nothing in here was disturbed."

"Interesting, don't you think? The kitchen is the one room with the most weapons: knives, long-handed utensils, heavy pots, glasses in the rack, that rolling pin."

"Now *that's* what I'm talkin' about." Janet gave a satisfied nod, her dark brown hair bouncing at her shoulders. "The vibe is alive and well. I hadn't even thought of that." She looked thoughtfully around her. "Beckman was either already dead and was put in here or incapacitated, and his killer didn't need a weapon to finish him off."

"Or there was no weapon."

Janet gave an insightful grunt. "Kowalski said that. You saw the autopsy report. Injuries consistent with a severe beating by either an unidentifiable weapon or it was done by hand."

"I know guys who can do that. And they're none of them good people. Yeah, I read the autopsy report. Antemortem contusions, as well as Perimortem and Postmortem, the bruising hat trick. They went over board on him."

Henry seemed intrigued by the details of the wounds. Showed no emotion in recalling them. Janet couldn't be that detached. She'd seen the body in person. Couldn't unsee the graphic autopsy photos and deep purple bruises. She could almost feel the ruptured blood vessels.

What she loved about police work was catching the bad guys and putting them away. The blood and guts stuff she could do without. At times she wondered if she were better suited to be a lab technician or analyst, a job removed from the violence of wailing victims and ugly crime scenes. Problem there was she'd have to wait for someone to bring her the evidence. Too limiting. As an investigator, she led the charge; she was the bloodhound with her nose to the ground. That part she loved and didn't think she could do without.

"Let me show you something." She led him along a short hallway to a small room with plush carpet and dark-stained wood paneling, a little too dark for her; it made the room feel more closed-in. There was a small profile white desk beside a two-drawer file cabinet. "This is how the attackers got in." She indicated the double-hung window. "The window screen was ripped out. Duct tape was placed on the top pane. The glass broken. Enough of it removed to let them undo the sash lock."

Henry's fingers touched the docking port on the desk. "And no computer, you said?"

"Right. It's missing. So are any notebooks, diaries, financial records. That file cabinet is half empty, though you can tell there used to be stuff in the file hangers. The killers cleaned him out. My guess is they didn't get what they came for and hoped Beckman wrote down where he'd put it."

"Whatever 'it' is."

Janet gave a heartfelt sigh. "Yeah."

Henry tossed her a sidelong look. "No checkbook records?"

"Nope. There is a Wells Fargo debit card in his wallet. We can check his bank records. I'm also following up with St. Luke's. He likely had auto-deposit somewhere."

"Good work."

Janet permitted herself a little smile. That tiny bit of praise meant the world to her. He gave her room to fail as well as room to succeed without continuously directing her. He encouraged her to take charge and didn't get pissy about it when she did. She loved him for that. It was such a boost to her confidence.

"One last thing," she said, motioning toward the hallway. She led him to carpeted stairs and up to the second floor. The bedroom was an IKEA showroom of Scandinavian style. In the corner was a wicker hamper. She popped open the cover. "One thing we missed the first visit was this. Guess nobody wants to check other people's dirty clothes." Janet made a face. "I almost drove away but remembered to come back to check this sucker and found this." From within, she pulled a black T-shirt with a stylized circle of tigers in the center.

Henry instantly recognized it. "The Five Tigers Martial Arts Academy."

She looked back with satisfaction. "That answers that question. You know it."

"Know it well. That's Mike Anderson's studio."

Janet dropped the shirt back in the hamper, suppressing the urge to say, "Eww." Not her favorite thing, handling a man's used workout shirt. Closing the hamper, she rubbed her fingers against her sleeve to remove any sweat kooties. "If we're lucky, Beckman's a student there. That may be where he got the old bruises. And maybe more," she added suggestively.

"Agreed. We can check them out."

"How about you check them out? I've got a list of Asian art experts in the area. There aren't that many. That was my plan for tomorrow. While I do that, you can visit the Five Tigers?"

"Will do"

"That's pretty much it," she concluded as they headed back down the stairs.

Henry paused on the landing. "There is one other thing, isn't there?"

Janet tried to decipher the crooked smirk.

He said, "Aren't you going to introduce me to our witness?"

"Oh, Barnaby. Right. I forgot."

After locking the front door, the detectives walked around the corner to the other side of the block where, among the orderly row of sedate suburban homes, their eyes were assaulted by a riot of bad taste in bold colors, as if a cat had coughed up a giant multi-tinted hairball. Before them stood a terra-cotta bungalow with neon yellow trim and purple shutters.

"My eyes," Henry squinted as if his retinas had burnt out. The bright sunny day intensified the color assault.

They barely got into the yard when they heard the excited barking of a small dog from inside.

"Arf. Arf. Arf. Arf. Arf!"

"There's your witness," Janet chuckled as they rang the front door bell, which, she realized, seemed pointless in that the canine early warning system had already alerted the homeowner of their presence.

They heard Mrs. Stademeyer before they saw her. "Quiet Barnaby! Behave." The door swung open, revealing an elderly woman in a leopard print blouse and shocking pink leggings. Some women, Janet realized with new understanding, should never, ever wear leggings.

"Yes?" A pair of curious eyes regarded them from the doorway. "May I help you? Oh, you're from the police." This last to Janet.

"Hello, Mrs. Stademeyer. It's Detective Lau again. I wonder if we could have another few minutes of your time?"

"Certainly." She stepped back to let them in.

The little sheltie backed up, eyeing the newcomers warily, especially Henry. "Arf! Arf!"

"Barnaby. Quiet."

The inside of the house looked nothing like the outside. The interior was sedate and tidy, the furnishings dated and careworn, though clean and comfortable looking. Janet introduced Henry.

"Another Detective Lau?" Mrs. Stademeyer looked between them.

They got this all the time. "Detective Lau is my uncle," Janet explained. "Though he read my report, I wanted him to hear your statement in person."

The old woman looked delighted by the attention. "Barnaby and I get few visitors these days. Glad to help if it means getting those awful people who killed Roger." Her pale, deeply-lined face took on a mix of sadness and anger, only to be wiped away the next instant as she noticed her dog.

Barnaby sat quietly, totally transfixed on Henry, who had sunk to a crouch and extended his arm in invitation. Barnaby cocked his head. Wary. Curious. Interested. Unsure. He inched forward and cautiously sniffed the outstretched hand. When no evil befell him, the sheltie attempted a tentative lick. Henry slowly reached over and stroked the side of Barnaby's throat, then rubbed the top of his head. Barnaby was ecstatic. His bushy tail trashed happily from side to side.

His owner straightened up with some astonishment. "Holy cow. He normally doesn't react that way to strange men."

Janet could attest to that. The other day when she came with Officer Kowalski, Barnaby didn't stop barking at him until Mrs. Stademeyer secured the sheltie behind a closed door. Seeing how the little dog reacted to Henry was no surprise. Dogs loved him. Clearly, they sensed something good about his man that humans didn't always get right away.

Henry rose to his full height and addressed the sheltie's owner. "Roger's house is directly opposite yours. You share a fence. How was he as a neighbor?"

"Good. He was good. I liked him. He'd look after Barnaby for me whenever I went to visit my sister in Santa Fe. He'd looked out for me too. He put up my new book shelf last year." Her mouth crinkled with appreciation.

"He sounds like a good guy. Did Roger ever talk to you about his work or hobbies?"

"Sometimes. I knew he was a college professor and liked Asian stuff."

"Then I suppose he didn't tell you much about his Asian art consulting work."

"Not really. Usually he'd tell me if he was traveling out of town so I could keep an eye on his house. Would you care to sit down? No? If you don't mind, I will. These old legs of mine get cranky if I'm on them too long." She shuffled across the hardwood floor in deliberate steps and eased into an armchair. The task took effort, but now that she was comfortable, the strain disappeared from her face.

Janet waited until she was ready. "Mrs. Stademeyer, I'd like to go over what happened Wednesday morning."

"Whatever you want, dear." Kind and caring eyes shined back.

Their warmth touched Janet, reminded her of her Nanna. She liked Mrs. Stademeyer. Janet decided she'd changed her mind about her leggings. This woman deserved to wear whatever she wanted!

"Wednesday was the day Roger was killed," Janet said. "Barnaby may have noticed his killers. He barked at something."

"You betcha! I let him out every morning to do his business. That morning I was in the basement doing the wash."

"This was before sunrise?"

"It was. I'm an early bird. Get up at five every day. Can't stay up much past nine most evenings, or I turn into a lump."

"As you said when I first spoke with you, it was unusual for Barnaby to bark like that so early in the morning."

Her head of stark white hair nodded vigorously. "For sure. Nobody's out that early. I was surprised. Barnaby doesn't like strangers. He was making such a racket."

Henry shifted his weight, his face hopeful. "Barnaby was outside?"

"He was."

"And the strangers cut through your yard? Not next door?"

"My yard."

"Is Barnaby a biter? Would he have chased after them?"

Mrs. Stademeyer glanced at the sheltie curled up by her feet. "No, the little darlin' is all bark and no bite."

Henry nodded.

"I heard the barking," she continued, "and went to see what all the fuss was about. Thought it might be a critter like a raccoon. It wasn't. It was a person."

"Just one?"

"One for sure. It looked like more. Maybe three. Hard to tell. It was still dark and they were running. Shapes were all I saw. Sorry I can't be more helpful."

Janet assured her. "You did great. You've been very helpful."

The old woman looked visibly relieved.

By now the sheltie had edged over to sit by Henry's feet, looking up at him with contented canine eyes. Henry reached down and stroked him behind the ear. Janet marveled at how docile the little dog was now compared to his brutish behavior toward Kowalski.

"Was there anything else?" Henry asked Janet, who shook her head. "Thank you, Mrs. Stademeyer," he said. "We've taken up enough of your time. If you think of anything, please let us know."

The old woman didn't react. She seemed lost in thought. After a second, her faded blue-gray eyes lifted toward them. "There was one thing…"

Janet's shapely eyebrow quirked. "Oh?"

"One of the people who crossed my yard said something. I couldn't understand it, so said nothing before. Now I think I know why. It wasn't English."

Janet was intrigued. "Any guesses what it was?"

"Chinese."

Henry gave a snort. "That's very specific."

Mrs. Stademeyer sat up in her chair and smoothed out a wrinkle on her leopard print blouse. "It is. The reason is last night I was watching a show on cable TV. It was on the Smithsonian Channel about the Chinese terra-cotta soldiers. They had some archeologists from Beijing talking. They spoke in Chinese with English subtitles." Her gaze shifted between them, the excitement of discovery radiating from her face. "You know how every language has a distinct sound? Well, as I hear these guys talking on TV, it comes to me that I've heard something like this recently. Then one of the archeologists said something I recognized. I'd heard it—or something like it—the other morning." She looked at them significantly.

"And what did you hear?" Janet coaxed.

"I forgot the whole sentence. One phrase was '*Gânkuài.*'"

"Hurry up," Henry supplied.

"Yes! That's what the subtitle said."

Henry's eyes narrowed on her. "And you're fairly sure that's what you heard outside early Wednesday morning?"

Mrs. Stademeyer nodded with conviction.

Thinking aloud, Henry summarized: "Predawn Mandarin-speaking runners cut across your yard. Later on, your neighbor's house has been discovered broken into, robbed, and he's left for dead. Yeah," Henry nodded, "I think it's fair to say the two events are connected."

CHAPTER 6

The following morning was a whirlwind of activity. Janet made phone calls and onsite visits to art dealers, which eventually let her to where she was now, sitting in a too roomy leather chair in an imposing office, with her insides wriggling like a bowl of earthworms.

Outside, though, she presented a calm, poised, professional exterior. It wasn't easy to maintain, for on the other side of the great desk loomed the owner of the office, a brawny man who sat like a medieval duke waiting to impart judgment on a peasant. Janet Lau being the peasant. Angelo Kasparian's lordly bearing was enhanced by an expensive suit of virgin wool fabric and fine tailoring that he wore like robes of high office. There was also the beard. Full, cropped, dark with a mustache. Sophisticated and foreboding, like something out of a fairy tale. A pair of wolfish eyes used to sizing up art objects leveled on her as if appraising her value.

"The police never come to see me," he said in a rich baritone voice that sounded disappointed. "To tell you the truth, Detective Lau, for a man in my line of work, I expected the police to come calling long ago."

"That almost sounds like an admission of wrongdoing," she said, intrigued.

"Not at all, merely an acknowledgment that my business has its unsavory side. Tomb robbers, the black market, fakes, thieves. Behind every transaction of important artwork lurks potential litigation. Where did a piece come from? Is it genuine? What's its provenance? Who is the rightful owner? I've dealt with quite a few significant pieces in my career. I half expect one of them will someday come back to bite me. Not from any wrongdoing on my part, you understand." A mirthless chuckle followed.

"I see what you mean."

"Fine art doesn't always breed fine ethics or fine manners, Detective. Greed is a powerful emotion. Speaking of manners, where are mine? Would you care for a refreshment? Coffee? Tea? Water perhaps."

"No, thank you."

"Pardon me if I help myself. My doctor wants me to keep hydrated."

Behind him was a walnut credenza against a wall of glass. Kasparian's office was on the forty-third floor of the IDS building in downtown Minneapolis. Every outer wall was a glass curtain that offered a sweeping vista of the urban forest far below punctuated occasionally by sky blue lakes. A god's eye view of the city. Kasparian opened a panel in the credenza to reveal a well-stocked mini-fridge from which he produced a chilled water bottle. "Sure you won't have one?"

Janet declined even though her throat was dry, a strategic decision. Sipping water in front of this man on their first meeting would have been a show of weakness, or so she believed. It may have been a silly notion, but she had the uncanny feeling that behind the hospitality was also silent judgment. She felt the need to be on her best behavior with this man. No slouching. Back straight. Shoulders square. And when she spoke, she formed her words with care. She didn't have his wealth or worldliness; what she did have was a thoughtful, self-possessed calm. Even so, the man made her feel small and insignificant.

Kasparian unscrewed the cap and took a long pull before setting aside the plastic bottle. Rubbing his hands together in a ready-for-action motion, he rested thick forearms on the desk and leveled mirthful dark eyes on her. "So, Detective, what brings you to my office in the sky?"

She ignored the attempt at humor and tried to bury her insecurity. "I've been visiting art and antiquities dealers in the metro area. Two of them directed me to you."

He sat up straighter, pleased by the attribution.

She elaborated. "I'm investigating a homicide. The victim's name is Roger Beckman. He was a professor of Asian Studies at St. Luke's and was also a freelance art appraiser."

Janet paused to see if Kasparian reacted to the name. He did.

"I read about Roger in the paper this morning. Shocking. A brutal death," he volunteered with a note of sadness.

She looked back with interest. "You knew Dr. Beckman?"

He nodded. "We'd met a few years ago at an exhibit at the MIA, Minneapolis Institute of Art. He knew me by reputation and introduced himself. We found we had a few mutual interests."

"Asian art and antiquities."

"Yes, it was during the MIA's China terracotta warriors exhibit. We crossed paths a few times after that."

Janet nodded, sweeping a quick eye round Kasparian's office, one that could have belonged to any upper-level executive, especially the contemporary décor. That piqued her curiosity. "Pardon me for saying this, but for a man who deals with works of art from around the world, your office is really...how can I put it?"

"Ordinary?"

"Well, yes."

"You were expecting to see Ming vases and pre-Columbian relics displayed on lighted pedestals, perhaps?"

"Yeah, I guess."

"Let me tell you something about the antiquities business, Detective Lau. Some people are collectors, some are brokers, and some are both. I'm a broker. My job is to acquire valuable pieces to sell, not to keep on display. My clients get to do that. I do have a gallery in Edina where I maintain some inventory—some rather choice pieces—though not as many as you might imagine. I'm not a collector. I appreciate the beauty and value of the items I find, but I make my living selling them or taking a percentage acting as an intermediary between buyer and seller. Those few items I own are far too valuable to keep here." He seemed to take pleasure in revealing this glimpse into his personal side, sitting back with his hands folded in his lap.

Janet moistened her lips which were dry as dust. She hated to admit it, but this man intimidated her, and she'd be damned if she'd let him see it. It took a moment to corral her anxiety before she could ask her follow-up question. "You've said you knew Dr. Beckman. He did freelance consulting work. Any ideas on what he was working on?"

Kasparian made a vague gesture. "I really couldn't say, Detective."

"Fair enough. What did you think of him as a person?"

"I'm not sure I understand what you mean."

"Was he impulsive or driven?"

"Ah, well, Detective Lau, it's probably fair to say that anyone who deals in antiquities on a regular basis is driven to some extent. At bottom, we're all treasure hunters. All of us dream of finding a lost city of gold."

She could tell Kasparian was a romantic. He may have liked to see himself in the jungle hacking a path toward a lost Aztec city, yet she found it difficult imagining him at a dig site hip deep in muck, tired and hungry. He was a dealmaker, a man who capitalized on other people's work, a man who never actually had to get his hands dirty. Or wanted to.

Kasparian continued. "Roger was a dedicated specialist. The Ming and Qing dynasties were his passion if you want to put it that way."

"Okay. How about this? Have you heard of S-A-C-H?"

She'd tossed that out like a hand grenade, hoping for a reaction. She got it. Kasparian gave a nod, his steel-gray eyes taking her in shrewdly. "SACH. The State Administration of Cultural Heritage."

"Sorry, what?"

"A Chinese government agency. They search for lost cultural treasures and stolen antiquities in hopes of recovering them."

"I see…" *Now things started to make sense!* Janet inched forward in her chair. "Beckman was working on a freelance project when he died." She paused to make sure he was paying attention to what came next. Not to worry. Kasparian hung on her every word. "It may have been a figure of a dragon," she said, "a bronze dragon."

An inscrutable half-smile spread across his lips. "I might be able to help you after all."

"Care to share?"

He paused. Realizing an instant later that she wasn't playing with him. "Oh, you actually don't know? I thought you were being coy."

"Trust me, Mr. Kasparian, I don't do coy. If you know what this bronze dragon is, I need you to tell me."

He acknowledged her by settling back in his chair. The rich leather groaned as he rocked slowly back and forth. "Bronze dragon is a generic description that could mean many things. However, for many collectors, *the* bronze dragon can mean only one thing. It's one of the lost treasures of China. Specifically, it's a superb figure of a dragon head constructed out of bronze in the eighteenth century, one of twelve such figures from the great fountain at Haiyantang."

"Sounds impressive."

"Very." His smile became almost beatific, as if he were to impart something precious and wonderful. "Would you like me to tell you the story? Or is it not relevant to your investigation?"

"I won't know until you tell me."

"A sensible answer. Around 1700 in China, Emperor Qianlong built a magnificent summer palace in Haiyantang known as the Hall of the Calm Sea. Inside the palace was an ornate fountain with twelve bronze animal heads that represented the Chinese zodiac. This magnificent fountain was a working water clock. Once every two hours, so the story goes, water would spout from one of the heads to indicate the time. Then at twelve o'clock, water would gush simultaneously from all the animal heads in a marvelous aquatic display."

Kasparian took a long pull from the water bottle to lubricate his throat. "The majesty didn't last. By the early nineteenth century came the Opium Wars, which was about Chinese isolationism versus free trade. The British killed thousands in the name of commerce. Not their finest moment. By 1860 French and British troops had overrun and ransacked the old summer palace, looting it of hundreds of treasures. Among these were the twelve zodiac animal heads which were once thought lost to posterity."

Janet, who'd been listening carefully to the story, latched onto one phrase. "'Thought lost to posterity.' I take it they aren't lost?"

Kasparian's eyes shined back with a hint of avarice. "Indeed they are not, not all of them. In the past few decades, several of the bronze fountainheads have reappeared. The ox, tiger, and monkey heads were purchased by the Chinese government from various sources. The pig and horse were acquired from private collectors. In 2009 the rat and rabbit found themselves in the collection of Yves Saint Laurent, the famous designer, and were put up for auction in Paris by Christie's.

The rabbit head itself was auctioned off at nearly twenty million dollars."

The hairs at the back of Janet's neck stood up. *Now here was a motive for murder!*

The antiquities dealer seemed pleased by her reaction, that she now appreciated the full value of what was at stake. Edging closer, his voice took on a conspiratorial air. "That left five zodiac heads missing: the snake, the sheep, the dog, the rooster, and the dragon. Again in 2009, the dragon head was located overseas and obtained by a Taiwanese collector who wasn't about to display it publicly, let alone donate to a museum."

Kasparian paused to let her process all this before he continued. "And then, curiously, in 2018, the dragon head reappeared in Paris at auction. Whether or not it was the same dragon figure, no one knows. However, after several rounds of heated bidding, a Chinese buyer bought the piece for a considerable sum. But, here's the thing, experts have doubts about the authenticity of the piece. The Yuanmingyuan Society of China authenticated the relic from *photographs* of the internal and external details but admitted they are not 100 percent certain. Repeat, the official Chinese delegation only saw photos, not the actual relic. Also, bronzeware experts haven't had sufficient materials from the piece to verify that the sculpture from the Parisian auction is the real Yuanmingyuan dragon head. And the Chinese buyer of the piece has said and done nothing since acquiring it."

She felt a rush of excitement. "That's some story! So the dragon head Beckman was asking about may be a copy or—"

"It could be the true lost fountainhead," Kasparian finished with shining eyes, savoring the moment.

Janet gave a slow nod, understanding it now. "That's what Roger Beckman was trying to establish."

"Yes, Roger started making inquiries last month. Antiquities are a fairly small community, Detective, particularly in the Midwest, so we tend to talk to one another. Dealers hear things. Rumors have a way of floating downstream. When a respected Asian scholar even raises the topic of an artifact like the bronze dragon head of Haiyantang, it makes one wonder why."

It made sense to Janet, who could see the curtain parting a little to reveal what was beyond. "Mr. Kasparian, you may have just told me why Dr. Beckman was murdered."

"Greed, it's that simple. Those who fiercely covet a great object of art often show no restraint in acquiring it."

She could add nothing to that. Treasure and plunder went together like bread and butter, whether in 1860 or today. People killed for any number of reasons, and financial gain was always near the top of the list. Which led her to another thought. "You wouldn't know the names of interested parties who've been searching for the missing zodiac heads?"

"Names? Not really. I have inklings. There's a London tycoon who expressed interest ten years ago but never got anywhere with it; the widow of an internet millionaire in Seattle with a passion for sculptures is another…and someone in Brazil whom I know nothing about. And then," he shot her a pointed look, "we have David Nakagawa. There's a name for you."

"Who's David Nakagawa?"

"A very—how should I put it?—aggressive collector, a man who goes after what he wants like a freight train. He's the CEO of Nakagawa Trading."

It was a failed attempt at diplomacy if it had been an attempt at all, suggesting a history between these two men.

Her eyes widened. "Where can I find him?"

"Minnetonka."

"That's close." Very close, she thought. "Thank you. I'll talk to him. That's a good start, Mr. Kasparian. Your information may be what breaks open this investigation. Thank you for your time—"

"Wait. Detective Lau, I'm disappointed. There's one question you haven't asked me. I thought for certain you would ask."

Halfway out of her chair, Janet eased herself down. "What question is that, Mr. Kasparian?"

"Aren't you going to ask me who Roger's client is? You clearly don't know; otherwise, you'd be talking to him rather than me."

She sat up. "You know who that is?"

"A pretty fair idea."

What sort of game was he playing? Earlier he'd made it seem he knew little. She'd had a teacher like that, a self-absorbed instructor who answered questions by asking other questions. Annoyingly Socratic. Angelo Kasparian reminded her of him, ensconced behind his showy desk, waiting to bestow his next gem of wisdom.

Kasparian said, "You want to talk to Leland Hatcher. He's your man. I'd bet on it."

"Lee Hatcher, the millionaire? Who was just in the news for acquiring North Star Airlines?" North Star was a popular large regional carrier.

"Entrepreneur, philanthropist, and patron of the arts. Yes, that Lee Hatcher."

Janet whistled.

Leland Hatcher was often in the news, if not for his latest business acquisitions then for his charity work. Hatcher, personable, photogenic, charming, had built up his business empire over two decades with savvy investments and the ability to turn around troubled companies. If Hatcher wasn't a household name in the region, several of the companies he owned were.

She wanted to believe the antiquities dealer but was wary. "And you know he has the bronze dragon because…?"

"Several reasons." He ticked them off on his fingers. "Roger has done appraisal work for Lee before. That coincides with the fact that Lee was in Shanghai this spring on a business trip and acquired some new pieces there."

"That's not much to go on."

"Perhaps. Unlike me, though, Lee Hatcher keeps his art collection on display at his headquarters building. To him, it's all about the prestige of having fine art, not the art itself. Last month I contacted an associate of mine who had recently visited Hatcher. Lee is involved in numerous charities. So am I. My contact had a meeting with Lee at his office. She told me she'd seen this dragon headpiece he'd recently acquired. Lee can't help himself. He likes to show off."

"Your contact saw a *bronze* dragon head on display?"

"She did, in his lobby gallery. How many of those can there be? That's good enough for me, Detective."

And good enough for her to visit Leland Hatcher, whose initials also matched the mysterious L.H. written in Beckman's appointment calendar on *the day he died.*

A cold chill ran through her. This was a breakthrough. Her excitement made her forget her anxiety. She had to tell Henry, send him a message the minute she left Kasparian's office.

CHAPTER 7

The mountain lake was smooth as glass and reflected the serene blue sky. Sunlight warmed the body while the burble of a nearby brook soothed the soul.

Henry Lau cracked open an eye. The cinderblock wall clock said two minutes to go. With both eyes closed, he submerged again into his standing meditation, sinking his spirit into a deep well of nothingness. To become calm, he must envision calm, listen to the aches and rumbles of his muscles, and guide them into the still waters of the mountain landscape. Each breath circulated his chi, his vital energy, through his body along ancient pathways. When he finished, he slowly opened his eyes and stood up to his full height, no longer on the shore of a clear lake but in the basement of his home in St. Louis Park, Minnesota. His fingertips tingled, his knees were numb, and he felt both energized and relaxed at the same time.

The pattern seldom varied. His kung fu regimen started every day at 4:00 in the morning: ninety minutes of working forms, followed by basic and specialized drills, ending in a twenty-minute run. Three times a week, he added thirty minutes for weapons work. The standing meditation increased his awareness of his body's center, which enhanced his fighting skills as well as his body's healing ability.

That practice had served him well in the intensive care unit when he was little more than a bag of broken bones and ruptured organs.

At first, Henry didn't tell his doctors what he was doing. They'd probably scoff. And to be truthful, he wasn't sure himself his plan would amount to anything. But he had nothing to lose. A Qigong master in Hong Kong had sworn by these methods. With nothing to do all day but lie in a hospital bed, Henry started mentally circulating his chi throughout his body. Hours and hours of deep mediation every day, visualizing energy flowing to his hip, legs, arms, and chest to stimulate blood flow. His vital signs greatly improved after two days. He surprised his nurses at the end of the second week by sitting up in bed with chart readings of a much healthier man. By the fourth week the doctors were astounded that he could stand on his own two feet with the assistance of a cane, so impressed that they transitioned him early into physical therapy. Within six weeks Henry was able to run again. Not particularly well, but that wasn't the point. Just the fact he could do it was more than his ER doctors had thought possible.

And here he was again, back in his training routine.

Henry moved to the sandbag mounted on the adjacent wall to do five hundred punches, Wing Chun vertical fist punches. Afterward, he went to the *mook yan jong*. Henry flowed through the wooden dummy form five times before ending with ten minutes of isolated drills.

The *jong* was an old friend, a souvenir from San Jose and the long hours of training. Like Henry, it had a few dents and nicks yet was still serviceable. His finger slid along the polished wood of the center arm and found the indentation he'd left after one angry session.

The week Kay died.

The week his life stopped.

The week he nearly lost his way.

The memory of that time was as vivid now as it was when he lived it. Emotions were dulled now, thankfully, though never the memory. The death of Kay had ripped out his heart. Overwhelmed by grief, he could barely manage to get through the day. Could barely cope. The wooden man, his silent training partner, was there for him, an outlet for his young rage and despair. He had plunged himself into it, beating his arms and shins against the teakwood until limbs were numb from pain and his heartache was dulled. Hollow comfort, though he was desperate for it. Kay McAdams had been the best thing that had ever happened to him, and he'd blown it. Supremely blown it.

When she had needed him the most, he wasn't there for her.

He could never forget that.

The passage of time had done little to ease the guilt, though it had sharpened his commitment to do what he could to help others in trouble. It was what made him such a tenacious investigator.

Time was up.

With a heavy sigh, Henry stepped back from the *jong*. Slow and easy breaths allowed him to lapse back into a meditative state for ten seconds, enough time to regain his calm. When he opened his eyes, they drifted to an old framed photograph hanging above the *jong*, a picture of himself and Alan Zhu taken when they were both nineteen. Their first time at the Golden Gate Bridge. Two best pals, young and happy, about to embark on new adventures in a new city. So full of promise. It was his favorite photo.

For a moment Henry let his thoughts linger on the memories of that day before heading to the shower. There was a lot to get done after breakfast.

You couldn't get away from the gym smell. That was the first thing Henry noticed stepping into the Five Tigers Martial Arts Academy. Disinfected floor mats and the muskiness of fresh sweat perfumed the air. Throaty grunts preceded the thwap of shins striking kicking shields met his ears.

The school was a spacious 9,000 square feet, nearly one hundred times the size of Alan's one-room closet *kwoon*, but then the Five Tigers was an old and respected venue with a national reputation, a full-time business compared to Alan's part-time school. Henry waited by the front door visitor area. A class was in session, led by an animated blond man roughly Henry's age in a T-shirt and a pair of canvas workout pants. He gave Henry a friendly nod. After class ended, the instructor ambled over with a white terry cloth towel draped over his shoulders.

"Henry, good to see you. It's been too long." Mike Anderson wiped his hand on the towel and extended it. He was marginally taller than Henry's five foot nine and beefier in the chest and shoulders. Had Slavic high cheekbones. Insightful eyes inspected Henry: lightweight bomber jacket over a blue police polo shirt and navy slacks.

"You look great," he said.

It took Henry a moment to realize Anderson wasn't complimenting his outfit.

"Back on the job, I see," Anderson added.

"About a month."

"You were really in bad shape. Incredible recovery."

"Thanks for the card, Mike."

"Sure. Wish I could've done more. Did they ever catch the guy who ran you down?"

"No."

"Any leads?"

"Only that the car was a dark coupe with racing stripes. No one got a license plate." Henry had shared the story so often he no longer had any emotion left for the telling. "It was late at night and most of the witnesses were either drunk or too freaked out when the car jumped the curb and nearly crashed into them."

Anderson shook his head in disbelief. "Man, you're lucky to be alive."

Henry made a vague gesture of acknowledgment. Yeah, he was. What else was there to say? He changed the subject. "Mike, got a minute?"

"Police business?"

"Yeah."

"Then this way."

Anderson led Henry to the far corner of the training area, far enough away not to be overheard by any of the students exiting the changing rooms.

"I'm investigating a murder, possibly a student of yours. Name's Roger Beckman. Sound familiar?"

"Sorry, it doesn't. I try to meet every student. I work out with many of them, but that's not so easy these days. We have over eighty regulars, not to mention the new people who come and go, the ones who drop out after a month or two when they realize they aren't gonna be Bruce Lee in six months."

Henry gave a little laugh. He knew all too well, as did all martial arts instructors. Typically these were young men who had no idea how many years of dedicated work it took to develop the skills they wanted, that it wasn't something they were going to pick up easily. Two years of tennis lessons would still get a novice player massacred by any Wimbledon professional, who practiced hours every day and regularly tested their skills on the court against other pros. Why should martial arts be any different? Beginners got disillusioned quickly.

Anderson asked, "You don't have a photo, do you?"

"I do." From inside his jacket, Henry pulled out his smartphone and showed the photo of Beckman's St. Luke's University ID. "He was a professor of Asian Studies."

Anderson pressed his lips together, studying the image. "There's a guy I'm thinking of. It was three months ago...Damn." He shook his head as the thought eluded him. "Let me get one of my assistants. I'll be right back."

As Anderson strode away, Henry's gaze wandered across the floor onto an upright bag that two female kickboxers took turns walloping with their shins. They were light on their feet, bouncing on their toes before unleashing each brutal kick.

Mike Anderson returned with another man. "Henry, this is my chief assistant, DeWayne Morris. Detective Henry Lau."

Morris, African American, mid-thirties, gave a curt nod. He had a firm handshake, a medium build, and well-defined shoulders and biceps under a tank shirt. He had the rough good looks of a professional athlete and the build of a man who likes to work out a lot with weights. "Mike said you're asking about Roger Beckman," he said in a husky voice with a hint of a Texas twang.

"You know him?"

"Yeah, he's in one of the classes I teach. What's this about?"

"I'm afraid I have bad news." Henry gave them the short version of Beckman's murder.

"Damn." Morris looked startled. "I can't believe it."

Henry looked back somberly. "How long was he a student here?"

"Maybe six months."

"What was he training in?"

"He was a regular in my Jeet Kune Do class, came every Tuesday and Thursday evening."

"How was he as a student?"

"A good guy. Paid attention. Was serious about his training. Good attitude." Morris looked to Anderson with a wry smirk. "Middle-aged students are my favorite."

Mike Anderson came back with a knowing chuckle, shifting his gaze to Henry. "The young guys have the passion but not always the patience to study. They want immediate gratification. Older students are more emotionally mature, easier to deal with."

"They don't have to show off," Morris summed up.

Henry eased a smile. Every teacher, no matter what subject, could appreciate that comment. *Was he ever that obnoxious? Probably.* In his younger days, Henry had been so driven and hungry to learn and to prove himself. Time, age, and experience do a lot to make a man humble. Henry glanced between the two men. "Did Beckman ever talk about his life outside of class?"

DeWayne Morris didn't have to think it over. "We never got into personal stuff. We keep it light. People might talk about where they live and what they do. Not much chance to really get to know the students."

"Did you notice a mood change in him recently?"

"If you put it that way, yeah. A week or two ago. I was doing a one on one with Roger, and he seemed...distracted. Quieter than normal."

"Like he had something on his mind?"

"Right. It was in the Level 2 Jeet Kune Do class. I was going over a trapping hands drill—" Morris stopped suddenly. "Maybe I should explain that."

Anderson stepped in. "It's okay, DeWayne. Henry knows what you're talking about. He does Wing Chun."

"Oh. Okay. It was a simple drill, but Roger struggled with it. Couldn't keep up. I asked if he was feeling okay. He said yes, so I dropped it. Now that you mention it, yeah, I think his mind was somewhere else."

"This was in the last week?"

"Yeah."

Henry thanked them for their time and shook hands. The two men watched him in silence as he crossed the mat to the front door. When Henry was well out of earshot, Morris turned to his mentor, puzzled. "Who was that guy? I get he's a cop. You say he does Wing Chun."

Mike Anderson, quietly regarding Henry as he opened the door and exited, said, "Henry's a good man. He's also a damn good martial artist. One of the best I know. You wouldn't want to mess with him."

Morris' dark eyes narrowed with skepticism. "Really. What else does he do besides Wing Chun?"

"That's it."

"That's it?" DeWayne Morris was a product of mixed martial arts. He avidly collected techniques and ideas from wherever he could from whatever style. If it was useful to him, he held on to it like a precious stone. The more, the better.

Anderson snorted. "I know that look. Don't underestimate him, DeWayne."

Morris grunted. "I think I could take him."

"Maybe you could. I should tell you he trained with Eric Kwan in San Jose. After that, he lived in Hong Kong for a few years and trained with some interesting characters. I heard he got into a few back alley fights. Fierce stuff, some of it. And Henry's got a knack for reading people's movements. Freaky good. Like he knows what you're gonna do before you do it. So, yeah, maybe you could take him. Let me put it this way: in a ring for five rounds with rules, I'd probably put my money on you. For five minutes on the street, I'd go with Henry Lau."

Morris gave a noncommittal shrug. He was confident in himself and his abilities, confident that he could size up the skills in other people by looking at them, and he wasn't sure what to make of this friend of Mike's.

Anderson read his expression. "Remember," he said in his instructor's voice, one meant to impart information, "it's not how many techniques you know that matters; it's how good you are at what you know. The depth of Henry's knowledge and skill in Wing

Chun runs deep. He doesn't need another fighting art. Remember Big Jerry Rathberger?"

For anyone who had attended the Five Tigers Martial Arts Academy during a certain period of time, it would have been difficult not to recall the human freak show that was Big Jerry Rathberger. NCAA wrestling champ in college, former bar bouncer, and Mike Anderson's best grappler owing to his ape-like arms. Big Jerry was a brawler. Big, strong, and tough as a gorilla but devoid of the great ape's refined social skills.

Morris shook his head. "Jerry the Meathook. Oh, yeah. Glad he's gone."

"The man was a handful."

"He was a thug, but—man!— he had a punch like a cannonball."

"I told you why he stopped coming, though it's been a while. You might not remember. It was four years ago, the month you were in Dallas visiting your sisters. We were doing one of our martial arts exchange weekends. Henry was here, speaking and demonstrating concepts from the Leung Sheung branch of Wing Chun. Well, Big Jerry, being the asshole he was, challenged Henry in the middle of his presentation. He said Wing Chun was shit and worthless in a real fight." Anderson shook his head, embarrassed at the memory. "Before Henry could reply, Jerry charged at him like a runaway train. He tried to grapple him to the floor but couldn't, so the idiot takes a cheap shot and smacks Henry in the face. Gave him a helluva black eye, as I remember."

Mike Anderson paused, remembering.

Morris winced in acknowledgment, having been on the receiving end of the Meathook's punch. "And that ended it."

"No," Anderson came back in a voice of wonder. "Henry staggered back in pain, straightened up, and went berserk. I'd never seen him lose his temper before. The guy was a demon, flew at Jerry, and punched the guy silly. Jerry grabbed Henry's arm, but Henry managed to land a kidney punch on him, broke free and kicked him in the chest. Sent Jerry flying on his ass. I swear the floor shook. Jerry cracked a rib."

Morris nodded in appreciation. It was no walk in the park to get the best of Jerry the Meathook.

"And get this," Anderson went on. "Afterward, Henry apologized to me and the students for having lost his temper. I told him, 'No, you got nothing to apologize for. I'm embarrassed by my student.'" Anderson's jaw tensed, still burning at the memory. "I told Jerry what he did was wrong, and he was no longer welcome as a student. He hauled himself up and left, holding his side and looking a little green."

DeWayne Morris had nothing to say after that.

CHAPTER 8

Henry emerged from Five Tigers into the cool October air. Neighborhood trees were at full color, the boulevard aspens a dazzle of bright yellow.

He glanced around. It had been a few years since he'd been back to this neighborhood; it hadn't changed much, the same single-story storefronts along both sides of the street. Though he could be wrong, having been preoccupied the last time he'd left Mike's *dojo* a few years back. That was the weekend he was a guest instructor for the seminar in which he was attacked by a monster truck of a student. *What was his name? Jerry something.* Without warning, the dude had charged at him like a rogue elephant on steroids; the tree trunk arms extended out to take Henry down. They had wrapped around Henry's hastily positioned *gaun sau* arms. He pivoted hard, only to check his pivot at the last instant, realizing if he completed it Jerry, already stumbling in a wide arc around Henry's center, would fly off into the nearby wall of mirrors. Broken glass. Lacerations. Blood. *What thanks did he get for showing restraint? An elbow in the face when he let down his guard.*

Blindsided, seeing stars, and knowing more was coming, Henry went into survival mode. Lost his cool and went on the attack. The black eye was sore for days. A stiff neck and sore shoulder required a visit to the chiropractor. Some satisfaction came a day later when Mike called him to let him know Jerry was banned from Five Tigers and was moving delicately and painfully with a cracked rib. Henry didn't enjoy inflicting pain on others, but, he had to admit, he'd found pleasure knowing Jerry the Meathook hadn't emerged unscathed from the encounter.

Henry's cell rang. He glanced at the Caller ID. "Hello, Janet."

"Oh, my God! You answered your phone. I can't believe it. I was going to leave a message, but you're live. I'm kinda thrown. What gives?"

"You caught me at a good time." He explained he'd just left the Five Tigers Martial Arts Academy. "Beckman was a student here."

"Bingo! Find out anything useful?"

"Too soon to say. Any luck with your antiquities people?"

"A big fat yes!" Janet said as if she'd been holding back and was ready to burst. "Angelo Kasparian was extremely helpful. He not only knows the background of the bronze dragon, he also thinks he knows who Beckman was working for." Overflowing with enthusiasm, she recapped her interview with the art dealer.

Henry whistled after she finished. "So Lee Hatcher may be the owner of the dragon sculpture, and he hired Beckman to appraise it. Easy enough to verify."

"You read my mind. I'm trying to arrange a meeting with him. What's on tap for you?"

A sign up the street had piqued Henry's interest. "I'm checking on something else here. I'll hook up with you after lunch."

The sign in question was large and ran the width of the storefront with English letters and Chinese characters. Silk Road Imports. It was next door to Glamor Nails Salon and a short walk up the block across the street from Caribou Coffee.

Passing through the doorway of Silk Road Imports, Henry was immediately enveloped in sandalwood incense. Above him came the lowing throb of an old-fashioned ceiling fan suspended from a green tin ceiling. Aisle after aisle of neatly stacked merchandise caught his eye: brightly colored paper lanterns, silk wall hangings, tiny human and animal figurines, furniture, vases, lucky bamboo containers. He maneuvered by a collection of teak end tables and hand-carved four-panel screens to contemplate a table covered in Buddhas. Small Buddhas, large Buddhas, Buddhas carved from marble or cast in bronze. Expensive Buddhas for a private temple, and cheap ones small enough to fit on top of a computer monitor. Henry's gaze shifted toward the front counter, where a middle-aged female customer in a quilted jacket gathered her purse and bag and made for the door.

The chunky Chinese woman behind the counter reached for a cordless phone and made a call. Early fifties, in a fawn brown dress, cascades of black hair piled on her head. She spoke animatedly in Mandarin with big hand gestures. There had been a time long ago when he would've understood what she was saying, a very long time ago. His Hong Kong years. Where Cantonese was the dominant tongue, but Mandarin was also spoken to a lesser degree. He was never wholly fluent in Mandarin, and she spoke too fast for him to follow much of the conversation beyond a few sentences. Biding his time, he wandered to a glass shelf of miniature animal figures. He picked up a rooster and turned it over, letting out a half-smile at the white sticker on the base.

SRI: $10.00.

The same sticker he'd seen on the Mongol jade piece in Roger Beckman's house. He'd wondered if it had been purchased here when he noticed the sign from down the block. Setting down the rooster, he paused to view a three-foot reproduction of the terracotta soldiers of *Shi Huangdi.*

"Hello, sir, may I help you?"

Darlene Chow was the name printed on a tag pinned above her sturdy bosom. She smiled with bright crimson lips.

"This is a copy. It's too short to be genuine."

"What's the matter with you? You think Emperor Qin wanted tiny soldiers in his tomb?" she came back in a heavily accented voice, mocking and flirtatious in one. "This is a hand-made reproduction. From the same clay as the original. Made at the Qin museum where the real statues are."

"I see."

"Very special. A bargain at two hundred dollars. Your friends would see what excellent taste you have." Her tone intimated purchasing the clay soldier would set him apart from the crowd and would ennoble him. When he hesitated, she pressed further. "If you want a life-sized statue, I can get one of those. I have connections overseas. Can get you a super deal." She leaned in for emphasis. "New statues made of the same clay, same process. Not the real old statues."

"Could you get one of the real terracotta soldiers if I wanted one?"

Darlene Chow looked offended. "Are you crazy? That would be illegal. You want to get me in trouble?"

Henry couldn't suppress a smile. She was working hard plying her trade and did it in a disarmingly honest manner. He showed her his badge wallet, and the proprietress stepped back and looked askance at him.

"You're not in trouble," he said, reassuring her. "I'm investigating a murder. The man I'm interested in was a student at the Five Tigers kung fu school down the street. I wonder if he ever came in here." He showed her Beckman's photo.

She squinted at the smartphone image for five seconds. "Hard to say. So many people come in here."

"His name was Roger Beckman. He was a professor of Asian Studies and an expert in Asian art. You're in the import business. He probably would've stopped in once or twice."

She shook her head. "If he did, I don't remember."

"Did you ever sell a small jade statue of a Mongol warrior on a pony?"

"Yes," she answered without thinking about it. "Two came in last winter from a dealer in Macao. I can get more—"

"Beckman had one in his house. It has one of your stickers on it."

"Maybe he was here," she conceded. "Or somebody bought it as a gift." She was pleasant, matter of fact, hitching her plump shoulders up as if to say 'that explains that.'

Henry mulled over something she'd said. "Do you have many contacts in China?"

"I do!" she said proudly. "My daughter Stacey flies to Hong Kong and China two times a year. I have a sister in Beijing, a cousin in Shanghai, and friends in Macao. Plenty of contacts. I can get good stuff. Not just cheap junk. Hard to find things. *Special.*"

He waited for the wink wink that didn't come.

She smiled at him coquettishly. "You looking for a gift for your lady friend? If I don't have it, I can get it for you."

The air currents from her hand gestures disturbed the rising thread of jasmine smoke from the incense burner on the counter, a green Tibetan snow lion. To Henry, it seemed like the slender white column was weaving and bobbing out of the way of her large red-nailed hands. He commiserated. He wouldn't want to be smacked by them either.

"You don't remember the name: Roger Beckman. He might've come in recently about a piece of art. Does the bronze dragon mean anything to you?"

Darlene Chow's face was blank. "Bronze? No. I have brass dragons, wood dragons, porcelain, and even stone dragons. No bronze."

"No, not to buy from you. This is a dragon head from an old zodiac fountain from the summer palace built by Emperor Qianlong." He looked to her for a sign of recognition. Nothing. *This was going nowhere. She was either too cagey or knew nothing.* He decided to switch gears. "Let's talk about the black market."

She waved a dismissive hand. "I don't do black market. I'm all legal. You can check."

"I'm not accusing you of anything. Just asking what you know. There's a big underground market for relics and artifacts. You must hear things, maybe even know people involved."

"Yes, I hear things from overseas. I don't touch. Not worth the trouble."

"What about people here?"

"People come here all the time trying to sell me junk." She scrunched her nose as if there were a bad smell.

"Has anyone tried to sell you a real antique?"

"Yes, but I don't buy from people, only dealers. Need proof of ownership. No fine art here. I sell home and office decorations. Most expensive thing I have is two thousand dollars. Not many of my customers want to spend $5,000 on an old vase."

"But people do ask you," he coaxed with a flirtatious half-smile.

"Sometimes." She regarded him carefully, sizing him up as if he were a prize chicken. "You a good-looking man. You seem nice, too. Are you married? I no see wedding ring."

"I'm not married."

That information swung open the gates of opportunity. Darleen Chow suddenly ratcheted down her personality to a quiet purr. "You should meet my daughter, Stacey. She's very pretty, not like me." She laughed. "And smart. Makes good money. Wonderful girl. You'd like her."

"Thanks, but I'll have to pass. I'm seeing someone." Which wasn't true but should have been enough for him to wriggle out of the wide net she was casting.

Chow sighed disappointedly. "Too bad. She's a great catch!"

Perhaps, except you come with the deal.

Henry dug out one of his cards and handed it to her. "In case you think of something later."

"Henry Lau," she read his name with approval. A well-manicured hand presented her card. It read: Silk Road Imports. Darlene Chow owner and manager. "In case you change your mind about my daughter." She smiled invitingly.

He held the card close to his nose. The scent of sandalwood and jasmine was strong. He tucked it away. "I'd like to go back to the jade statue, the one with the Mongolian warrior. Is there a way for you to check your sales records? Like you said, someone might have purchased it as a gift for him, and that someone might have helpful information."

"I wouldn't have names, only how many, dollar amounts, and the date sold. Sorry."

"Sure." He was about to turn away when he stopped. It was mid-October, jacket weather, although a month earlier, it was still warm. No jackets needed, meaning Beckman likely came in a short-sleeved shirt. Henry stepped closer to the counter and fixed his dark brown eyes on hers. "The man I'm talking about might have come in a month ago. He would've had heavy bruising on his forearms."

There was a flash of recognition—or something—in her eyes. She waved at his jacket pocket. "Let me see the photo again." She stared at the smartphone image for ten full seconds. "A man like you say came in last month and asked me about my contacts in China." She straightened up slowly as a thought came to her. "His arm was purple. And he was the same man who bought the Mongolian jade earlier in the summer. I remember now. This is a bad photo. Doesn't look a lot like him."

She'd just said something interesting, he realized. "Ms. Chow, you said this man asked you about your contacts in China. Is that right?"

"Yes."

"When was this again?"

"Three, maybe four weeks ago."

"Why did he ask about your overseas contacts?"

Darlene Chow replied, "He said he had something very rare he wanted to sell."

CHAPTER 9

The world headquarters of Hatcher Global International glistened on the hilltop overlooking Highway 494 like a jewel— a really big, garish jewel. The afternoon sun reflected off six stories of lavender-tinted glass, soaring towers, and sweeping neo-Gothic arches. Magnificently gauche. Janet imagined this was how Dorothy felt the first time she laid eyes on the Emerald City as she reached the end of the Yellow Brick Road.

And inside this palace of commerce was Oz, the Great and Powerful, the Wizard of Commerce known to most as Leland Hatcher. Securing an appointment with the industrialist dynamo for the same day she called had stunned Janet. Not only had Hatcher's assistant agreed to an appointment with no strings attached, but she'd also remarked that Hatcher was eagerly looking forward to their meeting.

How nice!

As she strode up the boxwood-lined walkway to the main entrance, she felt nervous, but in a different way. The butterflies in her stomach weren't gathering in defense against a confrontation; they were fluttering in anticipation. She was looking forward to laying her eyes on the famous entrepreneur.

She glanced at Henry, and her thin lips curled approvingly. He was dressed for combat. After lunch, he'd changed into an upscale charcoal gray power suit with a European cut. In it he looked stylish, handsome, and formidable. Like he belonged with the rich and powerful. He'd taken the extra step, changing clothes. Most cops wouldn't have bothered just to interview someone, but Henry had explained he liked having an edge wherever he could find one. If dressing up accomplished that, so be it. Or to put it another way: "If you're jumping into a pit of tigers," he'd said, "you don't want to look like a sheep." He'd gone on to say he didn't dress up often, just on those occasions when he felt it necessary. Some of Henry's colleagues thought he was nuts to do this. Janet wasn't sure she entirely bought into the strategy, although she could see some merit in it.

The detectives passed through the entranceway into a spacious atrium with a vaulted glass ceiling. On the wall hung a large LCD monitor displaying 3D flyover animations of various HGI holdings across the globe.

They approached the grand reception desk.

"Hello, may I help you?" greeted an attractive Hispanic woman, thirtyish with glistening straight black hair and a thousand-watt smile that made you happy just to be there.

Henry showed his ID. "Detectives Lau and Lau to see Mr. Hatcher. We have a three o'clock appointment."

The receptionist consulted her computer screen. "Yes, I'll let Mr. Hatcher's assistant know you're here," she purred in a warm hug of a voice. "Please sign in. Here are your visitor badges. Take the elevator to the sixth floor to Mr. Hatcher's office."

They exited the elevator into a large reception area where a polished, sharply dressed woman directed them in a posh British accent, "Mr. Hatcher is expecting you. Please go in."

Into the Inner Sanctum.

Janet rallied her courage. Purged a breath that went down to her toes. As she and Henry passed through the double doors, she half expected a volley of trumpets to announce them. No trumpets. No beat of drums. Not even garishly garbed sentries with pikes. Nothing. Only the sound of two people talking, a man and a woman.

Leland Hatcher sat on the corner of a sleek glass and chrome desk. Well-groomed and at ease with movie star good looks, he seemed like a man totally at home in his own skin. He was speaking to a young Asian woman standing a short distance away. Their conversation came to an abrupt halt the moment the newcomers entered the room.

Henry stopped in mid-stride. "Sorry to intrude. Your assistant said to come in. We didn't realize you had company."

"No, no," an ebullient Hatcher waved them in. "Minister Shen and I were just wrapping things up."

Minister Shen looked on politely. Janet guessed they were about the same age, late twenties. Shen was pretty, trim, and had an understated elegance about her that Janet envied if she were honest. She wore a tailored blazer, white blouse, straight navy skirt, and plain black pumps. Alert and businesslike, a flash of curiosity glimmered in her lovely dark eyes.

On his feet now, Hatcher made a sweeping gesture. "Let me introduce you. This is Minister Shen Jiang-Li of the People's Republic of China." He used the correct protocol, Janet noted, by presenting her family name first and followed with her given name of Jiang-Li. "And these are Detectives Lau and Lau from the local police."

Puzzled, the Chinese minister looked to her host. "These people are from the police?" Her soft, accented voice pronounced each word with practiced care.

"They're here about the death of an associate of mine, the man I was telling you about, Dr. Beckman. They also have some interest in the artifact."

"May I ask what interest the dragon head is to your local police?"

Hatcher seemed to relish the question a little too much, unable to keep the lid on his enthusiasm. "Dr. Beckman was murdered. He also had possession of what we both believed could be the summer palace dragon fountainhead. That's the connection if I'm not mistaken." A confirming glance toward the detectives, who nodded. "As I said to you earlier, Minister, the situation is more complicated now. The recovery of the dragon head is uncertain."

Shen's attractive oval face considered Hatcher. Straight black hair hung to her jawline in a blunt bob cut she made look chic. She wore little makeup. Didn't need much. Her natural good looks required little embellishment. There was about her a calm reserve that suggested she did not act on impulse but considered her options. Her long-lashed eyes—which Janet couldn't stop admiring—looked on with disappointment. "That is most unfortunate. Of course, the death of this man must be dealt with. I'm sure the two of you are very capable and will conclude your investigation quickly."

The words may have been intended for both of them, but, Janet noted, Shen Jiang-Li's attention was directed solely toward Henry. Her gaze lingered on him with a suggestive familiarity. The corner of her mouth pulled back into a winsome smile.

Was Shen flirting with Henry? Yikes!

Maybe Janet had misread the signal. She didn't think so. It forced her to reconsider the cultural minister. Shen may have been the emissary of a repressive political regime yet; apparently, the repression didn't extend to social interaction.

Lee Hatcher glanced between Henry and Janet. "I've been trying to explain the situation to Minister Shen. Perhaps meeting you will convince her I was telling the truth about Roger. Recovery of the dragon artifact is in limbo now. I don't know where it is."

Janet's eyes flicked toward Henry.

The bronze dragon was missing!

"Mr. Hatcher," Shen said, "the death of Mr. Beckman is most unfortunate. Regardless, my government expects your full cooperation."

"And you shall have it."

"Beijing also expects your help in reclaiming a lost cultural treasure."

Hatcher tossed his hands. "There's only so much I can do. Beckman had the relic. It's gone." He looked to Shen Jiang-Li for a hint of leniency and found none. With a shake of his head, he turned to the detectives. "The agency Minister Shen represents is in the recovery business, Chinese antiquities, as you may have guessed."

Dawn broke in Janet's awareness. "Of course, you're from the State Administration for Cultural Heritage. I should've realized."

A confused Shen Jiang-Li stared back. "You know about me? How is this possible?"

"Dr. Beckman made a notation about SACH in his desk calendar."

"I see. May I ask where this calendar is?"

She could ask, but she wasn't going to get an answer. Hatcher saw to that. He cut her off, ushering her toward the door. "I'm sorry, I need to speak to the detectives in private. This is an official police matter. I'm sure you understand. They have an appointment."

Unfazed, Shen Jiang-Li gave a curt nod. "A last question, please. In your investigation, have you come across a bronze sculpture of a dragon?"

Henry shook his head. "No, we haven't."

"You searched Mr. Beckman's home and his place of employment?"

"We did. And found nothing."

"His car?"

"Nothing there, either."

"Could someone have stolen it from him?"

"That's a possibility. We know an attempt was made, but it doesn't look like it was successful. Either he hid the dragon very well or…" Henry paused, reconsidering what he was about to say.

"Detective Lau?"

"I was about to say he either hid the dragon very well or disposed of it."

"Disposed of it."

Shen Jiang-Li repeated the phrase with some alarm. It was clear from her reaction that she hadn't considered this option. She shifted her weight to her other leg. Beneath the black skirt, a shapely calf muscle flexed. An athlete's leg, Janet assessed. A runner or a soccer player.

A tense silence followed.

What struck Janet was how Hatcher had failed to react to Henry's statement. Didn't he care that Beckman might have 'disposed' of the millionaire's potentially priceless artifact? *Maybe he was too cool for school? Didn't want to betray his emotions in front of the Red Chinese visitor? Or had the thought occurred to him already?*

With nothing left to discuss, Shen Jiang-Li presented Henry with her business card.

Only to Henry.

Janet's eyes narrowed into laser slits. *Hello? I'm over here! Don't forget me.* But Shen wasn't interested in her. The minister's gaze was for Henry only. The hair on the back of Janet's neck bristled. She hated antiquated old-world sexist customs and, under different circumstances, might have spoken up; however, this was a delicate situation with a foreign operative with potential political repercussions. Better to bite her tongue and play nice. For now.

Shen addressed Henry, "Detective Lau, if you should find the dragon fountainhead or learn anything about it, I expect you to contact me."

"Just a minute—" Lee Hatcher objected.

Shen brought up an open palm. "Mr. Hatcher, please, I insist on being kept in the loop. Isn't that how the saying goes? Detectives, I hope to hear from you soon." Shen Jiang-Li shook their hands and, with one final glance at Henry, left the room.

The three of them watched her exit in silence. The door closed behind her with a solid click. Hatcher waited three full seconds to make sure she was far enough away, then brought his hands together in one triumphant clap.

"That worked out well," he grinned with open delight.

Janet was taken aback.

Hatcher confided. "Shen's been chewing on my ass all week about the dragon piece. Wants me to surrender it to her. Donate it as a good faith gesture between our two nations. Like hell, I'll just hand it over to the fucking Chinese!" He slammed his palm onto his desk and glared defiantly at them.

Some transformation! Janet smiled. Seconds ago he'd been the composed Leland Hatcher she was familiar with from the media, the savvy entrepreneur who rescued failed companies, the generous philanthropist and all-around good guy. People ate up his story. As did she. Disadvantaged kid overcomes adversity to start his own business. Fails time and time again until he finally hits the winning formula. Eventually parlaying that success large scale. Along the way, the rough edges were softened, and the scrappy teenager with ambition and little else became the fiftyish, polished corporate tycoon. But now, alone with them, the curtain had been pulled back to reveal a man not quite as self-contained nor as polished as the public façade insinuated.

The faint lines around his eyes deepened. The smile faded. "Pardon me if I'm a little worked up. It's been a crazy month. Business issues have sucked up my time. The Chinese are threatening to cut off my access to key suppliers and partners, and then there's Roger's death." His brows knit thoughtfully. "What I can't figure out is how the fucking Chinese knew I had the dragon head. Hell, until three weeks ago, I had no idea what the damn thing was! Yet somehow, Beijing got wind of it and sent their fucking art cop to repossess it. That's why I wanted you to meet Shen. I arranged for her to be here, so you'd 'accidentally' walk in on us. I don't think she believed me. Thought I was stalling. Well," he laughed with satisfaction, "I think she believes me now."

He gestured toward a pair of plush visitor chairs. While his guests made themselves comfortable, Hatcher remained on his feet as though nervous energy would not allow him to rest, not even for a moment. Eyeing the detectives, the gravitas of the situation vaporized any lingering amusement from the well-chiseled face. Narrow shoulders sagged beneath an expensive twill sports coat. "But you didn't come here about my problems. You came about Roger."

Henry nodded. "We have. To be clear, it was you who hired Roger Beckman to determine the authenticity of the dragon artifact?"

"It was."

"A Chinese dragon?"

"Don't you already know this? From the way you and your partner spoke to Minister Shen, it sounded like you know all this."

"We had suspicions but didn't know for sure. That's part of the reason we're here."

"Gotcha. To make sure we're all on the same page, the figure is a bronze dragon head, a Chinese dragon." This last Hatcher added with a nod to Henry.

Confirmation! Janet felt gratified. Kasparian's information was spot on. Henry was pleased too; she could see by the faint smile tugging at his mouth.

Henry continued, "Mr. Hatcher, how well did you know Dr. Beckman?"

"Not well at all. I barely knew the guy. Saw him here and there if I needed a piece of art appraised. Even so, his death still sucks. People may think I'm a son of bitch businessman, but I'm not a heartless son of a bitch."

Janet's hands rested in her lap. "We don't know what Dr. Beckman did after he met with you that last time. Any thoughts?"

"Can't help you there. We just talked art when I met with him. The dragon head, yes, and other things. My collection is eclectic. Stuff from all over the world. Nothing *frou frou*. I don't care how 'important' a piece is, according to the critics. I have to like it. I brought Roger in to give his opinion on some Asian pieces I acquired earlier this year. Few things in my collection are high value. I have a Monet, for instance, mainly because it makes the art crowd happy. Gets you invited to high-class art functions where you can rub elbows with the big buck movers and shakers. It's all about networking."

The sparkle was back in his eye and the swagger in his voice. Janet felt she was getting a glimpse of the old street hustler from his early days, the scrappy kid who was always on the make. "You trusted his judgment," she said.

"I did. Roger was my go-to guy on Asian art. He knew his stuff. He also knew when to bring in someone with more expertise. Last year, for instance, he appraised this Tang Dynasty ceramic horse that was supposed to be the real deal, but he had doubts. Turns out an expert he consulted said the piece wasn't hundreds of years old but fifty if that. No treasure, just a nice replica."

Janet nodded. "When did you engage Dr. Beckman to examine the dragon piece?"

"Right after Labor Day. Is that how you found me, from some notation Roger left?"

"Actually, no. I spoke to a few local art dealers. Your name came up."

"*Angelo*," Hatcher said the name as if cursing. "Let me guess. It was Angelo Kasparian who ratted me out."

"I wouldn't quite put it that way."

"The man has tentacles everywhere. Last winter, I made a casual remark about a trip to Shanghai, an art junket, and somehow he put two and two together. It had to be him."

She neither confirmed nor denied it.

Hatcher noticed her reticence. "Yeah, he's the guy." Hatcher leaned in and lowered his voice. "Be careful with that man, Detective Lau. He's a wolf in sheep's clothing."

"How so?"

"Not in an overtly criminal way. He's more subtle than that. Let's say Angelo Kasparian is a swimming shark, always moving, on the hunt. His charity often comes with a price."

"Appreciate the warning. I will say the story he told about the emperor's zodiac fountainhead checked out. He was telling the truth."

The other gave a conciliatory shrug. "And that's what makes him dangerous. He gives you enough information to lure you in. It's what he does after that you need to watch out for."

"You sound like you have experience."

"I have," was all he offered.

Janet waited for him to elaborate. When he failed to do so, she nudged him on. "How did you acquire the dragon piece?"

"As I said, I did an art crawl during my last visit to Shanghai. Found this dingy hole in the wall shop. Lots of cheesy tourist souvenirs and other junk. The dragon head was hanging on a wall in the corner. The owner of the shop said the piece was at least a hundred years old. He didn't know much else. I liked the piece. Cost 36,000 Yuan. That's 5,000 US dollars."

Henry snorted. "And it might be worth millions."

"No shit! I thought it might be worth double what I paid for but had no idea it might be that much. I called in Roger to see if he could figure out what the thing was worth. After a few weeks research, he told me the story of the zodiac fountain and the missing animal heads and how my piece could be one of the lost treasures of China."

Janet's scalp tingled. That alone would be enough for some men to park their morals and take a stroll down Criminal Alley. She then asked the question that hung in the air like massing storm clouds: "Did Roger prove your dragon head is from the Emperor's summer palace?"

Hatcher came back with an elusive smile and raised his hands in an empty gesture. "I was on the verge of finding out. Roger had found a local contact who'd been at the Paris Christie's auction in 2009, the year the rabbit and rat fountainheads were auctioned from the Yves Saint Laurent collection. This guy saw them up close. Is a highly respected expert, so I let Roger borrow the dragon to show it to him."

Henry, who'd been listening carefully, sat up suddenly, puzzled. "Wait. You let Dr. Beckman leave the office with an object potentially worth millions of dollars?"

"Yes."

"Why?"

For the first time, their host seemed at a loss for words. Leland Hatcher moistened his lips and looked back sheepishly. "*Mea Culpa.* In hindsight, it was a mistake, perhaps the most boneheaded thing I ever did. At the time, it made sense."

Henry's eyebrow raised a fraction. "Care to explain? How did it make sense?"

"Simple. First, I trusted Roger. If he was going to fleece me, he could have done it before now. Second, and this is the main thing, I expected the dragon head to be found a fake like my Tang dynasty horse. It was always a long shot that the dragon piece might be valuable. In any case, I only paid five grand for the thing."

"Ha," Janet said in disbelief.

Hatcher stared at her.

Crap, did she say that out loud? Well, too bad. Perhaps a millionaire didn't bat an eye at losing five thousand dollars, but it would sure put a serious dent in her wallet. *Life of the rich! Write off the loss.* A new thought came to her. "Was the dragon head insured?"

"No. Before it can be insured, its value has to be determined."

Ouch.

This time Janet was able to keep her thoughts private.

Henry's brow furrowed. "Can we go back a bit? You let Roger borrow the bronze dragon. How'd that work? I mean, was in in a crate or something?"

"No, I helped him remove it from the display pedestal on the main floor. My collection is in its own little museum downstairs. The piece isn't that big, about the size of a basketball. We bubbled-wrapped it and placed it in a heavily padded canvas bag."

"No armed guards?"

"Yeah, that would've been a good idea. Like I said before, at the time, I didn't think it was necessary."

"Was there a reason Beckman's contact couldn't come here?"

"Roger said his contact was bed-ridden. He only reluctantly agreed to look at the dragon head from his sickbed. It was the only way."

Maybe that made sense. Janet wasn't sure. It was easy to judge decisions in hindsight, and she could see Hatcher was beating himself up over it. Henry had zeroed in on a few touchy points. He had a final card left to play.

"One other thing, Mr. Hatcher," Henry wondered, "after you learned about Dr. Beckman's death in the media, why didn't you contact the police? You must have been concerned about your property."

Lee Hatcher hung his head for a second and gave a short, self-deprecatory laugh. He was still on his feet; hands buried deep in his trouser pockets. "Why didn't I call the police? Shock, I guess. When I saw Roger had been murdered, I thought 'Holy Shit!'" Alarm, even a little self-preservation lurked behind those animated eyes. "I wasn't thinking about the dragon, a man I knew had been killed."

He cast his eyes down.

Respectful of that awkward moment, Henry waited a few seconds before continuing. "We could use some photographs and a description of the dragon artifact, so we know what we're looking for."

The millionaire nodded in a subdued manner as if a thought had occurred to him, but he didn't volunteer it. Odd, Janet thought. Lee Hatcher was no wallflower; he didn't seem the type to hold back, yet here he was walking on eggshells. Finally, she had to ask, "Mr. Hatcher, is there something else you want to tell us?" Appealing nut-brown eyes encouraged him on.

He waffled indecisively before caving in. "I trusted Roger," he admitted with regret and even embarrassment. "I think I got fooled. What if I was being played? What if this so-called expert of his doesn't exist, and it was part of a plan to get his hands on the dragon head?"

Janet sat up. "Are you saying Beckman stole it?"

"Maybe," came the bitter reply.

A shiver snaked up her spine. She thought of Darlene Chow and what she had told Henry only a few hours earlier. The import proprietor remembered a man who looked like Roger Beckman had asked her about her art contacts in China because he "had something very rare" he wanted to sell.

CHAPTER 10

Janet melted into her car seat and became one with the upholstery. Tired muscles began to relax as the clutter in her mind tried to untangle. Her car was parked, the engine off. No radio, no smartphone. Nothing but the sounds of nature as the crisp cool scent of autumn filtered in through her open window. She'd been on the go all day and relished this time after work to unwind and enjoy the tranquility of the sunset.

The art center was at the far end of the parking lot, waiting for her to go inside. Her class started in twenty-five minutes. For a moment, she reconsidered if she really wanted to watercolor tonight. Was it worth leaving the comfort and peace of her car? The answer, she knew, was yes. In a minute. Maybe five. She had plenty of time.

Rrrinng. Rrrinnng.

Her cellphone broke the mood.

"Hello?" she answered.

"Hey, Janet, it's Dani. Did I catch you at a good time?"

"Sure. What's up?"

"Just checking to see if you're still on the fence about Saturday."

Saturday…

That's right. Dani and her boyfriend Dustan were going out to dinner and wanted Janet along as company for a work buddy of Dustan's in hopes of rubbing two sticks together to make fire. Dani Montanado was one of Janet's oldest friends. She also operated under the illusion that she was a talented matchmaker.

"I don't know," Janet vacillated, grateful Dani couldn't see her sour expression. "I'm not good on blind dates."

"This isn't a blind date. It's four friends going out to dinner."

"Call it what you want, but everybody knows it's a setup between me and what's his name."

"Marcus."

"Whatever. It puts pressure on me—on both of us. Not the best way to start an evening. I'll probably trip over my best foot forward."

"Janet, honey, you're reading way too much into this. That'll ruin it for sure. Go with the flow a little. Imagine yourself having a good time."

"I don't know if I'm in the mood right now."

"Well, to be honest, Marcus kinda had the same reaction as you. He's a bit leery."

"Oh, this'll work," Janet mocked.

"It might if you give it a chance."

Dani was the eternal optimist, infectiously so. A hint of a smile pulled at Janet's lips. Doom was not a certainty.

"It's not pressure," Dani went on. "You'll be hanging out with friends, one you who haven't yet met. No expectations. Enjoy the moment."

Janet considered the idea. "It would be easier to do that if I knew this wasn't also a setup."

"Okay, next time I won't tell you."

"That's not what I meant."

"You like me, right? You love Dustan. You have fun with us. And there'll be this other guy along. No big deal. You got anything better going on?"

The only thing Janet had planned for Saturday was a date with a can of Dutch Boy to paint her apartment. The evening was free, as many of them were these days. She closed her eyes and set aside her misgivings. "Okay, count me in."

"Great! We'll pick you up at six."

Janet hung up. She tilted her head back against the headrest.

We'll see how this goes.

This would be good for her, she told herself. She needed to get out more. Do more stuff with different people.

The past four years had seen too much upheaval in her life. Some of it from her career, wanting to prove to Chief Bowman and her colleagues that she deserved this promotion. It was her nature to immerse herself into any new task, often at the risk of not allowing time for other interests. Like nurturing relationships. Or exploring new ones.

Janet's phone rang again.

She glanced at the name on the caller ID.

"Hi, Mom."

"Janet, glad I caught you. Is this a good time to talk?"

Why did everyone ask her if it was a good time to talk? Had she been cutting off people lately?

"My watercolor class is about to start."

"Then I'll make it quick. Your dad and I are driving up to Duluth on Saturday to visit your grandmother. Are you interested in coming along?"

Nanna Aileen had been moved into an assisted living home last winter. There'd been some discussion on whether or not to move her into the spare bedroom at Janet's parent's house, but Nanna didn't want to move to the Cities. She liked the North Shore, and two friends of hers were already at Spring Brook Acres. The curious thing about Spring Brook was there was no brook anywhere on the premises. Marketing fiddle-dee-do, as Nanna Aileen might say. Nanna had a wicked sense of humor. Smart, fiercely independent, she didn't take shit from anybody. She was a Scot. One hundred percent. An Aberdeen girl. It was tough seeing her with a walker, harder to see the sharp steel of her mind losing its edge. Janet hadn't visited her since helping to move her in. *Was that actually eight months ago?*

"When on Saturday is this?"

"We want to get there by noon, so it'll have to be an early start."

"Can we get back by five-thirty? I have a dinner date."

"No, dear. We won't get home till Sunday. We do want to spend a few hours with her and have dinner in Duluth."

It was a modest rebuke but a rebuke nonetheless.

"Oh…"

Of course, it would take all day. Janet knew that. Duluth was nearly a three-hour drive one way, counting rest stops. She was stalling, trying to figure out if there was a way to make this work. She didn't like disappointing her mother.

Abby Lau knew how to interpret a lengthy pause from her daughter. "Janet, I know this came out of nowhere. Don't worry about it. Your dad and I just talked about it this evening. You can go next time. We'll give you more notice."

"Thanks, Mom. Next time. Really."

"Are you okay? You sound frazzled."

"I am frazzled. But I'm fine. Super busy at work."

"Tell Henry not to work you so hard. Enjoy your class."

"Thanks. Say hi to Nanna for me!"

Janet put her phone away. She began to understand why Henry often kept his cell turned off. She closed her eyes and breathed in slow, deep breaths, held them for a few seconds, and let them out. Reverse breathing, as Henry had taught her. Expanding her diaphragm to extend her belly, filling her lungs. Calming, lowering her blood pressure, oxygenating her body.

She tried to find her way back to the tranquil oasis.

Mom.

There'd been a hint of disappointment in her voice after Janet told her she couldn't make it to Duluth. Her mother had hoped for a united family in front of Nanna Aileen, perhaps thinking it could boost the elderly woman's spirit if not her mental powers. Seeing so many familiar faces might help her thread her way through the shadows of old memories. It couldn't be easy watching a parent become frail and disoriented. Perhaps, Janet wondered, Abby Lau had invited her daughter along for her own moral support.

Now she felt guilty. Not from anything her mother had said. No, Janet had done that all by herself. Abby Lau was the most considerate, understanding, and generous person on the planet. Coercion simply was not in her mother's repertoire.

No, no, no. You're not going down that rabbit hole.

Janet shook off the thought.

Clear your mind.

Purge all negativity. Find your center.

Fooey. The negative vibes were like feeding hyenas circling back to their food source. *What should she do? Cancel with Dani and go to Duluth?* The truth was she wasn't sure she wanted to see her grandmother in her current mental state or watch its effect upon her mother. Janet needed more time to get her own life together. She'd dealt with so much in the past couple of years: Henry's health; the painful breakup with her cheating ex-boyfriend; her parked car getting totaled; the decline of her grandmother; the stress of her job—

One thing after the other. She was tired of *having to deal* with things. She wanted things to be normal for a while. Some quiet time. Time away from being on duty as a cop, on duty as a friend, on duty as a daughter.

Did that make her a crappy person?

Janet sighed. Being an adult was over-rated, she was starting to believe. All the responsibility, the hassle of trying to do the right thing, pleasing others while staying true to yourself.

The dashboard clock said her class was starting in ten minutes. Time to go. Art class suddenly looked very appealing. Watercoloring took her to another place, away from the real world with all its demands and ugliness, to a place of beauty and harmony. It was enough to get her out of her car with a budding sense of serenity, however fleeting.

After class ended, she jumped into her Mazda and drove across town into Minneapolis, parked, then strolled into the glass-walled lobby of the Minneapolis Institute of Art. Her badge got her past security but no farther than the lobby. A very private, important fundraiser was just concluding. She glanced at her watch. Just nine o'clock. According to the program, the well-heeled patrons should be filtering out any moment—

"Excuse me…"

Janet swung about. Behind her stood a pasty-faced, thick-set middle-aged woman whose inquisitive eyes seem to regard Janet as another work of art. She spoke tentatively. "I was watching you standing here. You have such an interesting face, so lovely. May I ask what nationality you are?"

Janet tensed slightly. Invisible fingers clenched her gut. *Not this again.* "I'm American," she replied in a put-out tone.

"No, I'm sorry, I meant where are your people from?"

"Plymouth, Minnesota."

The woman blinked. Janet smiled back pleasantly, intentionally obtuse.

"I mean what race are you, dear?" the older woman asked as if inquiring about the label on a fine garment.

And there it was! Why was it always white people who asked this question? Janet knew the answer. It was because they saw something they couldn't peg. The real sentiment behind their question was "There's something different about you. You don't fit in." This was so annoying. She'd gotten this question ever since grade school. It irritated her how perfect strangers felt entitled to walk up to her and question her ethnicity. They usually masked it with a compliment, except it still was racist. They had no clue how the question made her feel like an outsider, how it felt to be singled out as *different.* Janet wanted to tell this nosey woman to take a flying leap off a tall building but demurred.

"My father is Chinese; my mother is Scottish."

"Oh, what a delightful combination!" the other woman cooed. Her curiosity satisfied, she strode off as Janet imagined daggers in her back.

Noise snapped her back to the task at hand. A throng of people now meandered into the lobby through a pair of tall double doors. She scanned their faces. Two minutes later, she found her target: David Nakagawa. He looked like the photos she'd found on the internet. Even from across the room, Nakagawa looked like a big deal. Tall, angular, tuxedoed, he moved like he owned the place. A curvy brunette in a turquoise gown clung to his arm with the precision of a practiced escort. Impressive eye candy—

Wait, that wasn't fair. For all Janet knew, the woman was an accomplished brain surgeon who happened to look fabulous in a designer gown. *Don't pigeonhole people.* She hated it when others did that to her.

The fact remained, however, that the woman in turquoise was a looker. Nakagawa was no slouch himself with rugged good looks and a take no prisoners attitude. A seemingly endless crowd of patrons passed into the lobby. Too many people surrounded him for her to get close. She'd have to intercept him. Janet, feeling slightly underdressed in this crowd, smoothed out the wrinkles in her jacket and hustled after him.

"Mr. Nakagawa, my name is Detective Janet Lau." She flashed her identification. "Sorry to bother you. I was hoping to get a moment of your time?"

He waved her off, never breaking stride. "Sorry, I don't have time for this right now."

The heels of her shoes clacked loudly against the flooring as she tried to keep up. "I understand. Five minutes of your time. That's all I want. Can I make an appointment for tomorrow?

"Check with my office."

"Actually, I called your office this afternoon. Your assistant was the one who told me you'd be here tonight after she said your calendar was full. She said you were booked for the next two days."

"There you are."

It was a blow-off, plain and simple. Nakagawa didn't even look at Janet as he swung open the large glass door for his date—wife—friend—whoever the hottie was on his arm.

"I'm not going away, Mr. Nakagawa. This is a murder investigation. I need to talk to you. All I want is five minutes."

Irritated, Nakagawa stopped, handed a valet a ticket for his car while locking eyes with Janet. "Murder? Who was murdered?"

"His name is Roger Beckman."

"Sorry, I can't help you. I don't know anything. Goodbye," he said dismissively.

"*The bronze dragon*," she fired back.

Nakagawa hesitated. Something was going on behind those eyes. "Call my office," he said. "You got your five minutes. Tell them I said tomorrow at 2 p.m."

"Thank you."

He turned away without acknowledging her.

He knows something.

Janet did a little fist pump. She got her appointment. Would've been nicer if he could have deigned to spare her five lousy minutes right there while he was waiting for the valet to bring his car. But no,

Nakagawa couldn't do that. He needed to flex his power and inconvenience her.

"Self-important asshole!" she did not scream at his back and so desperately wanted to. It still felt good to think it, even if she couldn't utter the words aloud. It had taken all her courage to confront him. Barging into someone's personal space was way out of her comfort zone. The butterflies in her belly flapped hard. Still hadn't settled.

"Hello, Detective," greeted a familiar voice.

Janet turned to see Angelo Kasparian walking toward her. Like everyone else, he was dressed to the nines in a black tux with a white rose boutonniere.

"Mr. Kasparian, I guess I shouldn't be surprised to see you at a major art event."

He shrugged. "One is expected to make an appearance from time to time." He gave a nod toward Nakagawa, who was making idle conversation with a coterie of well-dressed art patrons waiting for delivery of their vehicles. "I see you took my advice about David Nakagawa."

Janet recalled Lee Hatcher's warning about Kasparian and found herself watchful of him but not particularly concerned. Truth was she liked the man. At least he wasn't too self-important to give her the time of day.

"He's a hard man to pin down," she said.

"David's definitely a person of interest regarding the dragon figure. He's been trying to get his hands on one of the fountainheads for years. Did you get the information you wanted from him?"

"No. He blew me off. Too busy to talk."

Kasparian looked disapprovingly at Nakagawa's back. "And yet he appears to be doing a lot of talking at the moment. None of it serious, judging by the way the others are smiling at him."

"Exactly! Gave me the brush off. Though he did toss me a crumb. I got an appointment with him."

"A small victory."

"Yes."

Kasparian leaned in. "If he continues to stonewall you, check his finances."

"Follow the money?"

"Definitely."

That came out too easy. Janet couldn't hide her suspicion. "Why are you being so helpful?"

The bearded face smiled. "Helping you helps me. David's a competitor, an often ruthless one. Anything embarrassing you uncover about him serves my interests."

She nodded absently, her attention elsewhere. A blond man was watching her from across the street. Tough looking with a surly mouth and harsh eyes, the kind of face you don't forget. Or maybe he wasn't watching her? Was it Kasparian he was interested in? She couldn't tell. Either way, the man gave her the creeps. A moment later, after a delivery van passed between them, he was gone.

CHAPTER 11

"Yes, what is it?"

The woman on the other side of the threshold eyed her visitor with thinly veiled irritation. Her body language declared disinterest in whatever he had to say. In her hand was a damp dish towel.

"My name is Henry Lau. I'm with the Gillette police. We spoke earlier."

The name sparked recognition.

"Right, about Roger. Like I told you earlier, I don't have anything else to say. We've been divorced for two years. We barely kept in touch. I can't see how I can help you."

"Anything may help. I only need a few minutes." His voice was calm yet insistent. Henry had a presence, in its unobtrusive way, that was hard to ignore.

Mary Jo Beckman considered him for a moment before capitulating. She stepped aside with a put upon look. "Come in."

Far from the warmest welcome he'd received. The ex-Mrs. Beckman reluctantly motioned him into the living room toward a sage gray sofa whose cushions had seen better days. She sat on the edge of a nearby armchair, the dish towel draped over the knee of her cotton slacks.

"What do you want?" she bristled, eager to be rid of him.

Henry lowered himself onto the sofa. "Mrs. Beckman, I'm investigating the murder of your ex-husband, and I must say you don't seem to care that much."

Her shoulders rose up and fell. "Like I said, Roger and I divorced two years ago. People who divorce usually don't like each other anymore. Excuse me if that offends you. I'm not going to pretend to be upset. I used up too much emotion in the divorce. I've got nothing left for Roger." She caught herself and added with more empathy, "I'm sorry he died. He didn't deserve that."

"Was it a tough divorce?"

"Yeah."

"How long were you married?"

"Nine years. What's this have to do with his murder?"

"Probably nothing. I'm trying to understand who he was, what kind of man."

"Well, there I can help you. Roger cared about only two things in life: Asia and old art. I came in third. Maybe fourth."

"Really?"

"It wasn't that way in the beginning."

"What do you mean?"

Henry looked back with keen interest. He was good at that, having a manner people seemed to trust. His non-judgmental expression was open to accepting whatever injustices she had to share. That appeared to draw her in. Mary Jo visibly relaxed. "In the beginning, it was all about me," she said, almost wistfully. "That didn't last. The thing you need to know about Roger is he was always trying out new things. For a time, I was his new thing. Then he lost interest. He does that, except for his interest in all things Asian. Come to think of it, I'm surprised he didn't marry an Asian woman." She laughed.

Henry considered her point. "If he was so deep into that stuff, why didn't he move to Japan or China? Immerse himself in the culture whole hog?"

She cracked a loaded smile. "He wanted to. I didn't. One of several reasons the marriage ended."

"That kind of move is a huge commitment."

"Roger spoke fluent Japanese and Mandarin. I don't. What was I supposed to do all day?"

"English is spoken in some areas, though that can still be a challenge. There's also the cultural difference if you're not prepared for it."

"And that was not what I'd signed up for."

A thought came to Henry. "You've been divorced for two years? He could've moved there anytime. Why didn't he?"

Her heart-shaped lips stretched with sarcasm. "Helps to have a job. Roger couldn't find work oversees, nothing decent."

"What about you, Mrs. Beckman. What do you do?"

"I'm a graphic designer. When you called this afternoon, I was in the middle of putting together a proposal for a big client. It's been an intense couple of weeks." Her eyes flicked to the front door then back at him. "Was there anything else?"

"Yes, can you think of anyone who'd want to harm Roger?"

She seemed surprised by the question. "No, I can't."

"When was the last time you spoke to him?"

"July. We owned a property together in Kentucky. It was on the market for a while. Finally sold this year. We had to sign the papers."

"How did he seem?"

"Seem? Same old Roger. No different."

"What about his friends or business acquaintances? Know any of them?"

"Not really. No one I'd remember."

"How about the Uptown neighborhood in Minneapolis? Can you think of anyone he knew there?"

That drew a blank.

Henry watched her carefully as he asked his next question. "Would you call Roger an honest man?"

"Yes."

"Was he ethical?"

"Hell, yeah!" she laughed.

"You sound very sure."

"The man was honest to a fault."

"Roger wouldn't do anything unscrupulous?"

She shook her head. "I had my issues with him, but dishonesty wasn't one of them. He was as ethical as they come."

"The reason I ask is that it's been suggested that your ex-husband might have stolen a Chinese artifact to sell."

Mary Jo Beckman handily dismissed that idea. "Steal an artifact? That's crazy. Roger would never do that."

"Never? Not even if it was worth millions?"

"Millions—" She seemed taken aback, turning the idea over in her head before abandoning it. "No, not even for that much money."

"Can you be sure? That's a huge amount of money. Too tempting for some to resist. People change."

"Not Roger," she insisted with an arresting certainty.

Henry didn't have a reply to that.

Seeing that, Mary Jo roused herself to her feet, her eyes glancing toward an ornamental clock on the fireplace mantel. "If there's nothing else, I really do need to get on with what I was doing."

"Thank you for your time."

In the Malibu later, Henry started the engine, circled the block and parked the car up the street from Mary Jo Beckman's Highland Park address. Too many thoughts were bouncing in his head; he wanted a few minutes to cull through them without the distraction of driving. He cut the engine and turned out the lights, settling back in the seat. The sun had set long ago. Nightfall dropped early in the Upper Midwest in October. His black sedan blended into the surrounding gloom. The tall trees obscured some street lights. He cracked a window to let in the cool evening air.

Beckman's ex-wife had issues with him yet was adamant about his upstanding ethics, a belief that contradicted Leland Hatcher's accusation. Henry also remembered Darlene Chow's comment. In her ID of Beckman's photo, she'd mentioned his reference to a piece of art he wanted to unload on the black market.

If that were true, how could he have expected to get away with it?

Under normal circumstances, he might.

That was the thing, though, wasn't it? Normal circumstances. What if this situation wasn't normal?

Blackmail was an old motive. Desperate people do desperate things. *Did Roger Beckman have a secret he didn't want revealed?* Henry parked that question for the moment in favor of a more important one: *What was Beckman doing in Uptown the night he was mugged?* Henry had checked. There were no Asian art galleries in the area, no import shops. Why was he there? Meeting someone? The thugs who jumped him weren't looking for money. They were after something else.

"I don't have it!" Henry could still hear the panicked voice pleading with his attackers. What was it Beckman no longer had? A bronze dragon head, perhaps? That fit into the general scheme of things.

A yellow glow flooded the front steps.

Mary Jo Beckman had just turned on her townhouse's front door light. Interesting, Henry wondered. Was she on her way out? As he was making his exit, she glanced at a clock. Perhaps she was expecting company. Why turn on the outside light?

He got his answer a minute later when a white station wagon drove by Henry's car and parked by the curb. A man got out and slammed shut the door. Hard soled shoes chuffed up the concrete steps to Mrs. Beckman's townhouse. Even in the dim light, Henry recognized Paul Rivera.

The door swung open, and Mary Jo ushered him inside.

"Well, well," Henry muttered. *Now things were getting interesting!*

He waited for a minute and returned to the townhouse, pushed the doorbell. The shock on Mary Jo Beckman's face when she swung open the door was satisfying.

"Hello, Mrs. Beckman. Sorry to disturb you again. I forgot to ask you a question. But I think I'm interrupting you. You have company."

Mary Jo struggled to find her voice. "Detective Lau…"

"Lau?" asked a concerned voice from inside. "Shit."

Henry stood on the doormat, eyebrows raised in innocent curiosity.

After a few uneasy seconds, Paul Rivera emerged from the living room to join Mary Jo by the door. Both looked as guilty as two teenagers caught making out in a high school janitorial closet.

The door closed behind Henry. This time he wasn't invited beyond the foyer, the meaning behind it clear: they wanted this visit to be brief. A single pendant light illuminated the space, a bluish-white glow devoid of warm tones and softness, like standing in an ice cave.

"This must look bad," Rivera finally said.

"It does." Henry agreed, looking to fan the flames of the others' guilt.

"I'm a friend," Rivera explained with a little too much urgency. "Mary Jo and I have known each other for years."

Henry wasn't buying it. "That's not really true, is it? You and Mrs. Beckman are more than friends."

There was an awkward silence.

Paul Rivera looked down at the area rug as if the right thing to say was woven in the pattern.

"You're right," Mary Jo confessed with a futile wave of her arm. "Paul and I are seeing each other. No point in hiding it. We were concerned it would make us look bad if you found out. That we'd be suspects in Roger's death."

"You are suspects."

Both looked back, startled.

"No," Rivera protested. "We had nothing to do with Roger's death."

Henry was stern. "The former wife of the murdered man and one of his co-workers are in a love relationship and acting suspiciously. Of course you're suspects. That doesn't mean I think either of you killed him. I do expect you to tell me the truth. So don't get cute with me, or I might change my mind," he warned in a voice as hard as flint. They thought they were being clever by hiding their relationship. It wasn't all that clever, and it only muddied the picture. "So," Henry's gaze shifted between them, "how long has this relationship been going on?"

Rivera cleared his throat. "About a year."

"The two of you got together after the divorce?"

"Yes."

"How did Roger feel about that?"

Another pause.

"He didn't know," replied the ex-Mrs. Beckman.

Henry raised an eyebrow. "Was there a reason for that?"

She nodded. "I told you before I'd seen Roger in July when we signed the papers for the Kentucky property. We got along fine. Roger was really good. A week later, he called me to talk." A stress-out Mary Jo Beckman crossed her arms over her chest. "He said it was good to see me again. Said he missed me. Said he'd changed and wondered if I'd be interested in getting back together with him."

Henry shot a glance at Rivera before turning back to Mary Jo. "I take it you said no."

She nodded. "Right. I told him I wasn't interested. It was too late for us, and that I was seeing someone else."

"How did he take that?"

"He was disappointed but understood."

"You didn't tell him that someone else was Dr. Rivera?"

"We didn't think it was a good idea. Too soon."

"And awkward," Rivera put in. "I see Roger fairly often. Who knew how he'd react, especially after what'd he said about still having feelings for Mary Jo?"

"We were going to tell Roger eventually," she insisted, "as soon as we felt he could handle the news."

"Well, thank you both. I won't intrude in your evening any longer." Henry reached for the door.

"Detective Lau," Mary Jo interrupted, "you said you forgot to ask me a question. What was it?"

Henry flashed an enigmatic smile. "You already answered it."

With that, he closed the door behind him, leaving that vague statement to hang in the air. The truth was there wasn't another question. He just wanted to see how the pair reacted when he confronted them about their relationship.

CHAPTER 12

The air was rich with the savory goodness of hamburger grease, grilled onions, and hot French fries. Henry Lau was tempted to put in a food order but didn't. Some temptations he could ignore.

"You haven't touched your beer," Alan Zhu remarked.

"Guess I'm not thirsty."

Alan looked at him. "It was your idea to come here."

"It was," agreed Henry with a self-deprecating nod.

From the adjacent table came the clink of bottles as the waitress gathered the empties. Twentyish, slightly on the plump side with pink hair, she seemed far older, as if weighed down by the job, life, or everything in between. She wore mascara and eye shadow like war paint, not so much to enhance her looks but, it seemed, as a mask. As she walked by, Henry met her dull gaze for a second, unresponsive to the smile of encouragement he offered, as if such pleasantries no longer mattered.

Henry rested his forearms on the small round table, his hands cupped around the amber bottle. He'd skipped Wing Chun that evening to visit Mary Jo Beckman. During the drive back from St. Paul, he realized he could detour into Minneapolis and get to Alan's *kwoon* before the end of class. He'd hoped to find Alan amenable to a quick beer at Omar's Bowl, a tiny bowling alley and bar two blocks from the school. The two friends sat near the large plate glass window under the glow of a purple neon sign. Beyond the glass loomed darkness and the headlights of passing cars.

"How're Mei-Yin and the kids?" Henry said, easing into the conversation, not quite ready to dive into the deep end of the pool.

"Mei-Yin got a promotion. Oh, she told me you need to come over for dinner sometime next month. Lori's learned to color in other colors besides red and black. And Stevie's in band now."

"What instrument?"

"The clarinet."

"Any good?"

"No, he stinks. But he loves it, and the kid practices his heart out." Alan rubbed the back of his hand across his mouth. "I have to say I didn't realize how much I hated the clarinet until two weeks ago. Sour notes are Stevie's specialty."

Henry cracked a smile. "That's too bad."

"He gets better every day."

"Then why do you make that face when you say it?"

"Because it's not true," Alan sighed. "Let me tell you something: a finished basement with decent soundproofing is a blessing."

Henry laughed. Alan's story wasn't that funny. Still, it was enough to amuse him and provide a needed distraction from what was on his mind. He could count on Alan, who could always lighten the mood.

And much more.

Alan was Henry's oldest and most devoted friend. They'd been pals forever, instant buddies since first sharing crayons in the second grade. Growing up, they did nearly everything together. When Alan got a chemistry set one Christmas, it was Henry who got the call to come over to help him make "cool stuff." That winter, they did experiments and made fuses out of cotton string and phenolphthalein. Not surprisingly, three months after Henry's seventeenth birthday, when he was bursting with excitement, the one person in the world he wanted to share the news with was Alan Zhu, who'd been away with his parents on vacation. On a sultry day in July after he had returned, the two friends hopped on their bikes and pedaled to Lake Nokomis.

It was early in the morning. The park was fairly empty, just a few runners and a woman walking her dog, which barked at the sailboats on the lake. Henry, ready to burst, patiently waited for Alan to tell his stories about camping in Yellowstone.

"It was fun, but, man, ten days is a long time to be with your family in the middle of nowhere!" Alan concluded, bright-eyed and full of laughter, a skinny Chinese kid with thick glasses and a mop of long hair whose ends danced on the shoulders of his Jackie Chan T-shirt. "So what did you do?"

Henry had waited his turn, which is not something an eager teenaged boy is usually good at. He knew when he got too excited, he could dominate the conversation and talk over people. He tried not to do that, especially with Alan, the one friend he had who appreciated his infectious enthusiasm, as Alan had called it. Henry leaned his ten-speed against the thick trunk of a nearby elm. For what he wanted to show, he needed his hands free.

"I'm doing the coolest thing ever! I'm learning kung fu!"

"No shit! For real?"

"Yeah."

"Way cool, dude!"

Way cool because the boys had played kung fu as kids, joked around a little in their early teens, though neither of them had actually taken martial arts lessons. The mere idea that Henry was going to a real marital arts school and learning real kung fu was the most exciting thing in their lives.

Henry stood within a few feet of Alan. "I've only been to four classes, but I'm starting to get the hang of it. Let me show you. Throw a punch at me."

Alan hesitated. "You sure? I don't want to hurt you. You can't be that good yet."

"Don't try to nail me. It's a demonstration. Go a little easy," he grinned suggestively.

That grin.

It was difficult to resist that grin. When Henry Lau was this jazzed about something, he sizzled like a Fourth of July sparkler. You may not have known the cause of the fire, yet you couldn't help but be dazzled by it.

"Okay," Alan agreed.

Henry tried to remember what he was supposed to do. He'd gone through the drill in his head a hundred times while his friend had been away.

Alan flicked out a left jab and followed it by a half-hearted right hook. Henry intercepted it with one arm and flipped down the other on top of it, causing Alan to jerk forward and down.

"Hey, that hurt!" He rubbed his forearm. "I went easy on *you*."

"Sorry. I got carried away."

"I know, you do that."

"I said I was sorry. C'mon, grab my arm now."

Alan, who could see into the future, eyed Henry with suspicion.

"Go ahead," Henry held out his arm, "I won't hurt you. I promise."

With some misgivings, Alan clamped his hand around Henry's forearm. Henry pivoted his body and flipped over his forearm. Alan looked down and was startled to see Henry now had a grip on *his* arm. Before that lesson had time to sink in, Henry moved in closer. Alan tilted backward and felt knuckles pressed against his windpipe. After achieving the result he wanted, Henry stepped back triumphantly.

Alan looked back with big puppy eyes. "Dude, that's awesome!"

"Yeah, and I probably didn't do it right."

"It was still awesome."

"It's called Wing Chun. It was Bruce Lee's original fighting system, the core of all the other stuff he did later. We practice at close range. Most martial arts try to keep a distance, but this one wants to get in close and stay close. It kinda freaks people out."

"It does," Alan nodded vigorously.

"So, what do you think? Is this good stuff?"

"It's freakin' awesome!" Alan nodded.

Henry had hoped for that reaction. A grand plan had formed in his young mind, one which his best friend would be a part of if he were willing. Henry eyed his friend hopefully. "If you joined the school, then we could train together outside class. Interested?"

Alan was. And with that was born a mutual passion for a martial art which had lasted for over three decades, one that had further cemented the bond between them.

Bowling pins crashed in the background. Fresh hamburger patties sizzled on the grill.

Henry fingered the bottle in his hand, picked at the label. "I'm thinking of retiring," he announced in a quiet voice barely audible above the buzz and din of people around them.

The pale amber bottle en route to Alan's mouth hovered in the air. He lowered it. "Did you just say something about retiring?"

"Yeah."

"Like hang up your badge and go fishin' retire or retire from Wing Chun?"

"Retire from police work."

"You just got back on active duty."

"I know."

"You spent all that time in the hospital and at home working to get healthy again. You're the guy who told me he couldn't wait to get back on the street." Alan adjusted his black-framed glasses to give

Henry one of his be-honest-with-me faces. "That's why you wanted to meet."

Henry bobbed his head, slumping against the wooden chair back. "I'm not sure what it is. Maybe I'm tired of the job, not sure I can do it anymore."

"Your back bothering you again?"

"Sometimes—but that's not it. Or my knees. Nothing physical." He picked at the bottle label with his thumbnail.

When nothing further was offered, Alan spoke up. "So, what's the reason?"

Henry took a pull from his bottle. Caught a glimpse of his reflection in the window and was surprised at how tired he looked. "I'm working this case," he began introspectively. "This evening I spoke to the ex-wife of the murdered man. They'd been divorced for a while. She said the reason for the split was because her ex was too obsessed with his work and hobbies. She got tired of coming in second." Shifting in his seat, Henry searched his friend's face. "Was that me? As a teenager—in college—would you have called me obsessed with kung fu?"

Alan opened his mouth to speak and held off as a young couple took the seats at the table next to them, happy with each other and oblivious to the world. The waitress—she of the heavy eye paint—handed them menus. Alan leaned forward and was blunt.

"Yes, that was you. You were obsessed with kung fu."

Henry replied with a slow, deliberate nod. It stung to hear the unvarnished truth, even if it was what he'd expected.

Alan continued, not mincing his words yet also delivering them with an air of understanding. "For years Wing Chun was the only thing you were passionate about. You were the guy who practiced two or three hours every day, six to seven days a week. That's the kind of dedication it takes to excel at anything."

Another slow nod.

"Remember," Alan said, "you're the guy who convinced me to move to San Jose with him so we could go to college together and study under Eric Kwan."

Henry's gaze dropped to the tabletop, where his forefinger traced out a pattern. "Doug thought I was being selfish."

"I remember."

Henry looked up and smiled. That's right; Alan was there for that, too. The move to California had upset his older brother far more than their parents. Douglas Lau had grown up with the dreams and responsibilities of being the firstborn son to his immigrant parents. He'd been pushed to succeed, encouraged to go into accounting because it was a respected profession that paid well, whereas number two son got to do what he wanted, didn't have the same pressure put on him. Henry knew that, even exploited it when he was a kid. Over time he did feel a little sorry for Doug, though that feeling dimmed as his brother continued to criticize his life choices.

"Kung fu is not a career," he took care to point out. "It's a hobby. What're you gonna do with that? Be a bouncer? Bodyguard? Grow up, Henry, get a real job."

Grow up and get a real job.

According to Doug, Henry's devotion to adolescent distractions were not the things real men—men with families and a sense of responsibility—indulged in.

Henry was brought back to the present by the scritch of a chair leg against the hardwood floor. A few tables away, a loud voice said something that got lost in the din of conversation. He didn't look up immediately, initially only noticing a pair of black boots. Black harness boots with straps and stainless steel rings sticking out from a pair of ragged jeans. The owner of the boots had shoulder-length dark hair and a hooked nose. Boot Boy had company, an oval-faced man with a blond crew cut.

Henry tilted back the bottle of Amstel Light and took a long drink.

Alan studied his friend with growing concern. "That woman really got to you, didn't she? So her ex-husband was obsessive. What does that have to with—?" He sat up suddenly at a realization. "This is about Kay, isn't it?"

Henry didn't answer.

"This month is the anniversary of her death," Alan remembered.

"This week," Henry corrected.

"Is that where this is coming from? You have to stop beating yourself up, man. That was over twenty years ago. You didn't mug her. You didn't kill her. Some weaselly ass punk did. There's nothing you could have done."

Henry's eyes flicked up and bore into Alan's like a hot poker. "I could have been there for her."

The silence between them hung heavily for a second.

"But you weren't there," Alan finally said delicately, not as an accusation nor bitter fact, just the plain truth. "You can't change history."

"I know."

"And it still eats at you. I know you'll never forgive yourself. You need too, a little."

Henry raised both hands in a vague gesture and let them fall again to the table.

Those first months after Kay's murder had been the toughest, the months afterward not much better. Henry had lost his way. Wing Chun had been his rock. No matter what else, his training regimen, his commitment to the classes, they gave him focus, a reason for being. Now that 'reason for being' left a bitter taste as he understood that his dogged devotion to his martial art might have cost him the love of his life.

His rock had developed a seismic crack.

But not Alan Zhu.

Alan, who was always there for him. Alan, who'd pulled up roots and moved across the country with him to share Henry's dream and adventure. Alan, who made Henry care about life again. Patient and perceptive Alan, who now sat across the table at Omar's, protectively watching over him now, as then, as he might an injured sparrow.

Henry tried to reassure his friend. "I won't get maudlin on you. This isn't about Kay, not really." That might not have been entirely true, he realized, not sure himself. His forefinger drew a line through the beads of sweat on his bottle as he looked for the right words.

"What's bothering you?" Alan finally had to ask, waving off the waitress. Bad time for an interruption.

Henry Lau ran a hand through his thick shag of hair and frowned thoughtfully. "All those years ago when we moved to San Jose, Doug chewed my ass for being frivolous, about not being serious about my career. I blew him off then. Was he right? Did I waste all those years training in kung fu? Did I sacrifice too much?"

Alan was taken aback. "I don't know what to say. Henry, being a top Wing Chun practitioner was your dream."

Best kung fu fighter in the world. That had been his impossible dream. A boy's dream. Vain and unrealistic. He'd known that as a teenager. Still, the young Henry Lau had fervently believed he might someday be counted among the top ten or twenty martial artists on the planet, and with enough hard work and dedication and the right teachers, he could achieve that goal. He was certain of it.

"I think I've been chasing a shooting star all these years," Henry confessed with more disappointment than he'd intended. "I put everything on hold so I could dedicate myself to being the best Wing

Chun fighter since Yip Man." He hitched his shoulders. "It never happened. Not even close. What do I have to show for it?"

From the quick shake of his head, it was clear Alan didn't like the direction of this conversation. "Where is this coming from? Look, I know you already know this, but I guess I need to say it again. Those top fighters you want to be among make their living as fighters. Those top martial artists spent decades learning and training. It's their job. They worked at it eight hours or more a day. Every day. A top tennis champion practices every day. A world-class dancer is no different. Unless you turn professional or live in a world where you could train all day and not worry about making a living, you're going to have to compromise."

Henry knew that. The problem with the heart is that it can't always accept the simple truth. Had he squandered his life in pursuit of an unattainable dream? Sacrificed a chance at a happy, comfortable life with a wife and family?

Alan looked his friend squarely in the eye, and there was iron in his words. "*You worked damned hard to get your dream.* You even moved to Hong Kong to train full-time for two years, trained like a demon. Like five hours a day, five days a week! Sparred like hell. Fought in a bunch of fights. You did your best."

"It wasn't good enough," Henry glowered back, the fingers of his free hand curling into a fist. I'm forty-four. My prime years as a martial artist are behind me."

"Well, I wouldn't be too sure about that," Alan countered. "Yeah, you're too old to be a professional brawler. But look at Eric Kwan. The guy's in his early sixties and he's still amazing. He can do far more with less effort than when he was our age. He understands his body can handle only so much. You know the lesson I learned a while back?"

"What?"

"That hard work and merit don't always pay off. Those things matter, sure, but hard work by itself doesn't guarantee success. Being in the right place at the right time can make a big difference."

And then Alan said something that made the back of Henry's neck tingle.

"We call the goals we desire most dreams," he said, "because they're out of our reach. A lucky few achieve their dreams. Most people don't. Do you know what my dream was?"

"To be taller and better looking?"

Alan lowered his head and considered Henry over the rim of his black frames. "Besides that. I wanted to be good at whatever I chose to do and enjoy my family and living my life. Remember when I was a manager at the CPA firm? I supervised ten people. Had a great title, made lots of money. Was rising up in my profession. It was killing me, putting in sixty to seventy hours every week. I had almost no life outside of work. Finally, I had to give it up. Two other guys and I opened our own CPA firm, took a twenty percent pay cut to do it. However, now I mainly get to work regular hours with less stress and spend more time with Mei-Yin and the kids. I get to enjoy my life instead of being a slave to work." Alan leaned in. He removed his glasses and pinched the bridge of his nose. Nearsighted, he'd always worn glasses as far back as Henry could remember. Sincere brown eyes searched deep into his. "I don't know what to tell you. Some dreams are catchable. Others not so much. The real question you have to ask is the effort worth it? If it is, then maybe the end goal doesn't matter. Not everyone gets to be an Eric Kwan, y'know."

Eric Kwan was a grandmaster who didn't call himself a grandmaster. Other masters and grandmasters used the term because they respected not only his skill but the man. His skills always seemed to improve. No matter how much better Henry got, Kwan had improved more. It was inspiring, showing how much he could attain.

However, there was a flip side to it. Henry had noticed that after all those decades Eric Kwan had been teaching, after all the students he'd trained, not one of them approached his level of skill. Not because he held back. A great truth had occurred to Henry some years earlier, echoing what Alan was saying, which was that not everyone who climbs Everest makes it to the summit. Most musicians never get considered for a Grammy. Most football players don't make it to the Super Bowl. Most scientists will never win a Nobel Prize, and not every martial artist can be an Eric Kwan or Bruce Lee.

And maybe, Henry had started to wonder; he shouldn't try to be. It had been a bitter pill to swallow. You can fool yourself, but you can't fool reality. There's a point after walking into a solid brick wall so many times that a person must realize there is no door.

Wisdom comes at its own sweet time and not always with the answers we want.

Alan regarded his friend philosophically. "Let me tell you something. Maybe you don't think you've achieved greatness. You have, though."

"Oh?"

"You've been a great friend."

Henry's eyes shot up to meet his gaze.

"I'm serious," Alan said from the heart. "I was a skinny, introverted kid. You pushed me into things that made me better and gave me confidence. When I was stressed out at my old job, you gave me the courage to quit and start my own business. That was scary, but you told me I could do it. I wouldn't be where I am if I hadn't known you. You even gave me money to help start my Wing Chun school. Didn't want it back."

Henry swallowed. Smiled back with affection. "You're my main man. Always have been."

The two friends talked further. By the time they left Omar's, Henry was no longer sure what he was feeling; his emotions felt like waves crashing against the rocks, going this way and that.

The night air had a bite to it as they stepped outside and parted ways. Henry shoved his hands into his coat pockets, kept his head down, and shuffled along on the sidewalk, lost in thought as he tried to sort through his feelings,

From behind came the muted scuff of hard shoes against the sidewalk. Had he not been so preoccupied, Henry would have noticed. Had he been walking at his usual brisk pace, those behind him might not have gotten as close. By the time he rounded the back of Omar's and stepped into the parking lot, it was too late.

A pair of rough hands shoved him violently into a parked Jeep Wrangler.

CHAPTER 13

Henry stumbled hard against the Wrangler. His head barely swung round in time to see the fist smacking into his face, followed by a gut punch. He dropped to the asphalt, back sliding against the door. Head throbbing, he blinked again and again, desperate to clear his vision, though not in time to stop a hard kick to his thigh.

He nearly passed out from the pain.

"Had enough, asshole?" taunted a raw voice.

Another kick flew in. Henry barely managed to raise a *kup jarn* smashing elbow to protect his head. A second attacker rushed in with a wide punch. Aching, confused, dizzy, Henry angled his arm to intercept the incoming fist, which collided with the edge of his forearm, a forearm hardened by years of *lap sau* and tempered against the *mook yan jong,* the wooden man.

"Gaaaa!" The puncher cried out, nursing his fingers.

Henry slumped against the Jeep, braced for the next attack as he fought rising nausea. The Wrangler's frame, he realized, was jacked up higher than usual. Flattening out, he rolled underneath. There was just enough room. Under the protection of the metal frame, his head had enough time to clear a little. He could make out two pairs of shins and feet. One set of legs terminated in black harness boots with straps and steel rings he recognized from Omar's. Boots kicked out at him, just missing.

"Think you're smart, fucker?" Boot Boy was saying. "You're dead meat. This'll teach ya to mess with us."

Who were these guys? What was this about?

Through the throbbing of his head, he remembered:

His sidearm.

Henry pulled the Glock 22 from his jacket.

"Back off!" he said, sliding his badge across the asphalt, the parking lot light glistening off its metal. "I'm a cop. And I have a weapon."

"A cop?" said a wary voice.

"Fuck." From the other.

"How do we know that badge is real?"

"Bend down and you'll see my sidearm aimed at your face." The shins stepped back, and the owner of them bent down. A pair of rough faces came into view. Henry's pulse beat in his ears like a bass drum as he presented his firearm.

"Shit! He does have a gun."

Without further comment the men tore off like spooked jackrabbits, their hurried footsteps receding into the night.

Henry's ears pricked at every sound. With a monster headache and screaming ribs, he wasn't sure he could've fired a clean shot in the cramped space. After a minute, the danger seemed over. Cautiously, he maneuvered out from under the chassis, watchful for another attack. None came. He groaned to his feet, anxious eyes scanning the dark streets. They were gone.

He limped to the Malibu, his thigh screaming the whole way. Across the street, a man and woman entered a convenience store. Henry did another quick scan. No one was watching him. Satisfied, he let his guard down and relaxed. Opening his car door, he climbed in with some effort and slumped against the seat, making sure all the doors were locked. He massaged his leg for two minutes until the burn diminished, then sat quietly for five more minutes to let the rest of him calm down. His vision cleared and his body feeling somewhat restored, he inserted the key in the ignition—

And paused.

Through the dull blur of images knocking about in his head, one idea elbowed its way to the front of the line. If he were to act on it, he should do it now, even though it would've been easier to give up and go home to soak his body in a hot bath and sweat out the lousy memory of the evening. But Henry Lau was stubborn and pissed off enough to do this one last task before calling it a day. He pulled out the key and grimaced as he climbed out of his car, then walked back to Omar's.

When he asked to see the manager, Henry was shown to a man behind the bar, a roundish man with curly black hair and a handlebar mustache. White shirt, open collar, sleeves rolled up to the elbows. He made a broad circular motion as he wiped down the bar. "I'm Omar Melish," he said with a welcoming smile. "What can I do for you?"

Henry showed his ID. "I was here this evening with a friend. We sat by the big window."

"Yes," Omar said without missing a beat, "I remember you. Has there been trouble?" His eyes drifted to the fresh abrasions on Henry's cheek.

"Two men jumped me after I left here. I don't hold you responsible," Henry assured, which immediately put the bar owner at ease. "They were also customers. They sat at that table. Early thirties, one had a blond crew cut. The other had long dark hair and beard stubble. Did you see them?"

"I did. Table nine. They weren't regulars. I really can't tell you anything else. Let me get the waitress."

A large metal pot clanked from the kitchen, nearly masking the laughter of a group of friends in the restaurant area, followed by the crack and tumble of bowling pins. Within seconds Omar appeared with the waitress with the pink hair and bold eye makeup. "This is Janine," he said. "She waited on the men you mentioned."

Henry tossed her a half-smile. Janine returned it unused. He gave a brief description of his two assailants. "Do you remember them?"

She shifted her weight and snorted. "Hell, yeah. The dark-haired dude asked me out. I said no."

Looking at her closely for the first time, he realized she couldn't be older than twenty-eight, yet she had the demeanor, posture, and world-weary attitude of a woman decades older. Looking beyond the thick makeup, Henry was surprised to see a sweet face hardened by too many rough dances with adversity. "You've never seen them before?"

"No."

"How'd they pay for their drinks?"

"Cash."

Too bad. A check or credit card, or phone app would give him a name.

"Did you catch anything they said?"

She shook her head. "Sorry. They stopped talking whenever I got to the table."

Another strikeout. Not surprising. This had been a long shot.

His thigh was throbbing from the abuse it had taken, and he was careful not to put his full weight on that leg. Henry leaned against the bar for relief, frowned at the floor before looking up again. "You said the dark-haired guy asked you out?"

"Yeah. Kept saying what a great a time he'd show me. Like I haven't heard that a gazillion times! Said he had this real sweet ride, a red convertible, and how fine I'd look riding in it." Janine looked like she was about to gag. "I've heard 'em all, believe me. I told him it was October, and riding with the top down in this weather would be kinda dumb."

"How'd he take that?"

"It shut him up."

Henry chuckled. He liked her take no crap attitude. "Anything else you can remember? Where they were from? That kind of thing."

She shook her head again when she suddenly recalled something. Her pouty mouth curved sideways, a spark of remembrance behind mascaraed eyes. "I can tell you one thing. The guy with the long hair smelled like gas."

"Gasoline?"

"Like he took a bath in it."

Henry's head cocked sideways. *Now that tidbit might be useful.* "Thanks, Janine, that might be helpful." He slipped her ten dollars.

He glanced at his watch. Just after ten-fifteen. One last thing to do before he could call it a night. Strike while the iron was hot, as the saying goes. Tomorrow might find him in a forgiving mood. In the warm sunlight of a new day, he might be willing to overlook having been jumped. Tonight, though, he was too pissed off and too worked up to forgive. He could turn the other cheek another day.

CHAPTER 14

Henry was early to work the next morning. The Gillette police station was unusually quiet, and he liked it that way. He was alone at one of the four desks in the Crime Room reserved for the detectives. Although the sign on the wall said Criminal Investigation Department, the space was commonly called the Crime Room, sometimes the Bullpen. The dispatcher's phone rang from down the hall. The murmur of the early shift gathering at the coffee station, the smell of fresh microwaveable popcorn. Ernie Sykes was making breakfast; the man practically lived off buttered popcorn.

Henry stared at his computer screen. The incident report would not fill out itself, no matter how much he willed it. Trouble was his mind was a dandelion seed in the wind, buffeted about by any undercurrent: Work. His health. Old friends he'd lost contact with. Last night.

His shoulder was stiff and left leg tender and sore from the attack, but he'd survived. He kept thinking about the conversations he had the night before with Mary Jo Beckman and Alan.

Henry grumbled. *Was life supposed to get more complicated as you got older? Wasn't it supposed to get easier with all that life experience?* Apparently not.

His arm brushed against a pen. It rolled off the desk. Reaching down to the floor, he felt a stab of pain in his abdomen just where the boot toe had collided into it at Omar's. He grimaced, retrieved the pen and sat back as a blast from the past invaded his thoughts.

The twinge threw him back twenty-three years, the second year into training with Sifu Erik Kwan in California. Henry had been a promising young student with a personal recommendation from his

Minnesota teacher and was allowed admittance into the much-coveted advanced sparring sessions. These special after-class sessions were for students whose behavior and ability had proven them ready. The sessions were intended to develop skills in more realistic, more intense situations and not degenerate into undisciplined slugfests. Henry's success early on was mixed. After one particularly rough encounter, Sifu Kwan took aside the achy, battered young student for a private talk. Kwan had a calm and helpful quality that naturally drew people to him. Beneath that calm—seen in the sparkle in his eye—was a hint of kinetic energy waiting to be unleashed. You paid attention to this man.

"You have skill," Kwan complimented Henry. "Chiang Li taught you well. I've been watching you spar, and I see a pattern. You try too hard to win."

Henry was all attention, soaking in every word from this respected master.

Kwan continued. "You do well against someone below or at your skill level. Against an opponent stronger than you or one with higher skill, you try to force a victory instead of letting it happen."

A confused Henry came back, "But aren't I supposed to be aggressive?"

It was then that Sifu Kwan spoke the words that would change Henry forever. "Yes, be aggressive when it makes sense. But not all the time. Only a fool runs into a closed door and expects to get through. You watch, you feel for an opening, let the energy tell you what to do and when to do it. Charge in when you know your opponent's defense is weak. Probe. Yet don't fully commit unless you feel you can make it collapse. Even then, you need to be ready to abandon the attack if your opponent puts up a strong barrier."

"You mean a counter move?"

"Think of the door, Henry. If it's open, you can run through. However, if the door is closed, do you still run into it? No, you have to be ready to change direction when you hit an immovable obstacle."

Kwan demonstrated, extending his bent arm. "Push," he instructed.

Henry pressed against his sifu's arm. It was springy yet did not collapse. From his experience, he knew better than to try anything.

Kwan said, "The door is closed. Don't force it open. Now try again."

This time when he pushed, Henry felt his teacher's arm give a little.

"Push hard," Kwan said.

Henry pushed harder and the arm collapsed. Henry rushed in to pin the arm against Kwan's chest. The impact made him teeter back slightly, robbing his balance. Henry stepped back.

Kwan nodded with approval. "Yes, the door was open. Now again, with the same pressure."

His bent arm came out again. This time when Henry touched it he felt a stiff energy. Kwan was pushing back with equal pressure. "More," the latter insisted. Obeying, Henry pushed harder—

And then nothing!

The resisting force had disappeared. But Henry's forward energy had nowhere to go except to continue forward. Before he could do anything, he stumbled into Sifu Kwan's other hand, which thumped him on the chest. Startled, he followed his teacher's eyes and saw that the hand of Kwan's initial contact arm now rested against Henry's stomach, poised to deliver a nasty palm strike.

Kwan smiled thinly. "This time you ran into a closed door and couldn't move out of the way of my attack. That's because you tried too hard to get through at the wrong moment. Behind the closed door was a tiger in waiting. See the difference?"

He did!

"Always remember, if your opponent's door is open, be fearless rushing in. If your opponent's door is closed, don't force it open; test it first. If his door is ajar, try to open it. But use caution in case there's a tiger on the other side."

Henry humbly thanked his teacher for this new insight.

Only a fool runs into a closed door and expects to get through.

Words Henry never forgot.

Words to live by outside the *kwoon*.

Henry fondly recalled the memory. Hard lessons from a special time. Lately, he'd found himself thinking back to those days more often.

He looked up, realizing he was drifting and needed to finish the incident report when he became aware of noise at the supply cabinet. Then something else: hard-soled shoes getting louder on the vinyl floor—

Stopping abruptly behind him.

Henry turned. Chief Bowman was surveying the fresh abrasions on his cheek and neck. "Please tell me the other guy is in worse shape."

With a deadpan expression, Henry replied, "I was helping a crippled old lady cross the street. She didn't want to go and put up one hell of a fight."

Bowman's dark mustache cocked as he smiled. He lowered one butt cheek on the edge of Henry's desk. "What happened?"

That was something Henry respected about Bowman: he liked getting his information right before offering an opinion. Henry recapped the incident at Omar's Bowl. Afterward, Bowman's bushy eyebrows sat up. "Lucky thing that Jeep was there."

"Yeah, lucky."

"I thought you kung fu guys could take on eight guys at a time."

"You've watched too many movies, Chief. Anyone can be surprised. No one is invincible."

"Glad to hear you say that. Some guys are too opinionated. You know Dick Puckett over at Minneapolis PD says Wing Chun doesn't work against boxers and wrestlers."

Henry had met Sergeant Puckett. A big man with a big mouth and a bigger ego who thought he knew everything about martial arts. Henry wasn't sure why Bowman thought it necessary to bring up Puckett. Was there a hidden message? If so, he had a ready answer. "Chief, you can make that claim against any martial art. There are so many fighting styles. Different schools emphasize different training. Some are more sport-based. Others self-defense centered. The person counts as much—if not more—than what he trains in."

Bowman nodded. "True enough. Glad to hear you're not as dogmatic as some martial artists."

Henry answered with a leisurely shrug. "I have a lot of real-life experience."

"So I've heard. I keep forgetting that."

There'd been a lot of fights and misadventures during Henry's Hong Kong years, a crucible of lingering anger and hard experience after Kay's death.

"*What the hell happened to you?*" broke in a new voice.

Janet had appeared from around the corner and came to an abrupt halt when she saw the scratches on Henry's face.

No one said a word.

Slipping off her jacket, she draped it over the back of her chair and, in one fluid motion, settled in the seat with rapt attention.

The conversation had skidded to a halt. In the pointed silence that followed, Janet glanced between the two men. "Did I interrupt something?"

"No, I was finished." Bowman hoisted himself up, smoothed out his trousers, smiled at them both, then sauntered off toward his office with the air of one who has done a great service.

After he was out of earshot, Janet tossed her uncle a meaningful look. "Are you going to tell me what little adventure you got into last evening?"

Henry repeated the story of Omar's Bowl. Janet's eyes went wide with concern.

"Sons of bitches," she said. "Did you recognize either of them?"

"No, never seen them before."

"So they weren't the same guys who jumped Beckman, the guys you fought off."

"Different guys."

Janet cocked a slender eyebrow. "Think they're connected to the dragon case?"

"No idea."

"Things are getting strange. I can't say for sure, but I think I'm being followed."

His eyes narrowed.

She added, "I first noticed it last night. I was at the Minneapolis Institute of Art, waiting to talk to David Nakagawa. Oh, I got us an interview this afternoon. Wasn't easy, let me tell you. The man's a piece of work. Full of himself. Anyway, I noticed this guy in the parking lot watching me. I ignored it, thinking I was imagining that was what he was doing. Well, this morning I stopped to fill up my gas tank, and I saw him again at another pump."

"Coincidence?" Henry posited.

Janet made a face. "I would have thought so, except it was the way he looked at me. Like I was a target. Not at all casual. Gave me the creeps."

"Did we stir up a hornet's nest with Nakagawa? Could this be one of his guys?"

"Nakagawa must be pretty uptight to sic a security guy on us for—what? I mean, I barely spoke to him." Janet's mouth turned down. A second later, she was taken by a new thought. "Those guys who jumped you last night. Were they robbers?"

"No. They just wanted to beat the crap out of me."

"Why?"

"They didn't say."

"Have you pissed off anyone lately?"

"Can't say. But I might have an answer soon."

"How's that?"

"An ID."

"Of your attackers? I'm impressed. How'd you swing that?"

He shared the story told to him by the waitress at Omar's. "One of them smelled like gas. There's a slim chance they'd filled their gas tank at a nearby station. I checked every station within a two-mile radius of Omar's. If you're curious, there are seven."

"And?" She looked back expectantly.

"I had a general description of the men and their vehicle. The night manager at a Gas America on Hennepin thinks he saw them. They have a CCTV surveillance system. I'm going back to view the DVR player."

"You did all that after Omar's? You must've got home late. No wonder you look tired. Did you get any sleep?"

"A few hours. Took a long hot shower first."

"Good detective work, partner." Her soft brown eyes rested on him with open affection. "I'm glad you weren't badly hurt."

I'm glad you weren't badly hurt.

The same words. The same inflection.

They swept in the ghost of a major milestone in Henry Lau's life: the day he met Kay McAdams.

Janet didn't resemble her in any way, not in face or form, yet when she uttered those words, they came out exactly as they had twenty-two years earlier. A different voice. A different person. A different time.

He'd been living in San Jose for two years, a junior at Stanford. It happened during week five of *CHIN 018: Culture, Spirit, and Warfare in Ancient China*. The highlight of his day was waiting for the Girl, tall and sleek, with sparkling eyes and a heart-catching smile. She'd walk the lecture hall steps to take a seat six rows down from him. Every so often, he'd catch her profile as she turned to her neighbor. She was lovely in a simple fresh-scrubbed manner. A cute yet elegant nose. Beautiful, expressive eyes beneath dark bangs. And a smile to die for. He'd count himself lucky if that smile were ever directed toward him.

Not likely. Henry was a nobody to her. He didn't even know her name. Once when she spoke up in class, he was delighted to learn the Girl had a voice as lovely as the rest of her. And then came the day Henry had answered Professor Cochran's question regarding the Ming Dynasty. Henry's grandparents had lived in Hunan then, and he told one of their stories. Several students had turned to look at him during the telling, including the Girl. That incident had been the Everest of their interaction.

Until the day of soreness.

When he moved to California to study under Eric Kwan, Henry had thrown himself into it, heart and soul. Among the teachings of the Leung Sheung branch of Wing Chun, as embodied by Kwan, was using only "just enough" energy to get the job done. No more. No less. More wasn't better. It could be wasteful and put you at a disadvantage. It was a fundamental teaching that sometimes eluded the younger male students with testosterone-driven muscles and excitable ambitions. After one class, Henry worked out with one of Kwan's advanced students and got too aggressive, too sloppy, ending up with an elbow in the face. The next day Henry wore the mark of that encounter. His back was also a little stiff. After Cochran's class ended, he gladly let the other students in his row edge past him to join the exodus in the aisle.

When he was ready, he slowly lifted himself out of the clothbound seat. Halfway up, he winced and became aware of a skirt and a shapely pair of legs standing in the aisle near him.

"Are you okay?"

His eyes flicked up.

It was the Girl. She stood on the step, clutching her book bag as other students angled past her toward the exit.

Henry grimaced from a muscle twinge as he stood, then flashed a crooked smile. "Worked out a little too hard yesterday."

"What kind of workout? Wrestling alligators?"

"Kung fu."

"Playing at kung fu?" she mocked good-naturedly. The tone was familiar to him. He'd heard it once from a middle-aged woman who'd thought he meant he was goofing around imitating some Chop Socky movie. The Girl was sweeter in her mockery, and he didn't mind.

"No," Henry replied, "real kung fu."

"Oh," came the response. With it, he could see in her face, a new understanding. "I'm Kay."

He gladly took the outstretched hand. Soft and warm, he didn't want to let go of it.

"Henry."

The ice between them was broken. They continued to talk as they walked out of the classroom.

"Kung fu, huh?"

"Yeah."

"Is your interest in kung fu why you're taking Cochran's class?"

"It's a break from my major, Criminal Justice. I guess it's a cultural interest. You may not have noticed, but I'm Chinese."

Kay laughed. "You're funny!"

She flashed him one of her smiles, and he felt like a million dollars.

The walk ended all too soon. Outside, Kay waved goodbye and veered off to her next class. Henry watched her lithe frame merge into the crowd, thrilled he'd been able to meet her, and lamented how brief the encounter had been, as well as how unlikely it was they'd talk again. A week later, he was convinced of it when Cochran's class started and someone else was sitting in Kay's usual seat. His heart sank. Had she dropped the class? Three minutes later an out of breath Kay quietly entered the classroom and, seeing her seat taken, slid into the empty seat in Henry's row, the seat next to him.

He couldn't believe his luck!

She settled into her chair and smiled at Henry as Professor Cochran began his lecture. It was going to be a good day, he knew, whatever else happened. As wonderful as that moment was, what he would always treasure above all else was her parting words to him that day when they'd met one week earlier after he'd gotten banged up a little. Words that did not promise anything, words he took care not to read too much into beyond their honest sincerity. As Kay had turned to go to her next class, she paused to say, "I'm glad you weren't badly hurt."

With that simple phrase, Kay McAdams had stolen his heart.

"Henry..."

The snap of fingers.

"Hello, are you with me?" Janet said, waving at him.

He blinked, focusing on her. "Sorry. I was thinking of something."

"I could see that. Having a breakthrough on the case?"

He returned a vague expression she couldn't quite fathom. Janet opened her mouth to press him further but stopped when Henry's cell phone rang. "Detective Lau," he said.

"Detective Lau, this is Shen Jiang-Li of the Peoples Republic of China. We met the other day at Mr. Hatcher's office."

"Yes, Minister Shen, I remember."

Janet sat up at the name, her face attentive.

"I've returned from New York," Shen said in her lightly accented voice. "I was wondering if there's been any progress with your investigation into Professor Beckman's death."

"Some." He knew what her next question would be. Henry suspected it was only out of politeness that she didn't lead off with it.

"Any luck finding the missing dragon head?"

And there it was!

"Not yet."

From the background noise, it sounded as though the Chinese minister was in a public place, perhaps even a restaurant. Henry caught a sense of voices in the background, the sound of dinner plates, the whirl of an electric fan.

Shen asked, "I want to talk with you on an important matter."

"Go ahead. I'm listening."

"No, not over the telephone. I don't trust phones. In person."

Henry didn't have any new information to share with the minister and was about to tell her as much when he learned that it was she who had news to share.

"There's something you should know about Leland Hatcher."

CHAPTER 15

Janet observed Henry's body language and his tone of voice. Direct. Polite with a touch of familiarity. Noncommittal. Her ears tingled at the words: "When?" and "Where?"

After the call ended, she made a loud clearing of throat. "I take it that was our new friend from Beijing."

"Yes, she just got back in town and wants to meet with us this morning. Says she has something to tell us about Lee Hatcher."

"What was wrong with the phone?"

"Not secure enough, I guess. She wants to meet in person."

Janet smiled a subversive little smile as she swiveled her chair toward him. "The lady likes you. She wants to see you."

"What are you talking about?"

"Seriously, didn't you notice the way Shen was flirting with you in Hatcher's office? She barely gave me a glance. Those seductive brown eyes were directed at you." Janet made a kissy face.

He stared at her.

"Admit it," Janet pressed.

His black eyebrows turned down.

"I'm right, admit it. And you enjoyed it. Shen Jiang-Li is young and pretty—"

"Too young for me."

True. The Chinese minister was close to Janet's age. An age difference but one not unheard of.

Stop that.

Janet chided herself for going down that route. She was letting her imagination run wild. In truth, she didn't believe Shen had romantic interests in Henry. Most likely, it was a ploy, a charm offensive intended to entice him to volunteer information about the missing dragon head.

Wasn't it?

Janet was disturbed by another possibility.

What if she were wrong?

The thought hadn't occurred to her. What if Shen Jiang-Li had flirted with Henry because she liked him? Not a very Chinese ministerish thing to do. But what did Janet know about cultural ministers from Beijing? China had seen changes and modernization over the last few decades. Shen was an educated, seemingly worldly young woman who was likely comfortable with both fashionable western attire and non-traditional Chinese mores.

Well, why wouldn't Shen Jiang-Li find Henry attractive? And why, Janet wondered, should she care if this minx from the old country tossed her uncle a coquettish glance or two? He was mature enough not to be swept away by such obvious tactics. Wasn't he? She reminded herself not to read too much into things.

Before the meet-up with the flirtatious Ms. Shen, Henry had another item on the agenda, which led them on a field trip into South Minneapolis.

A cold blast of conditioned air slammed into Janet's face the moment she entered Gas America. Sweater temps inside the convenience store while outdoors October clung in vain to summer. Feeling the chill, Janet nestled into the warmth of her sports jacket. The convenience store was typical of many businesses in early autumn in the Upper Midwest whose HVAC systems hadn't committed to the change of season.

The counter was strewn with colorful lottery card teasers for Lotto, Gopher 5, and Powerball. The scrolling LED sign of the nearby lottery machine proclaimed the jackpot was at 200 MILLION

DOLLARS!!! The clerk, a short, grandmotherly woman with a cherubic face and generous hips, handed her customer his change before shifting friendly eyes toward them.

"May I help you?" She glanced between Henry and Janet.

Henry presented his badge wallet. "My name is Detective Henry Lau. I spoke to the store manager this morning about a security DVR."

The woman gestured toward the rear of the store. "You must've talked to Marty; he's back there."

Henry nodded thanks, and the two detectives maneuvered between display racks of beef jerky and potato chips toward a stark white melamine door trimmed in aluminum. The sound of approaching footsteps brought a head of curly gray hair into view. Tortoise shell-framed eyeglasses perched crookedly on a slender nose.

"Marty?" Henry ventured.

"Yes," the other replied with a welcoming face as he stepped out of the storage room. "Is there something I can help you with?"

"I'm Detective Lau. I spoke to you earlier about a security recording."

"Right. Right. From yesterday."

Henry introduced Janet. Marty smiled back. "This way." He led them toward a cramped closet of a room with a tiny desk. The three barely fit in the space. Marty adjusted his glasses, then motioned to the PC. I've got the playback queued up. It's paused at 8:45 p.m. yesterday. I think that's what you wanted."

"Yes, thanks."

"The menu bar is there. That's your play button. Fast forward. Rewind. Stop. The four cameras display in the four boxes on the screen. Pretty straightforward."

"Got it."

"If you need me, I'll be outside by the propane tanks."

Marty took off, and Henry lowered himself into the solitary Samsonite folding chair and curled his fingers around the computer mouse. "When I visited last evening," he said over his shoulder to Janet, "the night manager thought he remembered two men who vaguely fit the description of the guys I'm looking for." The fast-forwarded figures paraded by as Henry soaked in the images.

Janet had no interest in the people on screen, didn't know who to look for. Instead, she studied her uncle's face, the intensity of his focus, and the fresh rust-colored abrasions on his cheek and neck. Banged up but still going, that summed up Henry's checkered life. There were aspects of his early years—the Hong Kong period—that she knew little about. He rarely spoke of those days and never in much detail. According to her father, Henry had struggled to find his bearings after Kay died, one of several reasons he'd relocated to Hong Kong. Janet never asked him about that time. Didn't feel she could.

Observing him now, she was struck by how worn out he looked. That startled her; for as long as she could remember, Henry had been a youthful whirling dynamo. Even after his near-fatal accident, you could still see his life ember burning hot. It had motivated him to recover faster than anyone had expected. Yet, she began to wonder if that effort had come at a cost. Perhaps he'd burned up too much of his reserves in pushing to reclaim his health, leaving little left for day-to-day existence. She'd read an article once, though she couldn't recall the source, where the author suggested that babies were born with a limited amount of life energy which was intended to be used up over their entire lifetime. A single tank of gas, if you will, that could not be refilled. Some adults burned up their life fuel too early, whereas others expired before their time and left behind petrol reserves. She didn't know if there was anything to this idea, but she was reminded of it now as she observed her uncle. The thought saddened her.

Henry stirred suddenly. "This might be it." He pressed rewind.

Janet's attention went back to the video screen. Rewind had changed to play mode. The scurrying images moved like normal people. After a few seconds, a car pulled up to the pumps. "Now there's a flashy red convertible," Henry said. The driver's door opened. A scruffy, long-haired man in black harness boots stepped out, a metallic sparkle at the steel rings. He gassed up the car; however, as he pulled out the hose, he jumped back slightly.

Janet squinted at the screen. "What's he doing?"

"Got squirted with gas. The waitress at Omar's said he smelled of it."

A passenger with a blond crew cut disembarked, and the two men entered the store where another camera displayed them in glorious high definition as Boot Boy paid the clerk.

"That's them," Henry grinned with a sense of triumph. "The guys who jumped me."

"You were right. And look, that screen clearly shows their license plate."

"It's gold." Henry agreed. He paused playback and took a few photos with his smartphone.

Janet wrinkled her nose. "I thought you were getting a copy of the video."

"I am. This is insurance in case there's a problem." He viewed the images with deep satisfaction. "Your asses belong to me, boys."

Downtown Wayzata Bay was flush with car traffic and pedestrian shoppers. Henry found the last open curb parking space near the Broadway Docks on Lake Street and pulled in. An unbroken row of high-end storefronts flanked the left side of the street while the blue-gray waters of Lake Minnetonka filled the horizon on the right.

Janet craned her neck and searched the docks between the parked vehicles. "I see her. She's not alone."

In the near distance, the Chinese minister and a male companion stood on the wooden dock and viewed the large empty lake, empty because sailboats and motor craft had been moored or put into storage for the season. Winter was coming. In three months, the lake surface would turn into a solid sheet of ice. Shen Jiang-Li was smartly dressed in a tailored pantsuit that was a cut above the average conservative business outfit. She had style. The man next to her, not so much. His ill-fitting gray suit looked off the rack. The man, also Asian, was short and blocky, with slicked-back hair and pointed eyebrows that gave him the look of a grumpy pit bull.

"Who d'you think that is with Shen?" Janet asked, stepping out of the car.

"Don't know. Shen's too relaxed to be his subordinate."

The detectives walked across the parking lot. As they neared, Minister Shen offered them an open smile of familiarity.

"*Nihao*," Henry greeted. "You remember my partner, Detective Lau."

"Your niece," Shen Jiang-Li replied with a smile toward Janet.

Recognition! And a smile! Janet was bowled over.

Shen gestured to the somber-faced man to her left. "Allow me to introduce Mr. Tong. He's a regional liaison"—she enunciated the words with care, displaying that English was not her native language—"from our Chicago embassy. He's accompanying me to another meeting after this one."

Apparently warmth was not an arrow in Mr. Tong's quiver. His dour expression remained unchanged as he offered a curt and silent nod.

Henry made a broad gesture toward the big lake. "Interesting place for a meeting."

"I grew up in Ningbo," Shen explained, "a coastal city. I like being by water. I find it...comforting." Darkly engaging eyes rested on him. "Mr. Hatcher brought me here to dine the first day we met."

Henry wasted no time. "Speaking of Mr. Hatcher. You had something to tell us about him?"

A sleek eyebrow quirked beneath lustrous black bangs. Shen Jiang-Li was blunt. "I wouldn't believe everything Mr. Hatcher says at face value. Is that right? Is that the expression?"

"It is."

A conspiratorial smile brushed her lips. "Mr. Hatcher is a wealthy, powerful businessman. Men like that often don't let obstacles get in their way, obstacles like ethics...or the law."

Too much innuendo for Janet. She had to cut in: "Are you suggesting Lee Hatcher had something to do with the theft of the dragon relic?"

Shen Jiang-Li was unequivocal. "Yes. Or he gave it to Mr. Beckman to hide for him."

Henry and Janet exchanged looks.

Seeing she had their interest, the Chinese minister grew more animated. "Has Mr. Hatcher notified the police that the dragon head has been stolen?"

Henry shook his head. "No, he hasn't."

"Don't you find that strange, Detective?"

"I do."

"Has he given a reason for it?"

"Hatcher thinks if word got out that the dragon relic was missing, it would start a frenzy of searching for it that might hurt its recovery."

"Does that make sense?"

"It doesn't. The more eyes searching for the dragon head, the better."

"Have you considered the idea that Mr. Hatcher may not want the artifact found?" Shen posited in her accented voice.

A gull soared over their heads and perched atop a nearby street lamp, eyeing them for food. A sparrow, either braver or hungrier, hopped close to them on the asphalt to peck at something.

Janet pressed her lips together, intrigued by Shen's accusation. Henry didn't quite appear to be on board.

"Okay," he agreed in a receptive though cautionary tone, "let's say you're right. Why would Hatcher do that?"

Shen laid it out plainly. "Who owns the bronze dragon figure is in dispute, as you know. If Mr. Hatcher tried to sell the artifact, the sale would be challenged." Her voice took on an undertone. "Doesn't it seem convenient for the dragon head to have disappeared during my discussions with him about returning it to the people of China?"

"I take your point. Hatcher can't surrender an artifact he no longer has. He even emphasized that point when we were in his office."

Shen nodded. "He did."

A group of young people strolled onto the boardwalk. Henry waited for them to pass by before he continued. "How certain are you the artifact is the genuine missing summer palace fountainhead?"

A breath of wind fluttered strands of Shen's hair across her face. A slender hand tucked them behind her ear. "We can't be absolutely sure until the piece has been examined by our experts, but our sources are confident." Once again, the cultural minister glanced at the grimly silent Mr. Tong as if to confirm her statement. Then she turned back to the detectives. "Mr. Beckman contacted a Mr. Chen in Shanghai who examined photographs and provided details that matched Mr. Hatcher's dragon head. It was Chen who notified our ministry that the missing relic might have been found and was in America."

Shen Jiang-Li took a step closer toward them, speaking her next words with care. "Detectives, I share this with you so that in your search of Mr. Beckman's killer, you don't overlook Leland Hatcher. How far is a man like that willing to go?"

Barely able to contain herself, Janet maintained a poker face all the way back to the Malibu. Once beside the black sedan, she let it out. "Well, what do you make of *that*?"

Pausing at the open car door, Henry tossed a last glance toward the cultural minister and her silent shadow, Mr. Tong. "She makes good points."

Janet nodded, feeling a rush of optimism. "Shen was not subtle, was she? The woman just accused Hatcher of engineering the disappearance of the dragon head and implicated him in Beckman's murder." She climbed into the car and closed the door, leaning back in her seat, reeling a little as she tried to make sense of it. Lee Hatcher, millionaire entrepreneur, philanthropist, and all-around good guy up to no good? The man was in the news at least twice a year, either promoting a new business venture or appearing at some charity gala, garnering good press and good feelings for his good works. Kind of a letdown, like finding out the Tooth Fairy was robbing banks to get the cash for all the kiddies. She knew one thing for certain. "We need to call again on Lee Hatcher."

CHAPTER 16

Before any return visit to Leland Hatcher, the detectives first had to fulfill a commitment with David Nakagawa. Later that afternoon, they entered the lobby of Nakagawa Trading Company five minutes before the hour. Once again, Henry had changed into his charcoal-gray power suit. An uncertain Janet remarked, "You may need that today. Whatever magic your suit has, let's hope it works on Nakagawa."

"He didn't treat you well at the MIA," Henry said disapprovingly. That makes for a lousy first impression on his part. I saw it as a warning of things to come. If this outfit gives us any luck, we may need it."

He was right, she realized. She had tried being optimistic about today. Had hoped Nakagawa would behave better. But why should he? Maybe she was too naïve. It hadn't been easy getting in Nakagawa's face and insisting on a meeting. It went against Janet's nature. She hated confrontations; they made her uncomfortable. But they were part of the job, and she'd have to get used to them or learn to get around them if she were to succeed. People pushed into a corner get defensive. She'd have to learn how to push back. For today, she was glad Henry was along for moral support and to take the lead if he had to. Safety in numbers, as the saying goes.

Janet straightened her jacket as the pair approached the reception desk. An attractive Asian woman sporting a Bluetooth headset greeted them. Janet put on her best spit and polish manner. "Detectives Lau and Lau to see Mr. Nakagawa. We have a two o'clock appointment."

The receptionist consulted her computer screen. "Mr. Nakagawa offers his apologies. A conflict came up. He asked if you could reschedule."

Henry and Janet looked at each other. She shook her head with an I-can't-believe-this-is-happening expression. Before she could respond, Henry intervened. "Last evening, Mr. Nakagawa specifically asked my partner to be here at two o'clock today. We drove all this way."

"I'm very sorry. Mr. Nakagawa is a busy man. Situations do arise that require his attention. Would you like to reschedule?"

"Is there an opening later today?"

"It appears his schedule is full for the rest of the afternoon....and tomorrow as well. The first available time slot I see for him is next week."

Janet let out an exasperated breath. Nakagawa had never intended on keeping this appointment, agreed to it only to get her out of his face last evening.

Henry maintained his calm, though his voice took on a harder edge. "I know this has nothing to do with you, but this is unacceptable. My partner and I are here on a murder inquiry." The receptionist reacted to the word *murder*. For added effect, Henry presented his ID. The brass detective shield caught the overhead light beautifully. "Time is important. Mr. Nakagawa may have material information relevant to our investigation. We need to speak to him today. Just a few minutes of his time. That's all we need. It would be much more disruptive to take him back to our station and question him there."

The receptionist's eyes widened. "I'll call Mr. Nakagawa's executive assistant."

Henry thanked her. Out of courtesy for her privacy, Henry and Janet stepped away a few feet from the desk as the young woman made the call.

Keeping her voice low, Janet asked, "Can we really do that? Take Nakagawa to the station?"

"That was a gambit, shoving a stick into a hornet's nest to see what comes out."

"Oh, you were bluffing."

"Look, Nakagawa agreed to an appointment today. I get he's busy. But to brush us off like that is just rude. My patience ran out years ago for entitled people who think it's okay to inconvenience others on a whim. We won't go away quietly."

The receptionist waved them over. They returned to her desk. In her perfectly poised and polished manner, she informed them, "Mr. Nakagawa's executive assistant is on the way."

"Thanks so much for your help," Henry replied sincerely.

Two minutes later, the elevator door slid open, and a short, stocky woman in a dark purple pantsuit strutted out. Not a hair out of place. Her jaw was set in a grim line. Her short legs drummed across the hard floor in a take-no-prisoners stride. "My name is Athena Kazan. I'm Mr. Nakagawa's assistant. I understand you're with the police. Is there something I can help you with?"

After Henry summarized the situation, Ms. Kazan came back sharply, "I apologize for the inconvenience, Detectives. Mr. Nakagawa, as I'm sure you realize, is the head of a multinational corporation; he often has to deal with situations at a moment's notice. I understand Ms. Watanabe already offered to reschedule."

Henry stood firm. "Next week won't do. We're aware of the demands on Mr. Nakagawa, just as we hope he appreciates the seriousness of a murder inquiry, of the urgency to get information while it's warm. We only need ten minutes of Mr. Nakagawa's time. *Ten minutes.* After all, it was he who specifically told my partner to schedule an appointment at two p.m. today."

"I wish I could help you, but Mr. Nakag—"

"*Ten minutes*," Henry cut her off, his voice losing all cordiality. "Or would Mr. Nakagawa rather waste a few hours in the Gillette police station?"

"Our lawyers might have something to say about that," Kazan countered icily, surrendering no ground. Neither did Henry.

He smiled suggestively. "I've dealt with lawyers before."

She glanced at the abrasions on the side of his face and neck.

He noticed. "You should see what the other guys look like."

She blinked.

Henry saw an opening. "Nakagawa Trading does a lot of business overseas. That includes China, if I'm not mistaken. You have several large trading partners in the People's Republic. Am I right?"

"We do. Why do you ask?" More to the point, her body language demanded, why are you wasting my time?

Henry's voice hardened. "How do you think the Chinese government will react when they learn that Mr. Nakagawa is impeding an investigation they have asked us to get resolved as quickly as possible?"

Kazan's flinty eyes betrayed a hint of concern.

Henry pressed. "Our investigation concerns a man who was in possession of a priceless relic which is now missing. The Chinese are very interested in having the item returned. A cultural minister from Beijing is in town and working with us. She's very keen to recover this national treasure. What do you suppose she'll tell her superiors after we explain Mr. Nakagawa can't spare ten minutes of his time to help? Perhaps the People's Republic of China will re-evaluate their relationship with Nakagawa Trading Company."

BOOM. The bomb was dropped neatly in her lap.

It took all of three seconds for Athena Kazan to process the implied threat and the importance to her employer. Trim eyebrows knit together. Peach-colored lips compressed in a tight line. "I'll find him," she came back in a conciliatory tone. "Wait here. I'll be back in five minutes." She wheeled about and strode off in hurried steps.

Janet couldn't restrain her admiration. "Not bad, partner. That was a nice bit of blackmail."

He made a dismissive wave of his hand. "When in the halls of ruthless corporate America, do as in ruthless corporate America."

She smirked. "Too long for a fortune cookie fortune, but I like it."

Minutes later, Athena Kazan returned with David Nakagawa, who looked ready to spit nails. Hard eyes rested on the persons responsible for dragging him out of an important meeting. Sizing them up for a moment, he brusquely motioned for them to follow, leading them into a nearby conference room with smoked glass interior walls. Nakagawa closed the door behind him with a decisive click, folding his arms across his chest. He did not invite them to sit.

"You have ten minutes." He looked to Kazan to act as timekeeper. "This had better be important. I don't like being threatened."

"And I don't like being jerked around," Henry came back in the identical tone, ceding no ground. Janet had to admit the tailored gray-stripped suit put him on equal footing with their host in a stare down of who looked the most imposing. The light scratches on his cheek and neck only made him appear like a man who didn't shy away from a fight. She loved it.

David Nakagawa stiffened, probably unused to being talked back to like this, she suspected.

"I have friends in the police," he warned in a clear attempt at intimidation.

Henry didn't bite. "What a coincidence. I have friends in the police too. More than you, I bet. And I have friends in the State Department and IRS. I could suggest they take a closer look into your business operations."

The muscles in Nakagawa's jaw tightened. His eyes brimmed with barely suppressed malice. "Ask your questions?" he grumbled, tenuously clinging onto civility.

Henry turned to Janet. She felt like she'd been handed a pissed-off rattlesnake. Swallowing her apprehension, she maintained a brave face. She wasn't going to let this guy get to her.

"At the MIA last evening, I asked you about Roger Beckman. You said you couldn't help. But you didn't say you did not know him." She'd been down this semantic road before with Kasparian and wasn't going to make the same mistake.

Nakagawa looked away as if determining how much to reveal. The rugged jaw, straight nose, fiery eyes presented a blank stone wall. Finally he admitted, "Yeah, I knew Roger."

There! Was that so hard? Janet was tempted to say but didn't. Out loud she said, "Let me guess. You didn't know him well. You used him for occasional consulting jobs."

"Yes."

"When was the last time you hired him?"

Nakagawa turned to Kazan.

Searching her memory, his assistant came back, "Eight months ago for our Sichuan project. Nothing since. To be precise, it wasn't for art; Roger was hired as a cultural liaison."

Janet couldn't conceal her disappointment.

An uneasy silence followed.

Nakagawa took that as a sign the interview was over. "If that's all," he reached for the door.

"*Wait.*"

No one moved. It was as if Henry had fired his Glock into the ceiling. Nakagawa glared back. His eyes raked over Henry, his posture, wardrobe, the command behind his expression.

"We're not finished," he shot back. "Did Beckman contact you in the last month about something he was working on?"

Athena Kazan said, "I talked to Roger last week."

"Last week?" Janet glanced at Henry.

"Last Thursday," Kazan checked with her employer for permission to elaborate. He gave a nod. "As you mentioned, Nakagawa Trading has holdings in China. We deal with officials and politicians and merchants on a regular basis. Roger asked if he could access one of our Macao contacts."

Henry shifted his weight. "Did he say what he was looking for?"

"Only that it was for a current project."

"Anything more?"

"No. And he wouldn't go into specifics. Because of that, I said no. I wasn't comfortable referring him to one of our overseas contacts if we didn't know what it was about."

"Sensible," Henry agreed.

Seeing an opportunity, Janet decided to swing for the fences. "Mr. Nakagawa, our information says that you've been interested in acquiring a piece of Chinese antiquity known as the bronze dragon. Is that correct?"

"It is."

David Nakagawa was shrewd enough to see how the dominos were lining up. A spark shone in his eyes. "Why are you bringing that up? Was that what Roger was working on?"

"It was," Janet confirmed.

"Hold on. Are you saying the zodiac fountain dragon head is in Minnesota?"

"Possibly. Beckman was authenticating it."

"Authenticating for whom?"

"I'm not at liberty to say."

Their host's face hardened, his expression priceless, like a dog whose favorite toy had been yanked from its mouth. You could almost see the gears turning in his head as he pieced together the reality that he'd been *so* close to the dragon fountainhead. "Do you know if Roger was able to establish the dragon's provenance?"

Janet shook her head. "That's unknown."

Nakagawa's face flashed with understanding. "That's why he wanted to use our Macao contact."

"There's more," she went on, enjoying having the upper hand for a change, "the artifact is missing."

"Missing! Like stolen?"

"Perhaps."

"Are you close to recovering it?"

"No. Which is another reason we're here. Your company deals with a large number of overseas dealers. Could you ask them if they hear anything about the dragon to let you know? And, naturally, you'll inform us."

A calculated smile parted Nakagawa's lips. "Be happy too, Detective. I'll have Ms. Kazan make a few discreet inquires." He looked pointedly at Henry. "And be sure to tell your Beijing friends of my cooperation."

"You were awesome in there!" Janet beamed at Henry the instant they exited the building. "I loved how you muscled a meeting with Nakagawa after he stiffed us."

It *was* sweet, particularly after the way he'd rudely dismissed her in the MIA parking lot. She relished the payback, would have given Henry a big hug if doing so weren't a breach of professional protocol.

Henry took the compliment in stride. "I didn't get a good vibe on the guy after you told me how he treated you." They were at their vehicle now and paused at the open doors. "So I did some research on

Nakagawa's business and saw it had major holdings in the South Pacific and China. Shen Jiang-Li's presence in town was too good an opportunity not to use as leverage."

"Yeah, that was handy. Is this a standard technique? Do you normally blackmail interviewees? I'm just curious in case I need to take notes."

"No, it's not something I normally do. Like I said before, I have no patience for self-important dipwads who think they have the right to treat people like shit."

"What if Nakagawa reports you?"

"Let him. I'm not angling for a big promotion. Don't need to play politics. I'm set in my ways."

Janet's face clouded. "I'm not sure I could face down Nakagawa the way you did."

"I'm not saying you should."

"I'm too nice," she sighed. Or timid, she wondered. "Maybe over time the job will harden me."

"It will, although I'd tell you to never lose that niceness. It's one of your best attributes. Each of us develops our own tools for the job. You'll find what works for you. You don't have to do things the way I do. One size does not fit all."

She flashed a heartfelt smile. "Thank you for saying that."

"Be firm, though," he advised.

"Right."

"Be firm without being an asshole."

She couldn't help but laugh. "Threatening Nakagawa with the Red Chinese or U.S. State Department or IRS wasn't being an asshole?"

"Well..." Henry conceded, "it was a bit over the line. I'm at an age where I don't care about the fallout if he complains. Like I said, sometimes when dealing with an asshole, you have to be one. However, take it as the exception to the rule."

The Malibu pulled away from the Nakagawa Trading Company onto Excelsior Boulevard, turning onto the ramp to northbound 169. Henry merged into freeway traffic. As an afterthought, he added, "And just to be clear, I only play the Don't-Shit-With-Me card with self-important jerks."

"Like David Nakagawa." She spoke his name as if it left a bad taste in her mouth.

"Yeah, and it doesn't always work."

"On him, it did."

"We got lucky."

"You saw how he reacted to the bronze dragon."

"When he realized that's what Beckman was working on, the man almost peed his pants!"

Janet laughed. "For sure. Think he'll really notify us if his Macao contacts learn anything?"

"He might."

"Or will he use the info to get the dragon relic for himself?"

"Or he might get it so he can personally return it to China for *beaucoup* PR."

"Yeah, he'd do that. He also might find the opportunity too hard to resist. The dude wants to get his own paws on the drago—"

She stopped and stared intently into her side mirror, twisting in her seat to look back. "There it is again! The black SUV I saw at the MIA. Same driver."

Henry glanced at his rearview mirror. "I see him."

"Good. Then you know I'm not making this up."

"He's drifting back a ways, hiding in traffic."

"What do we do?"

"Keep driving. See what happens." Henry snorted out a breath at a realization. "Interesting coincidence: you first saw this guy at the

MIA when you talked with David Nakagawa, and now we see him again after leaving Nakagawa's headquarters."

She nodded. "It was quick, but I got a good look at him. Short blond hair, thick dark eyebrows, ugly face. It's the same guy. This can't be a coincidence. We're definitely being followed."

CHAPTER 17

"This is precious!" Janet grinned at the old black and white photograph. "How old were you?"

"Ten, maybe eleven," her mother said. "I was all dressed up to go to Cherie Munson's birthday party."

"You look adorable." Janet had seen few photos of her mother as a girl, most of them having been destroyed in a fire decades earlier. Half of Abby Lau's dining room table was covered with papers and clippings, a stuffed old shoebox resting in a place of prominence, the late afternoon sun slanting through the dining room blinds. "Here's another." Janet held the small photographic print of an even younger Abby Campbell. She played in a sandbox and was engrossed in scooping toy shovelfuls of sand into her bucket. Janet turned over the photo. Faded handwriting noted: *Abby at Siesta Beach, Fla.*

"No date. This is Nanna's handwriting, isn't it?"

"Yes."

"Odd she didn't add the date after she already wrote your name and location."

"Mom wasn't much interested in dates. The who and where was what mattered to her."

"So I see." Janet rifled through the shoebox crammed with old papers and photos from a time before such things were digitized. These were original prints, heirlooms you could hold in your hand that had a real physicality and stories to tell. Janet was enthralled. "Where'd these come from?"

"I found the box stashed on a shelf in your grandmother's closet, buried under some old blankets. She didn't remember having it."

Abby Lau let out a prolonged sigh, one borne from the grind of dealing with a parent's dementia. In her youth, Abby had been an auburn-haired charmer whose shining eyes and ironic smirk rarely failed to captivate. Time had not faded her charms by much, and, as she rested still enchanting eyes on her daughter, she radiated warmth and safety, like a cozy winter blanket in front of the fire. Janet admired her mother's patience in dealing with Nanna Aileen, one of many things she admired about her. Abby Campbell Lau was one of the smartest people Janet knew, a *summa cum laude* graduate from Columbia University. Yet, for all her smarts, her mother was never condescending toward others. Her heart was too good for that. Her one Achilles' heel was her inability to suffer the blather of arrogance and cruelty. Abby was a daughter of Scotland, and the fire of the Campbell's blazed hot within her. Her mother was Janet's hero.

Abby contemplated the cluttered contents in the shoebox—receipts, old greeting cards, letters, photographs—with a look of accomplishment. Janet knew how much her mother had struggled to put Nanna Aileen's affairs in order in the three years since she was moved into memory care. Important legal papers were kept secure in a safe deposit box, yet every so often, a little stash of treasure was unearthed in some forgotten corner, such as this one. The photos were a bridge between generations. One, in particular, caught Janet's eye. It was a black and white glossy print of a young, vibrant Aileen Kerr Campbell, silken hair flying in the wind as she clutched ten-year-old Abby cheek to cheek. Aileen beamed as though this was the happiest day of her life.

"I love this!" Janet marveled at the photo. She'd seen too few photographs of her grandmother looking so young and full of joy.

A rumble of masculine voices drifted in from the kitchen. Henry and her father were having a discussion.

"Was this a special day?" Janet returned to the old photo. "Nothing's written on the back."

"We were at the Bronx Zoo. Just a fun day. Nothing special."

"Looks special to me."

Abby smiled and stroked the back of her daughter's head. "Thanks for dropping by. It was a fun surprise."

"Your house is on the way back to Gillette. We took a chance. To be honest, I didn't expect either of you home on a work day."

"Both your father and I took a few days off to take care of some personal stuff."

"Like Nanna?"

"One thing on the list." Abby perked up at a new thought. "Are you and Henry staying for dinner?"

"It's kinda early, don't you think? We should be getting back to the station." She felt a pang of guilt as she said it; it had been months since she'd last visited her parents.

Abby would not be deterred. "Maybe after you get off duty."

"I'll ask. See if Henry has plans."

At the mention of his name, Abby lowered her voice. "How's he doing?"

"Good. Better than good if you mean his injuries."

"Fully recovered?"

"Fit for active duty, as they say. He does have some lingering aches. Occasional stiffness in his back and legs. He doesn't complain, but I know."

Abby's voice was warm with admiration. "It's a miracle he's come this far." She leaned in, her shoulder-length reddish-gray hair dancing lightly on her shoulders. "How do you like working with your uncle?"

"I love it. He's a great teacher and partner. I'll enjoy it as long as it lasts."

Abby's brow darkened. "What does that mean?"

"It's a temporary assignment, Henry and me. Chief Bowman wants to ease Henry back on the streets. I'm like extra incentive for him. No telling how long the partnership will last."

"Oh, well, it sounds like you're enjoying the assignment."

"I am. Instead of seeing him a couple of times a year, I see him every day. We have a connection now we didn't have before—well, we always had a special connection between us since I was little. Knowing it's a temporary assignment makes me appreciate the time we have."

"That makes a difference," Abby said, averting her eyes.

Her mother's tone struck Janet as odd. "Sorry. Different how? I don't follow."

Abby Lau pressed her tongue against her teeth, struggling for the right words. She paused to admire her only child. "It's wonderful you're getting to know your uncle better. And no one is going to look out for you more than your own blood, so we're thankful for that...."

But? There was a "but" coming, Janet could tell. "But...?"

Abby said softly, "You are spending a lot of time with Henry. We hardly see you anymore."

"Mom, I've got a new job. I'm a detective now. Different responsibilities. My schedule's different, and, yes, Henry's my partner. I'm sorry I've been so busy. Be patient. In a few more months, I'll have the routine down. What?" Janet could see there was more in her mother's tight-lipped expression.

"Maybe I shouldn't say this..."

Which instantly got Janet's attention.

Abby hesitated. "I think your father's a little jealous."

"Jealous of what?"

"The time you're spending with Henry."

"Seriously?" A shapely eyebrow sat up. "Dad thinks I'm spending too much time with the guy I work with?" Incredulous eyes challenged her mother and softened at a new thought. "Wait, are you saying Dad wants to spend more time with me?"

Abby nodded.

"Oh, that's kinda sweet—"

They stopped, looked at each other. The discussion, which had been background noise in the kitchen, had suddenly amped up. Voices were raised. The two women edged to the doorway. The kitchen had new birch cabinets and marble countertops. Standing by them, Douglas Lau was in a defensive posture, arms folded across his chest. His short hair was thinning. His middle was thickening. Although three years older than Henry, he had the appearance of someone much older.

"That's bullshit," Doug said, annoyed. "What kind of answer is that?

Henry gave an indifferent shrug. His backside rested against a white-enameled dish washer. "What kind of answer? The only one I have. Take it or leave it. I'm healthier than I've been in six months."

"What you did was courageous," Doug conceded. "You practically came back from the dead. I give you that. I was proud of the way you fought back. Amazed. You proved your point. You're back at work. Maybe it's time to consider something less dangerous, a job that doesn't put you in danger."

"My job isn't that dangerous."

"Oh, really? Look at your face."

"That wasn't work-related."

Doug didn't relent. "You got jumped. Next time you may not be so lucky."

Janet saw Henry's posture stiffen as he struggled to keep his cool. From experience, she knew her father was building up to a point. It didn't take long. The hammer dropped a second later.

"The point is it's not about you anymore, Henry. You have a partner."

Henry's jaw dropped. "Is that what this is about: Janet?"

"Dad?" Janet barged in, no longer able to lurk in the shadows. "What's going on?"

Busted, her father squirmed like a kid caught with his hand in the cookie jar.

Henry was happy to enlighten her. "Your father thinks I'm a danger to you."

"*Danger*?" Janet retorted, fists on hips. "What danger? I work for the city of Gillette, Minnesota, population fifty-two thousand, seven hundred, not freakin' Chicago."

Doug didn't back down. "Crazies are everywhere. Cops get shot at just for being cops. You need a partner at the top of his game."

"I've got one, your brother."

"Not according to him," Doug countered. "If Henry does have physical limitations, he shouldn't be doing such a demanding job."

Janet heaved a sigh. Threw up her hands. Her father could be infuriating, and she didn't want to get sucked into a pointless argument. "Isn't that for Henry to decide? Are you sure my safety is what this is about?" From the corner of her eye, she saw her mother flinch. Janet wasn't going to reveal the secret her mother shared about her father being a little jealous of the time she was spending with Henry. She needn't have worried. The reference slid by unnoticed.

Douglas Lau was too wound up. "Harsh reality," his voice turned bitter. "I know my brother. I always had to be the responsible one. Toe the line. Henry got to do what he wanted, regardless of who it affected. Why should he start now?"

That was enough for Abby, who stepped closer. "*Doug,*" she warned in a voice that could freeze molten lead. "That's unnecessary."

Her husband stood unrepentant but held his tongue.

A stoic Henry took the verbal hit in silence. Why he did, Janet didn't know. Regardless, nothing prevented her from standing up for him. "Dad, that's not fair. He doesn't deserve that."

Her father was unmoved. "Life isn't fair, honey. You should know that by now. Shit happens."

"'Shit happens?'" A defiant Janet stepped closer, her shoulders square. "That's all you got? Dad, you got a tough break being the eldest son. Maybe it sucked. You also got advantages from it. Don't think for one minute Henry isn't taking his job seriously. I could tell you stories—Crap! I need to take this."

She grabbed her ringing cell phone. The call ended twenty seconds later. "Sorry, Henry and I have to go." She glanced at him meaningfully. "That was Maureen Levy. She got a letter from Roger Beckman, and she thinks we should see it."

Without further comment, Henry made his way toward the front door.

Janet glanced between her mother and father, searching for something to say, then gave up. Her shoulders slumped. "Well, this sucks. I'm sorry, we gotta go. Work." She made an apologetic gesture and took off after Henry, miserable for leaving the discussion hanging like this, yet also relieved she could get the hell away.

CHAPTER 18

The crunch of dead leaves punctuated the walk back to Malibu. In neighboring yards, the sugar maples still clung to their ruby red leaves. Other species were half skeletal with clusters of yellow and burnt orange hangers-on. By November, the flora of the Northland would go dormant as the fauna would prepare to slip into a long winter's sleep. Janet almost envied them. After the little drama inside the house on Crescent Lane, life in suspended animation didn't seem like such a bad deal. If only that were an option, she thought, to put your troubles aside for a long sleep. The reality was she'd have to smooth things over with her parents sooner or later. Much later, if she could swing it.

Inside the car, Henry closed the door, took in a deep breath, and shuttered his eyes. Not in a mood to talk. Janet watched the slow rise and fall of his chest. He hadn't uttered a word since they'd left the house. Abnormally quiet. She could practically feel the tension radiate from him. Normally he could shrug off verbal jabs, take them in stride. This time Henry held back, noticeably upset at his brother's tongue lashing and strangely silent.

Or was there more to it?

People reacted differently to hardship. It occurred to her that she really didn't know how well Henry dealt with bad news. She had an idea, but perhaps that idea was based on a misconception. *Had her father ripped the scab off an old wound? How could she ask him without making it worse? Or was she just too timid to upset him?* Janet sighed at her own lack of people skills. She didn't like rocking the boat. Fortunately, in this instance, she lucked out. Before she could dredge deeper for an answer from him, Henry snapped out of his reverie. Like a light switch had turned on. He sat up, eyes alert and ready for business, looking at her as if the previous twenty minutes had never happened. There was even the lopsided smirk.

He started the engine. "Where to?"

In a reserved voice, she answered, "St. Paul. Como Park." *Focus on the job. Maybe that'll lighten his mood.* But try as she might, Janet couldn't focus on the job. "Sorry about back there with Dad."

He said nothing; eyes keyed on traffic as the car turned the corner. The silence lingered.

Janet turned away. *Stupid! You shouldn't have gone there. Too personal.* She sighed.

They turned onto southbound 169.

Then, unexpectedly, Henry muttered, "Thanks for sticking up for me with your father."

His words lifted her. She felt a wave of relief. "You didn't defend yourself. I had to say something."

"I wasn't comfortable. Doug's house. His family. The men in my family are prone to tunnel vision."

"Yeah, he's not seeing the big picture."

"On the contrary, your father's big picture is you. Can't blame him for that."

"Sure, I get it. But that rant about you being selfish was over the line."

"Not by much. He has a right to complain."

Janet was caught off guard. "How do you mean?"

Navigating around a slow tractor-trailer, Henry was focused on freeway traffic. It was late afternoon and the beginning of rush hour. Crazy time. Henry kept his eyes on the road as he answered her question. "As you know, my parents put a lot of pressure on Doug. Had big expectations for him. He was the Boy Who Could Do No Wrong. Smart. Talented. Great with people. He was the yardstick against which I was measured. My father would complain to me, 'Why aren't your grades better? At your age, your brother was a straight-A student.'"

Henry grumbled at the memory. "For the record, I got excellent grades, just not perfect. I couldn't live up to Doug, so I stopped trying. I went my own way. After a while, my parents gave up and let me do my own thing." He shrugged. "It let me pursue my passion. Doug never got to do that. He has a right to complain."

That she knew. Knew how hard her father had worked to secure his career and make a good home for his family. He wasn't a whiner, never complained, just put his shoulder to the grindstone and kept going. Janet had always known him as the loving, patient, somewhat uptight, funny man who'd encouraged her and supported her life choices. *Her choices.* Probably because it had been done to him, he had never tried to push his personal agenda onto her. It suddenly occurred to her what a gift that had been, and she felt guilty for her harsh words.

By now, the car had transitioned onto eastbound 394 and was rolling toward St. Paul.

"Doug was right," Henry admitted out of the blue. "When I was younger, I was selfish...at times."

It was almost inconceivable for her to believe that of her Uncle Henry. For her entire life, she had known him as someone to look up to. Gazing at his profile, she felt a flush of affection for him. She turned toward him as far as the seat restraints allowed, ears burning to hear what else he might be ready to share.

He glanced at her. "I was a handful as a teenager and my early twenties. Knew exactly what I wanted to do and how I was going to do it. Nothing and nobody was going to get in my way." Hindsight filled his voice with irony. "I also disappointed a few people."

She heard the regret in his voice and let it pass without comment. What could she possibly say? He seemed about to unburden himself, and she was disappointed when he offered nothing more. She wasn't going to pry. Not here. She didn't feel comfortable pressing the issue, so the two of them rode in silence for the next few minutes.

Janet checked her side mirror for the umpteenth time. "We may have lost our tail. I haven't seen him since after we left Nakagawa Trading."

"Maybe he gave up."

Eventually the Malibu exited the off-ramp onto north Dale Street and made its way into the Como Park neighborhood. It didn't take long to find the brick-faced rambler with the orange door and half-moon window, which was illuminated by the amber glow of a bronze carriage lamp. It wasn't yet sunset, but Maureen Levy was taking no chances.

"Thanks for getting here so quickly." Levy closed the door after them. She led them to the dining room and paused before an old walnut table which, going by appearances, was seldom used for actual dining, its surface covered in an array of binders, books, papers, an iPad, and scattered number 2 pencils. In the one open section left bare was a white envelope with Maureen Levy's address at the university written by hand in block letters.

"It's been a hectic few days." She heaved a frazzled sigh, running her fingers through unruly, rust-colored hair that refused to be tamed. She adjusted an oversized torn sweatshirt in an attempt to look more presentable. "Crazy week. I was barely in my office the last few days. Hadn't looked at my mail. So today, I scooped it up and stuffed it in my satchel to read after dinner, in between correcting some badly written term papers. I swear students' writing skills are getting worse thanks to all the texting they do." She caught herself digressing and shook it off. "Anyway, I finally managed to catch up. Went through my mail and found this. It's from Roger."

Both Janet and Henry zeroed in on the envelope. Henry carefully picked it up by the edges. "Postmarked three days ago," he noted. Inside it was a half sheet of notebook paper with one handwritten line: *Maureen, hang on to this for me. Roger.* Henry looked into the envelope then tilted it. A small brass key tumbled out onto the table. Etched on the bow were the numbers 933.

Henry snorted with satisfaction.

"The note is definitely from Roger," Levy volunteered. "I recognize his handwriting."

Henry motioned to the key. "Know where this goes to?"

"Sorry, no idea."

Janet's thin eyebrows drew down. "It's not a house key or for a standard padlock. More like something you'd see for a strong box or a locker."

A locker.

Janet blinked, training big eyes onto Henry. "Could it be a locker? Beckman was worried enough about his safety to make sure this key was protected."

"A key to something important."

"You thinking what I'm thinking?"

"The dragon head."

Levy looked back with interest. "Oh, have you confirmed Roger's freelance gig was about a Chinese dragon relic?"

"Yes."

"Hmmm."

"Does that mean something to you, Dr. Levy?"

She seemed distracted for a moment. "Oh, don't mind me. I was just sorting it out. I'm a scholar. We like to find connecting threads to things." She gave a little laugh.

"Back to the key, then. Speaking of lockers, I take it St. Luke's doesn't have faculty lockers."

"I couldn't say. Roger and I had offices. We wouldn't need lockers."

"Makes sense." Henry picked up the key and ran the edge of his thumb along the teeth. "If this opens a locker, where is it? A bus station? MSP airport? A health club—"

He stopped abruptly with a strange glimmer in the back of his eye.

Janet saw it and felt a surge of hope. "What?"

In a far-away voice, he said, "Don't quite have it yet. A thought flashed through my head before I could make out what it was."

With a lull in the discussion, Maureen Levy stood up and remembered her duties as hostess. "Would either of you like a cup of tea? I'm stewing a pot."

"I'd love a cup," Janet said wistfully.

"Detective Lau?" Levy looked to Henry, who shook his head, lost in thought.

Excusing herself, their hostess returned with two steaming mugs. Janet breathed in the warm peppermint vapor that reminded her of cozy nights in her first studio apartment out of school. Coffee reminded her of the police station brew pot and stressed-out coworkers, whereas tea conjured memories of winding down and relaxation.

Levy luxuriously inhaled her tea before taking a sip. Her shoulders unbunched. Her face and voice mellowed. "Please, sit down." She motioned to the wooden dining room chairs. "There was another thing," she said in a tone that grabbed their attention. Levy shifted her gaze between the two detectives. "I was thinking what you asked me the other day about how Roger was the last few weeks." Another, longer sip. A curl of steam wafted past her face. "I think I want to amend my original answer. I told you how excited Roger was about that consulting gig." A glance at the key on the table. "That thing makes me believe Roger was in trouble. Even afraid for his life. He's never done anything like this before." She cast a wary eye at the envelope and its unsettling contents.

A thoughtful silence followed. Janet clasped her fingers around the ceramic mug and basked in the warmth.

As if sharing a juicy tidbit, Henry said, "I visited Mary Jo Beckman last evening. Paul Rivera showed up. The two of them were not happy at me seeing them together."

The ball was lobbed out of the blue to see how it would bounce. Janet recognized the tactic. Henry often did it to see how someone would react. There was a reaction. Levy giggled, a crinkle of delight behind her eyes. "That's funny. Paul thinks he's so discreet. Tries to hide the relationship from me. I really don't know why. He's not doing anything wrong. They're both adults." She lifted her cup and took a long sip, chuckling. "I wish I could have seen the looks on their faces."

Henry settled into the wooden chair and changed the subject. "I believe Dr. Rivera's niche is Pre-Columbian art."

Levy bobbed her head. "That's right."

"Off the record, we can tell you the artifact Dr. Beckman was working on is missing, perhaps stolen. We're looking for any leads to distributors of ancient relics who might have an interest, any kind of distributor."

"The black market," Janet put in, in case there was any doubt.

Levy shot her a disapproving glance. "What are you asking?"

Henry tread lightly. "I'm not suggesting Dr. Rivera is involved in anything illegal. Because of their disciplines, there may be an overlap of interests where he and Roger may have shared contacts. Has either of them ever told you about questionable art dealers they know?"

"You should ask Paul that."

"I plan to. First, I wanted to know if you've heard anything."

"No." Levy tightened up.

Henry pressed. "Roger never gave you any reason to suspect he had dealings with illegal sources?"

"No. He hated that. You're talking tomb raiders and non-sanctioned digs. Happens all the time for dinosaur bones and Native American relics. That kind of digging destroys the integrity of an archeological site. We all hate that. Roger's only interest in the black market was trying to understand what was being sold and what to be careful about. Like counterfeits—" Levy looked up, remembering. "The reason I know this is because eight months ago Roger was upset at some local art dealer who he suspected had acquired a piece through questionable back channels."

"Any chance you remember a name…?"

"Ohhhh, I don't. It's on the tip of my tongue. What I remember is it sounded like an old cartoon character. Um, Caspar! Y'know, the friendly ghost."

Janet felt an electric shock. "Kasparian?" she blurted.

"That's it! That was the name."

On the way to the car, Janet noticed an extra bounce in Henry's step. "That was productive," he said with a little swagger.

She agreed. "Yeah, I'll make a return visit to Angelo Kasparian tomorrow. I knew he wasn't being totally honest with me!"

"Good."

"How about the key? Your flash of inspiration ever gel?"

"It did. This could be a health club locker."

"Did Beckman have a health club membership? I don't remember anything in his bank statements."

The corner of Henry's mouth pulled back. "A health club of sorts. One with five tigers."

CHAPTER 19

The following morning came with fresh optimism. Henry sailed through his two-hour predawn workout. His forms and weapon work were fluid and precise. His training drills and legwork spot on. His kicks brutally efficient. He shadow-boxed like a wraith and smashed through his morning run. Hours later, that optimism still charged through him in south Minneapolis as he parked near the front door of the Five Tigers Martial Arts Academy.

He felt ready to take on the world.

Ten students stood in two lines in the main workout area, doing their best to mimic the precise movements of a spiky-haired Latina who slowly guided them through a form. Henry removed his shoes, set them against the wall with the others, and unzipped his bomber jacket.

The students powered through their form. Henry smiled inwardly. He could watch martial arts students for hours. The style didn't matter. Watching a skilled practitioner in action was a thing of beauty.

He turned at movement in his periphery. A well-built, broad-shouldered man approached with a welcoming smile. "DeWayne Morris. We met the other day."

Henry took his extended hand. DeWayne had a firm grip with calloused knuckles. Old calluses and new ones, a signal DeWayne liked to pound things. A lot. Henry caught DeWayne's gaze sweep over him, sizing him up with a fighter's eye. It was a subtle move but noticeable.

Henry said, "I texted Mike last night. He's expecting me."

"Mike's in the back with some students. Should be another five minutes. I'll let him know you're here."

"Thanks."

DeWayne strode away with easy grace, broad shoulders and well-developed biceps straining at the fabric of his T-shirt. He'd be a formidable opponent. Henry could see that not only was he in outstanding physical shape; he was also highly skilled. The last Henry took for granted. For DeWayne Morris to be one of Mike Anderson's assistants, he would've had to earn that position by being a hardworking, accomplished, trustworthy student.

Nearby, a student was repeatedly slamming knuckles into a sandbag. The chunky young man pounded with everything he had. Decades of study and personal insight had sharpened Henry's perception so that he could usually tell how skillful a practitioner was after watching him for a minute. Head and foot movements revealed much, told him whether he'd be able to move an opponent with two fingers or if the other was an intractable mountain. The young man's rhythm was off. So was his center. He was trying to kill the sandbag.

"Too much," the ghost of his first teacher, Sifu Chiang, echoed from the distant past. *"You hit too hard. You get it wrong. Waste energy. You don't have to punish the bag or yourself to develop a powerful punch. I show you."* Sifu Chiang had placed his fist two inches from the seventeen-year-old student's abdomen. *"Cover your belly with your hands, or this will hurt."* Henry had obediently complied, and Chiang's punch from two inches away had knocked him flat on his ass. The young student looked back with confusion and awe. *"Relaxed energy very powerful. You want to hit hard; you practice soft."*

Henry cracked a smile. The chunky man murdering the sandbag reminded Henry of himself. So young. So intense and hungry to learn yet impatient to fully digest new information. Always wanting the next thing before he'd mastered what he'd already been taught. A punch from his first *sifu* had opened Henry's eyes to the true nature of his objectives. Speed and power were not important to begin with; what he needed to focus on was mastering body alignment and his sensitivity to energy, both his and his opponent's.

"Henry!" greeted a cheery voice. Mike Anderson, a white towel draped across his thick neck, extended a hand. The silver-gray eyes crinkled with warmth. The gray T-Shirt was blotched with perspiration stains. "Two visits in one week. What gives?"

"What can I say? Luck of the draw."

"What d'you need?"

Henry held up the brass key.

Anderson recognized it. "Yep, looks like one of mine. Locker rooms are this way." He led him across the floor mats out of the main training area into a smaller space dedicated to heavy bags, weights, and two Wing Chun *mook jongs*. Changing rooms were at the end of a short hallway. The clang of metal doors and buzz of gym bag zippers bounced off white-washed cinderblock walls. Anderson paused in the doorway. "What's the number on the key?"

"933."

"Over here. I have seventy lockers in the men's changing room, shared by all the classes. Ten lockers have keys. Those who want a private locker pay a monthly fee. Roger Beckman had one. Hadn't remembered that. I checked after you texted." Anderson stopped before a metallic door painted a dull institutional green. For a moment he wavered between staying and going. "You need privacy?"

Henry almost laughed. Privacy wasn't practical in a locker room, not with three men close by in various stages of undress. One man, heavy set, fortyish, with a brush mustache, sat on the bench in his boxers. Another man zipped up a pair of canvas slacks. The third was four lockers away, lacing up his shoes.

Henry motioned for Anderson to stay. "Stick around; I might need you."

Inserting the key in the lock, Henry felt a rush of anticipation. Would he find the face of a metallic dragon staring back at him? Probably not. The locker was too narrow.

He lifted the handle. The clang of locking bars shifted in their sockets. He swung open the door.

And nothing.

Nothing but workout clothes. A black T-shirt and gray sweat pants hung in the back. On the floor was a pair of sneakers resting on a folded terrycloth towel.

No dragon.

Henry released the breath he'd been holding. His optimism crashed to the ground like a kite caught in an errant wind.

Anderson noticed the reaction. "Not what you expected, I take it."

"No."

"Too bad."

"Yeah." He tried not to sound disappointed. Didn't want to give away too much. He trusted Mike Anderson, though they'd never been close friends, more like chummy, long-term acquaintances. A thought came to him. "Mike, is this the only key?"

"Yes, except for the master."

"Who has access to the master key?"

"Me. My assistants."

Henry made a noise. Decided not to ask how easy it was to access the master key. It didn't matter. There was no way of knowing what had been in Beckman's locker in the first place, let alone if someone had taken anything.

"Thanks for the help. You'll get the key back. Right now, it's evidence."

"Understood."

Habit compelled Henry to look again at the locker contents. He lifted the sneakers and examined the toe space for valuables. Nothing.

A shadow under the folded towel caught his eye. It didn't look right. Lifting the towel, he saw a small 4 X 6 spiral-bound notebook. He flipped it open and saw notes in Beckman's handwriting. At the top of the first page was written: *Dragon figurehead.* The words made his heart pound faster. Page after page followed with notes. And dates.

Was it the notebook Beckman was protecting?

A surge of hope caught his breath.

Anderson peered over his shoulder. "That what you're looking for?"

"No, but it might be useful." Henry closed the notebook and casually slipped it into his jacket pocket as though it were nothing. He stood to his full height and thanked Mike Anderson.

Outside the Five Tigers academy afterward, an energized Henry considered his options on his way back to his car when his gaze fell upon a large black SUV parked across the street. A tight-faced blond man in a dark suit jacket watched him from the driver's seat. The man and vehicle matched Janet's description. Henry decided to check it out. He got as far as four steps before the driver peeled off like a bat out of hell. The SUV roared down the street.

Henry shouted after him, "Was it something I said?" He tried to read the license plate yet couldn't get a good bead on it.

Crappy surveillance, but whose? he wondered.

With an indifferent grunt, he returned to the sidewalk and suddenly changed direction. His car could wait. New developments require quality think time. Instead, he strode half a block up to Caribou Coffee, whose sign had beckoned him on a chilly morning. Inside, he was put at ease by the comforting aroma of fresh ground coffee beans and the timber-framed Northwoods décor. Latte with skim milk in tow, Henry found a small table by the front window and settled in. Two sips later, he flipped open the spiral notebook cover and scanned the contents. Notes, dates, comments, some quick sketches. Names. Luckily the professor was an avid note-taker. If electronic versions of this info existed, they might never be found. Beckman's home and work computers nor his smartphone had turned up. His killer had taken them. Janet's examination of his work email had turned up nothing of value.

Henry went back to page one. The first entry was written in a fluid cursive style. "August 3. L.H. wants advice on a new piece he acquired last winter. Wants it authenticated. Good money. Piece is a bronze Chinese dragon head. Size of a basketball."

Taken by a thought, Henry flipped through the notebook pages. Beckman never mentioned Lee Hatcher by name, only by initials. Others he named but never his client.

Outside on the sidewalk, a young couple and their toddler strolled by. The boy pressed his head against the glass and made a face at him. Henry stuck out his tongue. Behind him came the growl of a bean grinder. He took a long sip of his latte as his eyes drank in the notebook. "August 5th. Met with L.H. Saw his art collection. Impressive. Mostly European art. Some African, some pre-Columbian baskets. L.H. has three Asian objects: a 20th-century jade horse, a silk banner, and the dragon head. He let me hold the dragon piece. Damage at the neck, as if it's incomplete. Like it's been torn off something. Took detailed photos."

A comment later: "Know nothing about this piece. Check with Richardson, Yang, Kasparian."

Kasparian.

Henry caught his breath.

So Beckman had talked to Kasparian about the artifact.

According to Janet, the antiquities dealer had denied that had happened.

More pages turned. Nothing special until September 10th and in bold letters: "Yang saw the photos. Thinks the dragon head could be from the zodiac fountain from Yuanmingyan Garden!!!" The next was underscored three times. "Yang: seven of the fountain zodiac heads have been recovered. Five remain missing. Although the dragon head was allegedly found in 2009 and auctioned in 2018. Questions about its authenticity. Is it a fake? Could Hatcher's be genuine or a copy?"

A few false leads followed. Then on September 14: "Chen H.F. in Singapore has a contact who's an expert on the zodiac fountain. He could authenticate. Kasparian returned call. Very interested in the piece. Offered to help. Need to be careful with K."

The writing was more rushed now. Henry flipped to the last page of notes. "September 24: Chen H.F.'s contact believes the dragon head may be the real deal! OMG! Must get authenticated. Need to tell L.H. the news."

Then this: "October 7: New wrinkle. Contacted by a Chinese cultural assistant minister, Shen Jiang-Li from S.A.C.H. About the dragon piece. Claims it belongs to her government. Not good! How the hell did she learn about it all the way in Beijing? Maybe Yang or Chen associate? Ugh. This complicates things."

"October 8: Told L.H. about Shen. Not happy. It was inevitable. Word gets out on this stuff. Shen flying to Minneapolis in a few days. Wants meeting with L.H."

"October 12: Meeting with Shen J.L. in L.H.'s office. Cordial but tense. Shen insists the dragon head must be returned to the People's Republic of China. She'll involve the U.S. State Department if necessary. This could get ugly."

And it did.

Henry's eyes lingered on the two final entries, scribbled in haste. Beckman was anxious. Henry flipped through the empty pages after them to the end. Nothing more, only a doodle on the back cover. Too bad Beckman had stopped there. It would've been too easy if Beckman had written down where he'd stashed the relic.

Bothered by that thought, Henry returned to the doodle on the back cover: a stick house next to a bumble bee or hornet. What either meant—if they meant anything at all—were lost on him. That it was the only drawing in the book not of the dragon head made it stand out. Even so, did it *have* to mean anything? It was a doodle. So what? Except it was the *only* doodle in the notebook. And that bothered him.

Slouching in his chair, he lifted his coffee cup and downed the remaining contents as he examined the notebook again, bothered by that scratchy drawing and wondering if there was some clue to it in the notes. The clatter of porcelain dishes and the hiss of a milk steamer filled his ears as he flipped through the pages. Lee Hatcher had off-handedly accused Beckman of stealing the dragon head under the ruse of getting the artifact appraised. Minister Shen had suggested another option: that Hatcher had intentionally given Beckman the relic to keep Beijing from getting their hands on it. The more Henry chewed on the suggestion, the more he liked it. His thumb ran along the coffee cup edge, thinking through different scenarios, considering which were the most likely. Before he traveled too far down that road, he thought it prudent to text Janet ahead of her meeting with Kasparian.

Message sent, Henry heard a car door slam outside and looked up. Two Asian men climbed out of a silver-gray minivan; the movement got a passing glance from Henry. An indescribable feeling flashed through his consciousness. It made him look again, this time harder. One of the men seemed familiar for some reason, yet he couldn't place him. Then, when the taller man glowered at something the other said, Henry felt a jolt of recognition.

Mr. Tong! Shen Jiang-Li's associate.

The same pit bull face and pointed eyebrows. Although today the man he'd met in Wayzata Bay wasn't decked out in an ill-fitting suit, he sported a faded University of Minnesota hoodie, jeans, and black high-top sneakers. The pair hustled across the street and entered Silk Road Imports.

Henry got up to follow.

CHAPTER 20

The clang of a little brass bell and a whiff of sandalwood greeted Henry as he entered the import store. Only one customer was inside, a plumpish middle-aged woman in a faux leopard jacket who seemed indecisive about a miniature blue porcelain Buddha. Should she buy it? No. Yes. Maybe. She put it down and tried to step away, only to be lured back by the smiling figurine an indecisive moment later.

There was no sign of either of the two men whom he had followed in.

Odd.

Henry scanned the shop. Nothing. Just to be certain, he walked the aisles before approaching the check-out counter. The proprietor looked up and smiled when she saw him.

"You come back," said Darlene Chow. Her bright crimson lips parted generously, and the thin, curving black eyebrows rose over dark eyes that sparkled at his approach. "You decide to go out with my daughter?" She chuckled, tidying her printed blouse, primping for him a little. "You forget her number? I get for you double-quick," she added with motherly encouragement.

Henry politely waved her off. "No, thank you. I'm here for another reason."

Chow winked. "Oh, don't be embarrassed. I give you her number again. You'll like Stacey. She's very pretty."

Tempting as the offer may have been, Henry let it pass. "I'm looking for the two men who just came in."

"What two men? I no see them." Her pudgy hand made a sweeping gesture around her.

Henry met her gaze and held it. "I saw them come in. I was right behind them. Where did they go?"

She paused to collect her thoughts. "I no see anybody," she repeated with an odd tone of voice.

Something was off. Henry wasn't sure what. Just to remind her of his position, he displayed his badge wallet again. "This is a police investigation, the same one I mentioned when I first came here. I'm not playing games."

Her black-dyed hair jiggled as she shook her head. Henry noticed a CCTV camera mounted on the wall above her and wondered if anyone could be watching. He motioned at a divider bamboo bead curtain hanging at the rear of the store.

"That's the back room?" he asked. "Is there another door?"

She nodded.

"Mind if I take a look?"

The easy smile evaporated. "That private. You no go there."

"I need to see what's behind the curtain."

He saw her hand drop to the edge of the counter as if pressing a button. As Henry moved to the bamboo curtain, he heard the clatter of shoes running up steps. The sound didn't feel right, so he drew his Glock and pushed aside the curtain. Across from him stood rows of metal racks, their shelves stuffed with inventory items of all shapes and sizes. He nearly bumped into a tall stack of cardboard boxes labeled and ready for shipping. In front of him, off to the side, was the back door, half-open. Two men had just run up from downstairs; one with his hand on the knob wore a U of M sweatshirt with the hood down.

Mr. Tong.

From a dozen feet away, there was no doubt. It was the same man.

"Police! Don't move." Henry stood in a low ready stance; his sidearm pointed at the floor yet ready to bring up in a blink. His eyes zeroed in on each man for a weapon. Both seemed to be calculating the odds of diving through the back door before Henry could react. "Listen up," he ordered. "Put your hands above your head and keep 'em there."

The pitbull was indignant. "We didn't do anything." He spoke in perfect American English, a peculiar look in his eyes.

"Then why were you running?"

"We thought you were robbing the place."

"Really?" Henry said, amused. "I thought I was more memorable than that. Don't you recognize me, Mr. Tong?"

The other shook his head. "You got me mixed up with some other dude."

"I don't think so, but there's an easy way to resolve that. We'll just check your IDs. Both of you move away from the door. Now."

The men hesitated as if planning their next move.

Henry raised his weapon. "Step away from the door."

Reluctantly, they edged forward and to the side. Henry pivoted to keep a bead on them. "A little more."

Tong's eyes flicked to the stack of boxes near Henry.

Uh oh.

An instant later, an explosion of motion and cardboard engulfed him. Henry stumbled back. His left arm flew out to steady himself, grabbing a handful of dangling bamboo bead strings. The curtain rod ripped from the doorframe when he pulled on it. Somehow he managed to regain his balance, standing awkwardly and facing the wrong way. He couldn't see the door, just large boxes and the floor. And a brown shoe. The shoe was attached to a foot crashing into his shin.

The blinding pain short-circuited his ability to stop the savage thrust kick to his chest that hurled him back and down to the floor. Large boxes were thrown on top of him. Unable to see or think straight, Henry frantically tried to clear his head. His ears caught running hard-soled shoes from behind.

"*Zǒu kāi! Zǒu kāi!*" a familiar voice interjected, Darlene Chow's. She spewed in her native Mandarin. "Go away! Go away!" Henry understood the words. She wasn't finished. She was pissed, boldly chasing the men out as she railed after them as he struggled to get out from under a mountain of heavy cardboard. He heard the door squeal open. The intrusion of traffic sounds. Hasty footsteps and a door slamming shut. Henry elbowed the box over his face, realizing the Glock was still in his right hand.

"Are you okay?" Chow said, concerned. She lifted another large box off his pelvis; the broken contents shifted inside. Henry saw her anguished face bent over him. "Bad men go away. They run outside. You hurt?"

"I'm okay." He struggled up with a groan. His chest felt like it had been hit by a sledgehammer.

Chow looked relieved. "You come with me. Have tea. Tea make you feel better."

"I'll be fine."

"You need tea," she insisted.

Tea didn't interest him, though he did follow her out of the back room to the front counter. No one else was in the shop, the female Buddha enthusiast having made a hasty exit at the earlier commotion.

Henry felt his ribs to make sure none were broken. He looked at Chow. "Who were those men?" he asked again. Something was going on. Tong and the others had been in the basement. She must know something.

Chow fingered her blouse collar. Her face clouded. "They threaten me. The men came in here like you said. They show big gun. Say they want a piece of art, head of a dragon made of bronze. The men say they know I have the dragon here. They want it. I tell them I don't know what they're talking about. I no have dragon. They no listen. They say a man told them I have it." She tossed up her hands in frustration. "I tell them they're wrong. No bronze dragon here. They no believe me. They want to search the basement. They say if I tell anybody, they'll kill me and my customers."

Now Henry understood what had happened earlier. "That's why you said they weren't here. They were watching you from the CCTV."

"Yes, they watch from the basement monitor."

That reminded him. "When we talked earlier, it looked like you pressed a button on the counter."

"Buzzer for downstairs. You show me your badge, camera would see it good. I buzz, so men downstairs look at monitor. Maybe scare them away."

Good thinking on her part, he thought. And it had worked. Although their getaway was spoiled by his untimely appearance.

"Thanks for your help," Henry said, "You stood up to them. That was dangerous. Thank you."

Her chin jutted out, hands resting on sturdy hips. "They come into my place and boss me around. That not right. They were hurting you. I was mad!"

He laughed. "You scared them off. That's all that matters."

Swelling her chest, she said, "I tell them the video cameras record them too. The longer they stay in my store, the more video of them I show the police. The one man got angry. He said he'd shoot me and take the tapes. I tell him tapes not here; they go to alarm company on the internet!"

"And they left right after that."

"Yeah."

"I'd like to see those tapes."

Now it was Darleen Chow's turn to laugh. "No tapes. I make it up. Close circuit TV is live only, for me to see what's going on in the store when I'm downstairs or in back. Helps on days when I work alone like today. My other employee is on vacation this week."

She'd bluffed them and won. Clever, he thought, and resourceful. He couldn't help but smile back. "Have you seen any of these men before?"

She shook her head.

Which reminded him. Both Tong and his friend had been in Henry's view the whole time. Someone else had been in the back room with them, that someone was the one who'd pushed the stack of boxes at him. "Someone else was with them. Did you see him?"

Another head shake. "Sorry. The men opened the back door and let him in. I no see."

"These men thought you had the dragon head?"

She nodded.

"Why did they think that?"

"They say someone told them I had it."

"And you have no idea who that was?"

"No. I sell plenty of Chinese dragons. You see all around you. None like they looking for. Maybe someone got mixed up."

"Well, that will have to do. You still have my card?"

"In the cash drawer."

"If those men—or anyone else—contact you again about the dragon head, let me know."

Darlene Chow offered a motherly smile. "Happy you not hurt. Too bad I no have video for you."

"It's okay." He patted the pocket of his bomber jacket. "I should still be able to identify them. I took a photo of their car license plate with my cell phone."

She looked back, impressed. "You smart!"

Yes, he was smart. Though maybe not as smart as he thought, Henry would realize much later. For now, he had a prior commitment. Somewhere he really needed to be. A debt he needed to honor, one that nothing or nobody would prevent him from honoring.

CHAPTER 21

"What brings you back, Detective?"

Angelo Kasparian eased into the leather chair and adjusted his suit jacket. His large hands rested on his desk as he patiently waited for Janet to get down to business.

She wasted no time. This could be a very short visit. Henry's text message had given her a stick to poke him with. If he didn't respond, she had nothing else to get a rise out of him. "Mr. Kasparian, I don't believe you were entirely forthcoming during my first visit." She paused, not for dramatic effect but to rally her courage. Not only was she being confrontational, she was going for the jugular. "Last time I asked if you'd had any recent dealings with Roger Beckman, and you said you hadn't." She skewered him with a look. "We've found his notebook. It's a log of his activities with the dragon head relic. Names. Dates. Your name comes up a few times."

An innocent smile spread across Kasparian's bearded face. "Given our working history, I wouldn't be surprised to find my name in Roger's notebook."

"This was recent. Less than a month ago. He asked what you knew about the dragon artifact."

"He did," Kasparian conceded. "That's when I told him the story of the missing fountainheads from the Garden of Eternal Spring."

"You didn't mention that last time."

"Didn't I?"

"No."

"As I recall, Detective, you never specifically asked."

Okay, now she was pissed off and had no qualms letting him know it. "This isn't a game, Mr. Kasparian; this is a murder investigation. You could have said something."

Armani-clad shoulders lifted dismissively. "I'm a merchant of information. I don't give it out freely. Since I didn't kill Roger, the question of when I last saw or spoke to him wouldn't have helped you. I saw it as irrelevant."

"That's for me to decide, not you."

"Perhaps. In any case, you didn't specifically ask, and I decided not to volunteer what I knew."

Janet stared back with laser eyes. A lesser man would have flinched. Not Angelo Kasparian, who, she thought, was too cagey for his own good. A straight question deserved a straight answer. People who dodged a question were hiding something. She cleared her throat, carefully phrasing her next words, not bothering to hide her impatience: "Mr. Kasparian, did Beckman talk to you—either verbally or in writing—about his work on the bronze dragon?"

"He did."

A lengthy pause followed.

That was it?

It was all she could do from reaching across the desk and slapping the smug smile off his face. Of course, she wouldn't have actually done it. Verbal confrontations were difficult enough; physical ones were out of the question. Still, the idea of it satisfied a primal urge. Instead, she kept her wits and pursued a more diplomatic path. It was a struggle. "Can you elaborate?"

It couldn't have escaped someone who indulged in wordplay as much as Angelo Kasparian that Janet was irritated. After a reflective moment, his manner changed. "I apologize if I've been too circumspect. A second visit from you makes me wary. Contrary to the old nursery rhyme, sticks and stones may break my bones, but words *can* come back to hurt me." He cocked an eyebrow. "But I like you, Detective. I think I can trust you. Allow me to start over. Roger contacted me in early September. He mentioned a freelance appraisal he was working on. He asked what I knew about the water clock fountain at Haiyantang. A passing knowledge, I told him. I'd read about it years ago. I knew most of the looted fountain heads had been recovered and that a few were still missing. After what seemed a reluctant pause, Roger said his client might have acquired one of them." Kasparian's eyes gleamed like a kid opening a Christmas present. "When I heard that my heart almost skipped a beat."

"I'm sure it did."

"Roger was trying to determine the artifact's authenticity. He was cautious, starting with the assumption it was either a cheap copy or an outright fake. He asked if I knew anyone who could authenticate it. Metallurgists. Period specialists." Kasparian paused to reach for a water bottle. He chugged half of it. No sipper he.

"What did you tell him?"

"That I have contacts in China, none with special expertise in the Garden of Eternal Spring or the fountain, although one of them may know someone who does. I gave Roger a couple of names out of courtesy."

Janet shot him a sidelong glance. "You didn't happen to express your own interest in the dragon head, by any chance?"

He folded his hands across his belly. "I did ask Roger to pass along my services to his client, should he be interested in disposing of the piece. If the item turns out to be genuine, it will fetch a pretty penny on the resale market."

"If the Chinese government doesn't seize it first."

"True."

Nothing more needed to be said. Janet made to stand up. "If that's everything, I'll be one my way—"

"Just a moment, Detective." Kasparian motioned for her to remain seated. His voice and manner grew personal. "Last time I saw you was at the Minneapolis Institute of Art. How did your meeting go with David?"

She made a sour face. "I was not impressed. Nakagawa tried to wiggle out of it the next day."

"Yes, I heard you and your partner rattled David. Got him to answer your questions. Nicely done."

Janet raised an eyebrow. "How do you know that?"

Angelo Kasparian answered as one sharing a privileged secret. "Let's say I have friends in many places. Word gets back to me, especially when it concerns my rivals and a juicy tidbit like that."

Friends? More likely well-placed informants. The meeting with David Nakagawa was held at his company, not a public venue. Some employee at Nakagawa Trading Company must have notified Kasparian, she figured. Janet looked at the man sitting across from her with new respect. Along with his other talents and abilities was Angelo Kasparian also a spymaster? She wondered how far and how deep his web of informants reached.

"We were at a standoff," she volunteered. "My partner provoked a reaction from Mr. Nakagawa."

"I wish I could have been there to see it. David can be difficult."

"So I've seen."

"He views himself as a major player in the business world. That's not exactly fair; he *is* a major player in his niche. His holding company has strong ties to or outright owns several Fortune 500 companies. But I will say he does get full of himself at times. Thinks he's John D. Rockefeller or Bill Freaking Gates. Puts himself on top of a pedestal and looks down at everyone else. Be careful."

Janet managed to drown a rising snort. First, Kasparian had warned her to be careful with David Nakagawa. Then Lee Hatcher had warned her to be wary of Kasparian. Next, Shen Jiang-Li cautioned her and Henry not to trust Hatcher. Now Kasparian was once again telling her not to trust Nakagawa. Nice bunch of crooks, she thought.

Kasparian's paternalistic tone made Janet think of her father. A timeless image reared up. She was sixteen and standing in her living room, about to go on a date with Steve Fanucci and being lectured by Douglas Lau on the perils of dropping her moral guard. For crying out loud, they were just going out for ice cream!

She managed to suppress her amusement.

"...he can be cutthroat when he has to be," Kasparian was saying.

"How cutthroat?" she asked. "Are we talking criminally?"

"Hard to say."

"Would he kill?"

"Kill? No..."

"You don't sound convinced."

"Who can say? I don't know David that well. He has stepped over the ethical line from time to time."

"How so?"

Kasparian reached for the water bottle and took a long pull. "I have an associate in Singapore. His brother had dealings with Nakagawa Trading. The brother makes integrated circuits and was working on a deal to supply one of David's companies with chips and microprocessors. The deal had been in the works for a while. At the eleventh hour, David's man tried to sabotage the deal, demanding below-market costs."

"Sounds ruthless."

"I've no doubt David knew about it, probably even engineered the whole thing. He's a fierce competitor."

Janet nodded. Point taken. "If Nakagawa really wanted the bronze dragon head, would he have gone behind Roger's back to acquire it?"

Kasparian scoffed, "David Nakagawa would sell his grandmother if it got him what he wanted."

"And you wouldn't?"

"I wouldn't. Detective Lau, my reputation *is* my business. One whiff of a dishonest deal is enough to kill a career. No reputable dealer would go near you again."

"What about disreputable ones?"

"It may come as a shock to you, but I have had no experience with disreputable dealers."

"That doesn't answer my question. Surely a man of your experience has heard things or is aware of illicit transactions."

He looked back modestly. "You flatter me, Detective. I may not be as well connected as you believe."

She wasn't buying it. "C'mon, you have associates worldwide. Am I right?"

"You are."

"You're honestly telling me that not one of them has ever been involved in or had contact with a disreputable seller? Aren't even aware of the players? I find that hard to believe."

Kasparian's voice turned to flint. "If anyone ever asked me to do anything like that, I'd tell them they have the wrong man. As I said, once a reputation is tarnished, that's the end of a career. And I value my reputation."

"I'm sure you do." Although that didn't mean she believed it was beyond him to dip his toe into a few gray areas from time to time. What she didn't know was what Angelo Kasparian valued more: a spotless reputation or being a man who could get you anything.

As soon as she got back to her car, Janet called Henry's number. It went straight to voice mail. She sent a text. No reply. That didn't surprise her. Henry was not a heavy cell user. In fact, she'd been surprised to get a text from him that morning. She started her car but didn't shift the gear out of Park. She kept thinking about Henry. Had a niggling urge she should check up on him, though she didn't know why. It occurred to her he may have told her earlier in the week that he'd be taking an extended lunch today. Some private errand. At first she thought he might be attending one of Alan's late morning Wing Chun classes until she realized it was the wrong day. Alan was at work.

On a whim, she decided to call Alan, who was like another uncle to her. She'd known him her entire life. She cut the engine and sat back.

"Janet!" he answered on the first ring. She could visualize his wide grin. "Are we going to see you in class sometime soon?"

"I hope so. I'm trying to work it in my schedule."

"Somehow, I don't think you called me about kung fu. And you're too old to be selling Girl Scout cookies."

"I'm looking for Henry. He's not answering his phone. You haven't talked to him today, have you?"

"Sorry, I haven't. Is something wrong?"

"No," she answered. "Just a feeling I should talk to him." To anyone else, she would've added, "Weird, huh?" Not to Alan Zhu, whose ability to appreciate the intricacies of the human heart was second to none.

"If the feeling is that strong, it must mean something. If I hear anything, I'll let you kn—"

He stopped abruptly.

Silence.

"Alan?"

"Is today October 15th?"

"It is. Is that significant?"

"It's the day Kay was killed."

Jesus! She should have remembered.

Kay McAdams.

Henry's college girlfriend. Now Janet wished she knew where he was. What did the day mean to him? The death anniversary of a loved one could be emotional. With no idea where he was, she could only hope for the best.

CHAPTER 22

The falls at Minnehaha were a raging cascade thanks to an unusually wet spring and summer. Its tributary creek was swollen for its nearly twenty-two-mile journey from Lake Minnetonka in the western suburbs through the heart of Minneapolis to its terminus.

Henry watched the torrent from an observation deck near the base of the falls. Close enough to smell the damp spray and feel the mist. The creek waters rushed close by. Fallen leaves, propelled by a strong current, sailed rapidly into the densely wooded park where they would eventually spill into the Mississippi.

There were few visitors at Minnehaha Park that October morning. Henry had the place mainly to himself. He needed that, to be away from people, alone with his thoughts in nature. Nature asked for nothing except to be left alone. Nature offered serenity and gave him a comforting space in which to reflect, to grieve, and to heal. He needed a place special to him in order to pay respect to the memory of someone special: Kay McAdams. That much he owed her, for it was on this day twenty-two years ago that the love of his life was murdered in cold blood.

And he could have stopped it.

Henry gripped the fence rail and stared into the foaming white thunder of water as the memory pulled at him. So long ago yet still so fresh. What continued to gnaw at him was knowing that his final moments with Kay on that last day had not been his finest hour.

They'd been dating for nine months, the last four seriously, more or less. Unfortunately fall quarter that year was an intense one, with conflicting class schedules that had left little time for them to be together. To mitigate this, they had arranged to meet at Rusty Bob's for lunch between classes. The café was near campus, a throwback to a 1950s diner, complete with Formica pink counters and a jukebox. They ate lunch at a small table beneath a black and white photo of James Dean in a leather jacket.

"How'd your test go?" Henry's face contorted around a jumbo cheeseburger with a youthful disregard toward eating decorum.

Kay wrinkled her nose. "Let's just say aerobic bacteria metabolism and I are not friends. But I think I passed."

"Good," he said between chews. "You studied hard for that."

"I did." Kay's sensuous lips brushed against a French fry and engaged it. He was mesmerized.

She noticed the vacant expression. "You okay?"

"Uh, yeah. For a moment, I was envious of that fry."

Enchanting dark eyes warmed with affection. Kay said, "You make me laugh."

He smirked wide, glad to be appreciated. Classy, kind-hearted, and bubbly, she lit up any room she entered. In his heart of hearts, he knew she was out of his league. She could have had her pick of beaus. Many had made a play for her, which she skillfully managed to deflect. Somehow, for some reason he never fully understood, Kay had chosen him above the others. Him! How was the possible? Smart as he was to grasp this, a young and naïve Henry Lau wasn't yet smart enough to know how to keep her.

Kay shook her head. "Been a tough month with the books. I barely passed that test. I'm dreading the final."

"You're smart. I have faith in you."

"Thanks. It means even more extra hours studying. Little time for anything else." A hint of sadness colored her voice. "Just school and part-time jobs until break."

"Yeah."

"I miss you."

"Miss me? You saw me last week."

"For just an hour."

"I miss you too," he replied in kind.

Kay looked back, struck by a thought. "There's that Mexican restaurant Amy was telling us about. Food's supposed to be out of this world. Let's go there for dinner tonight," she said with a longing in her voice.

He didn't pick up on it. Henry took another bite of his cheeseburger. "Bad timing. I have Wing Chun tonight. We could go after."

"They'll be closed by then." She looked deflated. "Henry, you're always in kung fu class. Can't you take a day off?"

"Kay, I'm not *always* there. Just three days a week."

"What I meant is when you're not there, you're practicing. It's like a part-time job. We've hardly seen each other this month."

"I know things are crazy now. Next quarter it'll be better. I promise."

An elegant eyebrow arched skeptically. "You sure? To me, it seems like you're spending more and more time with kung fu. Whenever there's an opening in your schedule, that's where you go. If you could get a degree in Wing Chun, you would."

Henry swallowed. "You know the chance to study with Eric Kwan is the reason I moved to California," he said defensively. "Wing Chun is my passion."

She regarded him with a look he didn't understand then and replied in words that would come to haunt him for years afterward. "I wish you had that passion for me."

"I do, Kay." He reached across the table for her hand.

"It doesn't feel that way. I feel I'll always have second place in your heart."

Henry set down his sandwich and met her gaze. "I'm sorry. I do get too involved. Kung fu is my life, the only thing in my life that ever made me feel special...until I met you. You *are* a passion with me, Kay." He lowered his voice. "I'm not good at showing it."

He also wasn't good at shifting priorities. Over the past few years, he'd had one goal that burned like a white-hot ember: to be the best martial artist in the world or, failing that, in the top tier. Achieving a goal like that meant he had to be extremely dedicated and focused. Training was everything. The more he trained and sparred, the better he got. A day not training was a day lost. Each day stacked upon the other. Each day got him closer to his goal.

It was then Henry noticed it. The brightness had dimmed in her eyes. A realization whispered to him that he needed to address her concern straight on. With contrition, he admitted, "I do need to do better. Promise, I'll work on that."

Hope filled her eyes. "So we've got a dinner date for tonight?"

"How about Saturday? We can spend the whole day together. You've been talking about going to Monterey. We'll drive there. Whatever you want."

Kay withdrew her hand from his. "I really was hoping for tonight."

"Saturday's not that far away," he said, selling the idea with a wink.

Disappointment—and something else—hardened in eyes that had always embraced him until then. Bitterness edged her next words. "I've supported your kung fu. I've not complained because I knew how important it is to you. But Henry, you need to think about what really matters. Am I important? I won't be patient forever."

Kay let her words sit heavily upon him. She rose without further comment and exited Rusty Bob's, leaving Henry alone and confused as *Earth Angel* played from the jukebox.

Go after her. The voice in his head urged. *Go. After. Her.* But Henry just sat there, reviewing the conversation, the self-absorbed logic of a twenty-two-year-old justifying his comeback to her. Yes, he could see her point, and he would do better from now on; it just didn't seem important enough to change his plans for tonight. He thought he'd been reasonable by offering a compromise. Saturday mornings were his favorite training day, and he'd been willing to give up this coming Saturday for her.

The irony was Wing Chun class that evening turned out to be a disappointment. Eric Kwan was unable to attend, something to do with his second daughter getting in a fender bender. Only five people made it to class, none of the senior students, which meant he didn't have anyone at his level or above to spar with. Even Alan Zhu didn't make it. Comparing notes with Alan after a workout was one of the best things about training. Class turned out to be nothing special. After making such a big fuss about going, he could have skipped it and gone to dinner with Kay and not lost any ground. The first thing he did after he got home was to call her. Even though she wasn't happy with him, he knew Kay was too sweet-tempered and too good a person to stay mad at him, especially after he apologized for screwing up.

The landline receiver rang. On the fourth ring, the phone was answered.

"Hello…"

It was Jo, Kay's roommate.

"Hi, Jo, it's Henry. Is Kay there?"

"Henry—" She nearly choked on his name.

"Jo? What is it?"

She didn't respond. Instead, a disturbing silence.

"Jo, what's wrong? You're making me nervous."

She inhaled sharply, barely able to utter the next words. "Henry…Kay's dead."

"*What?*"

"She was mugged. Kay was out shopping and some guy attacked her in the parking lot."

"How….how did she die?"

"She was shot."

"Oh, God."

"She died at the scene."

It was a gut punch that he had no defense against. He barely got out the next words. "Did they catch the guy?"

"No."

He tried to form a reply but was at a loss, his heart too heavy.

Jo came back with a stifled sob. He felt guilty for putting her through this. She struggled to compose herself. "It was awful. I found out forty minutes ago. The police just left. All I know is what I told you. I was going through Kay's address book when you called, looking for her parents phone number. Oh, this'll destroy them—"

"Jo, you okay? You need company? Want me to come over?"

"That's nice of you, Henry, but Evan's on his way. Oh Henry—" She choked.

"I know," he replied in a muted voice. Too numb to say much else. "If there's anything I can do, let me know."

Henry replaced the receiver and stared at the phone for a while as if he couldn't believe any of it had actually happened. After a moment, he trudged zombie-like to a chair and fell into it as the world around him crumbled, one thought swirling in his mind: *I should have been there.* If he'd gone to dinner with Kay, this wouldn't have happened. She'd still be alive if he hadn't said no to her. All that stupid training. What was it good for? To do cool things? To protect people? Yet when she'd needed him the most, Henry wasn't there to help Kay.

Kay McAdams was dead. Sweet, beautiful Kay. He'd never see that glorious smile again, would never hear that melodic voice or feel the warmth of her touch. Henry bowed his head, realizing for the first time in his young life that actions have consequences. When the sobs finally came, they rose from deep within.

A heavy melancholia settled in that lasted for days. For weeks afterward, he could barely function, going through the motions of his life without actually engaging in them. He attended classes. Scarcely able to pay attention. For a time he even avoided Wing Chun. It somehow felt tainted. His heart wasn't in it. His heart had been torn out, and the wound was still raw. It was Alan Zhu who helped guide him out of his depression. Alan suggested his rage and pain needed an outlet. Punching the snot out of heavy bags soon became Henry's new favorite thing, though it was all wrong for Wing Chun. All external. All anger-driven. Except it felt so damn good!

Over time, slowly, the pain started to dull, dull enough for Henry to start caring again. Years of training had guided him; lessons intended not only to make him a better fighter but a better human being. These took on new meanings. Or had he finally understood what they'd always meant?

Codes of conduct like:

Practice courtesy and righteousness.

Learn to develop spiritual tranquility.

Abstain from arguments and fights.

Use martial arts skills for the good of humanity.

Help the weak and very young.

Help the weak…Use his skills for good.

That he could do. By protecting others he could, in some way, make amends for having let Kay down and also honor her memory.

Laughter pulled Henry back to the present. A young couple walked below the falls along the dirt path by Minnehaha Creek. They kicked through the fallen leaf clutter as they went, young and in love. Henry smiled. They reminded him of good times with Kay.

Damp green moss clung to the shale rocks on the grotto. The roar of the falls, though not the still mountain lake of his standing meditations, soothed him by masking out sounds of the world beyond so he could reflect without distractions. In honor of Kay's death, the fifteenth of October was the one day of the year Henry made sure he took stock of himself and what positive effect he had on the world.

And would she approve?

CHAPTER 23

"Thanks for coming. I know it was short notice." Abby Lau greeted Janet in the lobby of the Rich Harvest Cafe. Hugs were exchanged.

"You caught me at a good time." Janet motioned toward the order counter. It was close to lunchtime, and this location was on her way back to the station. The call from her mother had surprised her. In all the time she'd worked for the City of Gillette, her mother had rarely called during working hours. The conversation was brief, a request for a short meet-up.

Mother and daughter got down to business after they had their food. Their table was near the gas fireplace, which added extra warmth and ambiance on a cool October day. Black cardboard bats hung from the menu sign, and bright plastic jack o'lanterns glowed by the coffee airpots. Halloween was two weeks away.

A few slurps into her baked potato soup, Janet broached the subject. "So, what did you want to talk about?"

Abby lowered her coffee and dabbed her mouth with a paper napkin. "You can probably guess. It's about yesterday. That whole thing between your father and Henry. I'm really sorry."

Janet, tuna fish sandwich in hand, gestured in futility. "Mom, you have no reason to apologize. It was Dad."

"I know."

"Where did that come from? Is Dad having a mid-life crisis?"

"Funny you should say that."

"Wait. I'm right?" A startled Janet said with a mouthful of tuna fish.

Abby waved the comment aside. "I'll get to that. Look, what happened yesterday wasn't fair to Henry, nor to you. After you left, I had a chat with your father. He didn't want to, but I didn't let him off."

"Whoa!" Janet sat up. "You got Dad to talk about his feelings?"

Douglas Lau tended to be a closed-mouth man who didn't waste his words, particularly when it came to his emotions. It wasn't so much that he wouldn't share his feelings; it was the limited depths to which he'd share them.

An impressed Janet eyed her mother. "Really? You got him to talk?"

"Yes," Abby confirmed in a note of pride, "I told him what he said to Henry was unfair, that Henry had done nothing wrong."

"What did he say to that?"

"Nothing at first. He clammed up. Then I said I wasn't putting up with his silence. If he didn't talk, he'd get no sympathy from me."

"How'd that go over?"

"He gave me that look of his. Said he was protecting you."

"I know that look," Janet nodded, the ghost of icy stares from her teen years reared up in her memory.

"Your father bottles up his feelings, the negative ones. He and Henry were brought up that way."

Janet smirked. "Unlike you."

Abby smiled, swallowing a bite of her grilled cheese sandwich. "My mother was a cranky Scottish woman who'd shake her fist at the clouds if it rained too much. She couldn't hold back. Ever. Let's just say I grew up in a lively household." Abby, distracted by something on her plate, brushed away a strand of rust-colored hair that had fallen from her head. "I like to think I'm mellower than your grandmother."

"You are, Mom, you are!"

"I look for the positive in people and don't complain just to be negative. However, I have enough of Aileen Campbell in me to yell for the train to stop when it pulls into Bullshit Junction. *If yer bum's oot the windae I hafta say something.*"

The last was spoken in a Scottish burr. Abby had nailed her impression of feisty Nanna Aileen. Abby Lau, lovely, educated, poised, was as gracious as they came, and you'd be well-advised not to mistake her good manners as a license to steam roller her or anyone or anything she cared about. Abby was a redhead and a Scot, unafraid to speak her mind to power. God, Janet thought, when I grow up, I want to be her!

"Dad gave you that look." Janet guided her mother back on topic.

"He did. I told Doug I share his concern about the dangers of your job. Every parent of every cop feels that way. You go after bad people. That's the career you chose. We have to respect that. It's like Doug is blaming Henry for putting you in danger. I told him that wasn't right."

"And?"

"He came back with some bullshit about how I wasn't looking at the big picture. I stared him down and told him to cut the crap. Yeah, he was being overprotective of you. I sensed there was more going on."

"Like what?"

"Your father feels trapped."

"Trapped? By us?"

"No, no. His job."

"Oh."

Abby moved her tray and empty soup bowl to the side. In the distance came the gurgle of the soda dispenser filling a cup. Abby's melodic voice spoke in confidence, rising barely above the low din of conversation at the surrounding tables. "His day job's gotten more demanding these last five years. Being a controller takes up all his time. He often comes home exhausted. Has no time for other interests or even much time to unwind."

Janet nodded. She got that. She barely managed to touch her watercolors outside of class. Other interests had fallen by the wayside thanks to the demands of her job.

Her mother looked off in the distance, remembering. "Your father never wanted to be a CPA."

This was news to Janet, who looked on with interest.

"He wanted to be a carpenter or cabinet maker," Abby said. "His parents pushed him into being an accountant. Your father loves working with his hands."

"Yeah, he made those wooden toys and play boxes for me when I was little. He was always puttering in the basement on some woodworking project."

"He hasn't touched those tools in years."

Janet wiped her hands on a paper napkin. A lump swelled in her stomach as she understood the depths of her father's sacrifice. She knew she wasn't the first child to suddenly come to the realization that her parents had had actual lives when they were young with dreams of their own and disappointments.

Abby was saying: "I think your father lashed out at Henry because he's jealous he got to follow his own path."

That much Janet had suspected. "If Dad's frustrated by his job, tell him to find another one."

"Exactly what I said. Go to a smaller company. Give up finance. Do something else."

"I bet that didn't go over well."

"Nope. Too much like starting over." Abby gave an indifferent shrug. "I told him I was okay with that. We don't have to live in a big house or in a fancy neighborhood. We can scale down."

"He won't do it, though."

"No, he's afraid to start over. He's at the top of his career. It's a lot more difficult for a middle-aged man to change careers than someone half his age. It feels like failure."

The noisy lunch crowd was thinning by now. The decibel level had dropped. Janet looked at her coffee mug and realized it was empty. She wasn't motivated enough to get a refill. Janet's inquisitive face searched out her mother's. "What happened when you suggested Dad get another job?"

"He agreed that's what he should do. But he's scared. Feels he's too old to start over. I told him if we have to downsize, we can. If a less stressful job makes him happy, he should do it. We can move to a smaller house. Live more simply, if that's what it takes."

"Good!"

"He thanked me for saying that. Then he called Henry and apologized."

"Wow..."

Abby leaned in slightly. "He's going to apologize to you, too. He's working up the nerve to do it."

"Huh?"

"Honey, you're his daughter. He knows you always looked up to him. Admitting he has faults to you is difficult."

"I am an adult now, not a girl."

"He knows. Give him a little time. That's why I wanted to meet with you, to give you a heads up."

When Janet returned to the station later, she had hoped to find Henry at his desk. He wasn't back yet. No messages, either. She logged onto her computer and eyed the paperwork waiting for her with a sense of dread. From behind came the rumble of a familiar voice.

"Hey, Detective Lau."

Officer Kowalski stood tall and large behind her, a bull moose in police blues.

"Hi, Dan."

"How's your 10-89?"

In Minnesota, a 10-89 was code for a homicide. Kowalski had been the first officer on the Beckman premises and had secured the crime scene for Janet. Because of that, he kept an interest in the case.

"Still sorting through leads," she said, offering nothing further. One thing Henry had taught her was to be careful showing all their cards prematurely, even to colleagues. It was better that way, if difficult for Janet, who was trusting by nature. And she liked Dan Kowalski.

"Hope you find something." The low voice rose as if from a deep cavern. "By the way, Ginny loves the watercolor set you gave her. It's her new favorite thing."

"Great! I'm so glad she's enjoying it."

"She's painting a picture for you."

Janet's face brightened. It was an old watercolor set she'd found at the bottom of her art box, a starter set with half the colors used up. After Kowalski had mentioned that his eight-year-old was dabbling into art, Janet remembered the old box.

Kowalski added, "After Ginny's done with the picture, I'll bring it in. She's doing an 'extra special' job on it."

"Can't wait to see it."

He returned a nod, his smile fading. "Bowman wants to see you."

Janet followed his gaze to the back of the roomy squad room, expecting to see Chief Bowman standing outside his door waiting for her. He wasn't. That was a relief. Still new to the job, she always felt under scrutiny. She found Bowman in his office, looking out the window at the row of Norway spruce in the parking lot.

"Close the door, please, and sit down."

A worry worm squirmed through her gut.

Bowman eased into his chair and looked across his desk at her. "The mayor wants to see me tomorrow, which means my meeting with you got moved up. You have a few minutes, Detective?"

"I do."

"How's your case load?"

"I've got five open cases. I should wrap up one of them today."

"Good. Just the one homicide?"

"Yes."

"How's that coming along?"

"We've got a new lead. Henry found a notebook left by the deceased. It has names and information." It was probably a measure of her insecurity that she wanted the chief to know they were making progress.

For his part, Bowman gave a cursory nod but didn't seem all that interested. It was then it occurred to her that perhaps the chief hadn't called her into his office for an update on her cases. His next statement confirmed it.

"Let me ask you something," he said. She sat up a little straighter. "How is Henry?"

"Fine. He's fine."

He gave her a reassuring smile. "Be honest. Don't think you need to say that because he's your uncle. I want your honest opinion."

"That is my honest opinion."

"Good to hear it."

She shot back a pointed look. There had been something in his tone. "Why do you ask?"

"Just curious. You've known him your whole life. Now you're working with him, what's your opinion of how he is? I mentioned before he seemed different after his injuries."

"Yeah, you said something about a spark missing. I'm not sure I'd call it that."

The chief's eyes drifted to a framed photo on the wall, an autographed 8 x 10 of basketball legend Michael Jordan standing next to a much younger Bowman as if the ball player could help him coalesce his thoughts. The chief looked back at her. "Maybe I didn't put it well. Perhaps it's better to say he's more thoughtful, more guarded."

"He's been through a lot."

"I know. It's more than that." Bowman's fingers tapped the edge of his desk. "Most guys who'd been run down by a car and left for dead would be obsessed with finding the son of a bitch who did that to them. Henry never talks about it. It's like he doesn't care."

"I don't think he does."

The chief's face was slightly incredulous. "Seriously? He doesn't care? That's a little hard to believe."

"I've never heard Henry bring it up. Not once."

"Then all I can say is that kung fu meditation shit he does must be paying off."

She waved him off. "If you want a real answer, you'll need to ask him. There are some things he's good at. Other stuff, not so much." A slender eyebrow lifted. "Maybe he's too focused on getting better to dwell on getting even. I think I know him, yet even I can be surprised. It's like he has two sides, the calm, thoughtful exterior and the black mamba."

Bowman nodded. "Nasty African snake. Fierce mothers. Saw them on a nature show. The fastest snake in the world. You get bit by one of them, you die." Bowman grunted at an amusing thought. "It's like when Henry goes ape shit on some asshole."

"You've seen him do that?"

"Not me personally. But I've heard things."

Heard things....

Janet had never seen Henry go apeshit on anyone. Nor had he ever spoken about it. Nor Alan. Was this a case of rumor exaggerating her uncle's temperament?

For a moment, Chief Bowman seemed lost in thought. "So it's your opinion that Henry's handling the transition back to work."

"Yes."

That pleased him. "Henry's good at what he does. The thing is, he doesn't always ask for help when he should. He can be stubbornly self-reliant. Don't let him get away with that. Make sure you help him if you think he needs it. That's an order."

"Will do."

"Good. Keep me posted on any changes. That'll be useful when it comes time for his assessment."

Crap. Janet realized she might have said too much. She trusted the chief and hoped her words weren't going to be used against Henry. Good thing she hadn't expressed her concern that she had no idea where her partner was or had misgivings about his current emotional state.

CHAPTER 24

After Janet returned to her desk, she noticed a new email from Angelo Kasparian. She read it and her eyes grew large. *Oh My God.* She settled into her chair, shutting out the groan of the paper shredder in the next room and idle chit-chat from the coffee station. Scooching closer to the display, she carefully read the email again to make sure she'd gotten it right. The content didn't change. Janet grabbed her cell phone. Now she had a reason to call Henry.

That proved unnecessary when, two breaths later, he appeared from around the corner, looking his usual energetic, cheerful self, although she noticed the cheer was turned down by a few notches. Only someone who knew him well would have picked up on that cue. He slipped off his jacket and hung it on the coat hook on the back wall, then dropped into his chair with a friendly wave. She could tell something was on his mind. Most likely Kay McAdams. Trouble was it was too public here to ask such a deeply personal question. Instead, she offered a supportive smile and hoped for the best.

It was then that she noticed the angry red welt along the side of his neck that disappeared into his shirt collar. "I see you've been busy."

A pair of muscular shoulders lifted and fell. "Had a little run-in with some bad guys."

She sat up. "The same guys who jumped you at Omar's?"

"Different guys. It was after I texted you from Caribou Coffee."

He explained the encounter at Silk Road Imports with the man they knew as Mr. Tong and his friend. "The proprietor managed to chase them off. Or they realized it was to their advantage to hightail it while I was buried under a pile of boxes."

Janet nodded with satisfaction. The pieces fit together nicely. Dark eyes latched onto his and didn't let go. She had to be sure. "You're positive this was the same guy we saw with Shen Jiang-Li in Wayzata Bay?"

"Yup. We got up close and personal. There was a look on his face when he saw me."

"A look?"

"Recognition. And something else."

Her face was a question.

There was a glint in Henry's eye. "Panic at being found out. The Oh Shit Look. He saw my reaction. Knew I knew who he was. Makes you wonder about our Chinese minister, doesn't it?"

Janet rubbed her hands together. "Funny you should bring that up." She'd been chafing at the bit to spring the news on him.

Henry eyed her suspiciously. "You found out something?"

Her soft voice carried the words on a tide of excitement. "Just a minute ago, I got an email from Kasparian. Maybe he thinks he owes me after my visit this morning. I'll tell you about that later." She waved it off to get to the juicy stuff. "Kasparian has an associate in San Francisco with a pipeline to Beijing. The message from official channels is there is no record of a Shen Jiang-Li working for SACH or any department of the Chinese government. Shen—or whatever her name is—is an imposter."

There was a silence.

"Well, well," Henry said at last. "The thought had crossed my mind after my run-in with Mr. Tong." Henry frowned thoughtfully at his desk blotter. "The whole thing was a con. Somehow our bogus SACH minister learns that Lee Hatcher has acquired one of the lost bronze fountainheads. She appears before him as a representative of the Peoples Republic of China with a threat of reprisals against his Asian business interests if he doesn't return the stolen artifact to her government. Even if Hatcher has the law on his side, he believes refusing to cooperate will risk pissing off the Chinese. But, as Shen suggested, if he generously donates the relic, he'll be a hero and will get loads of positive publicity worldwide and will gain the gratitude of the people of China. Brilliant!"

"And gutsy," Janet agreed.

Henry clasped his hands behind his head and stared at a ceiling tile. "The question is if our Ms. Shen is the mastermind behind the operation or just the frontwoman and someone else is pulling the strings."

"Could she be behind the Beckman killing?"

"Yes. No. Maybe. Hard to say. One problem with that."

"They jumped too soon," Janet supplied.

A nod from Henry. "Right. They were on the verge of success. Why kill Beckman if Hatcher was on the verge of handing over the relic? Why kill the expert who was about to prove the relic was authentic?"

"Doesn't make sense." Janet brushed back a stray lock of hair from her face. "What about Beckman's alley thugs? Any connection between them and our Chinese friends?"

"Good question. My gut says no."

"And the SUV guy who's been tailing us? I didn't see him today. We still don't know who he's working for."

"Oh, I saw him this morning. I was leaving the Five Tigers. He was parked across the street. He drove off the moment he saw me walking towards him."

Janet scrunched her face. "How many people are after this statue thing?"

A blank look from Henry.

"Back to Tong," she said, intrigued. "Odd that he went to the import store for the dragon head. Why would he think it was there?"

"Maybe he thought Beckman left it there for safekeeping."

"Why would he think that?"

"No idea. Maybe bad intel."

She considered that, her lips pressing together. She grabbed a pencil and tapped the eraser-end on her desk. "We're missing something. Like you said, who's the mastermind pulling the strings? Could it be Tong?"

"No way. I've seen the man in action. He doesn't strike me as mastermind material."

"That brings us back to the lovely Ms. Shen."

"I wouldn't rule her out. She has the smarts and manner for it."

Janet heard the approval in his voice, almost like admiration. Her mouth stretched into a full smile. "You like her, don't you?"

Henry made a self-deprecatory motion.

She read his reaction. "I think you're disappointed she's a fake."

"I am," he sighed.

An honest reaction and understandable, which is why she chose not to pursue the topic. She didn't want to tease him further. The attractive Ms. Shen's come-ons to her uncle were now clearly a patent attempt to curry favor with him so he'd talk freely about the dragon artifact. Janet had distrusted Shen from the beginning. Had never been quite able to figure out why. Now she felt vindicated, though she didn't want to gloat in front of her partner.

She needn't have worried; he wasn't about to let that slide. An annoyed Henry voiced what they were both thinking. "We need to figure out who Shen Jiang-Li really is."

"Agreed."

"She gave me her card. Let's see if I can arrange a meeting."

"Good idea."

Henry fished out the card and punched in the numbers. After a few rings came a recorded greeting and voicemail. "Hello, Minister

Shen. This is Detective Lau. I have a lead on the dragon figurehead. We know where it is. Call me back."

Janet laughed.

"Don't hold your breath. I'm sure Tong informed her of our encounter at Silk Road Imports. She might avoid us."

"Unless she also likes to flirt with danger." Janet made the kissy face again.

Henry rolled his eyes. "I have something for you." He got up and retrieved a small spiral notebook from his jacket, tossing it onto Janet's desk. "Beckman's notebook. I've gone through it. See if you notice anything."

Janet plucked the curly metal spine with a fingernail. "Will do."

"There is one thing. Might be nothing. Go to the inside back cover."

She flipped the pages back to view the doodle. "What's this?"

"I don't know. May be nothing. Or it could be important."

"It's a bee and…a building."

"Yup."

She turned the notebook this way and that. "Looks like a house. A house and a bumblebee. Is that supposed to mean something?"

"It could just be a doodle. People do doodle. We don't want to read too much into it."

"True."

"What bothers me is it's the only one in there."

"I'll give it another look later." Janet closed the cardboard cover.

Henry nodded. "While you're working on that, I'll work on finding Mr. Tong. We find him, and we may find the elusive Ms. Shen."

She looked back, surprised. "You got a lead on Tong?"

Henry dug his smartphone out of his pocket and showed her the photo of Tong's car license plate in sharp focus. "He conveniently parked on the street in front of the coffee shop. The DMV should tell us who the registered owner is."

Janet laughed. "Nice!"

Just then, Henry's cell ringer went off. He swiped the answer button. "Henry Lau," he said, listening for half a minute. After which, he burst into a grin. "Thanks, Rudy, I owe you one!"

Setting down the cell phone, Henry continued to grin at Janet, a triumphant, highly satisfied grin. Her earlier concern about his emotional well-being was not abated by the delight in that grin.

"That was Rudy Chavez from MPD," he said. "The VTR image we got from the gas station paid off. He found the assholes I was looking for."

"Which assholes? The alley thugs?"

"No, the guys who jumped me at Omar's."

"That was fast."

"Pays to have friends with database access."

"What happens now?"

"If you're not busy this afternoon, you can go with me for a little field trip."

"Sounds interesting. I believe I can free up my schedule."

"Great. First, I need to reply to a message from Lee Hatcher."

Janet's eyes flashed open.

"Oh?" she replied with a raised eyebrow. "What does Mr. Hatcher want?"

Henry spelled it out. "The other day, we talked about a follow-up visit to Hatcher. I tried to set one up. Left a message. There was a chance it could happen today. Hatcher emailed to say he had to back out. He has a conflict that just came up. Hopes to get us in tomorrow." A jazzed Henry tapped furiously on his keyboard. "I'll tell him not to worry about canceling, that we have a breakthrough on some goons we need to follow up on."

CHAPTER 25

Large posters hung on nearly every wall. Posters of polished steel motor housings, gears, heat sink fins. Flanges. All products manufactured by Precision Machined Products. The detectives sat in black vinyl guest chairs in the lobby.

Janet appraised Henry. "You're enjoying this, aren't you?"

"I am."

"May I ask why you're doing this?"

In a quiet, measured voice, he replied, "Most crime victims don't get to do this."

"I see."

"Any particular reason you ask?"

"Just curious," she said in a non-judgmental tone, thinking back to her meeting with Chief Bowman a few hours earlier. "We've gone out of our way for this confrontation. I'm not saying I'd do it differently. Just askin'."

"Think it's too much?"

"No. Just trying to understand how things work in the Big Bad World. I'm still young and inexperienced." Janet batted her eyelashes at him.

Henry chortled. Not that inexperienced, he knew. Although Janet had been brought up in a sheltered upper-middle-class suburban home, Abby Lau had gone out of her way to ensure her daughter was not naïve about the ways of the world, had made sure she grew up with respect for all people and creatures. That education included working with the less fortunate and disabled. Entitlement was a foul word in the lexicon of Abigail Campbell Lau.

A door creaked open.

A hooked-nosed man with dark stringy hair entered the lobby. Black harness boots with stainless steel rings walked over to the receptionist, who pointed to the visitors.

"I'm Dave Nagy. What's this ab—" Nagy cut himself off in mid-word, staring at Henry.

"Well, hello." Henry smiled, getting to his feet. He displayed his ID. "Detective Henry Lau from the Gillette Police. This is my partner, Detective Janet Lau."

Nagy swallowed. "Y-you're a cop?"

"Yeah. I told you that the other night outside of Omar's after you and your buddy jumped me. Remember?"

Nagy's eyes darted between the detectives. Worry lines creased his brow. "Shit," he muttered.

"There's the look I wanted to see. You do remember. I'm so glad."

"You've got the wrong guy."

"Shut up, Dave. It was you. You know it and I know it. I have a video of you from that night. How do you think I found you?"

Cornered, Nagy grew defensive. "Okay, but you started it. You cut me off in traffic, ran my car off the road."

Henry paused. "First, even if that were true, it wouldn't justify what you did. Second, that wasn't me."

Nagy's breath caught in his throat. He looked like he was going to crap his pants.

Henry went on. "I take it someone ran you off the road or mouthed off at you. When was this?"

"A month ago."

"Where?"

"The on-ramp to 694 in Maple Grove."

"What kind of car?"

"A red sports coupe with mag wheels."

"Wasn't me, pal. I drive a black Malibu, and I haven't been near Maple Grove in months."

Confusion clouded Nagy's face as he tried to parse the significance of this information. Henry didn't give him time. He took a half step closer to fire a hard look at Nagy that went to the back of his eyeballs. "You know what you did? You mistook me for some other Chinese dude. Didn't bother to confirm I was the same guy before you jumped me."

Nagy shifted uncomfortably. "The light at Omar's wasn't that good, and I'd had a few beers."

"That's not gonna cut it, Dave. Aggravated assault. That's what I can charge you and your buddy with. I could haul your sorry ass to jail right now."

Nagy swallowed hard.

Henry waited, giving him time to digest the threat. "But I'm not going to do that."

"You're not?"

"No, I'm going to let you off with a warning. However, if I *ever* hear about you pulling shit like this again, I'll be all over you." Henry harpooned him with a look. "Stay out of trouble. I know where to find you."

A cowed Dave Nagy nodded.

"I wasn't expecting that," Janet said with approval as they stepped outside into the cool afternoon. "Well played." Their shoes chuffed against the concrete steps as they descended onto the black asphalt parking lot.

Henry shrugged. "What were you expecting, me going 'ape shit' on him?"

She gave a neutral smile. Ape shit. The same phrase Chief Bowman had used.

"I know my reputation at the station," Henry added. "It's overblown. A disgruntled troublemaker started it before he got suspended and left."

For some reason, that pleased her. "Well, to be honest, I was expecting a more in-your-face confrontation with Mr. Nagy."

"I think I made my point."

"You did."

"And I didn't rough him up. Didn't lay a hand on him."

"Nope."

"Did I ever tell you why I first got into kung fu?"

She looked back with interest. "No."

"When I was a kid, I was picked on. Bullied. Some of it was usual stupid kid stuff, some it was racial. Got beaten up a few times."

"Oh."

"The bullies were bigger than me. I stood up to them. That didn't always go well. I didn't know what I was doing. I had spirit but no fighting skills. That's what got me into martial arts. I wanted to be able to beat those guys. Make 'em shut up and leave me alone."

Even now, decades later, she could hear the echoes of those bullies in his voice. You never forget getting picked on.

Henry said, "There are bullies everywhere. All kinds. A lot of people aren't able to stand up to them. You don't always need to be violent to fight back."

On their way to the car, Henry thought the large black SUV parked in the next space looked familiar but dismissed the idea. It was a common make and color. As he and Janet got within a few yards, the driver's door to the SUV flew open and a man emerged. Dark suit, white shirt, black tie. Sturdy build. Short blond military cropped hair, thick black eyebrows, and a surly lower lip. Henry immediately recognized him as the man outside the Five Tigers. Same ugly mug. The man who'd been tailing them.

He strode over to Henry and Janet like a bar room bouncer. "FBI," he barked. "The two of you need to come with me."

It was an order. Henry didn't like being ordered by a big-mouthed jerk who'd just walked up to them without so much as a "pardon me."

"FBI? Really? Show me your ID. Any fool in a suit and a bad haircut can say he's FBI."

"Don't make this difficult." The blond man grabbed Henry's forearm.

Big mistake.

Henry's hips snapped a hard rotation as his elbow pivoted into *tan sau,* which lurched blondie forward just as Henry's free arm exploded a knife-edge *fak sau* into his throat, then circled round to the other side to pinch his carotid artery. Blondie grimaced in agony as he sank to his knees. Janet drew her sidearm as a precaution.

"Whoa! Whoa!" shouted a voice from afar. "Stand down!"

Henry saw a man running toward them, arms trying to flag them down. Medium height and build in a tan overcoat, his rugged, square-jawed face was filled with concern that a disaster was underway.

"Lower your weapon! FBI." He slowed as he neared, hands still out front and empty, his voice apologetic and desperate. "I'm Special Agent Glenn Redding. I'm going to reach into my jacket for my ID. Okay…?"

Henry nodded, releasing Blondie, who collapsed to the asphalt, gasping for air. "Janet," Henry said, "cover our friend here."

Slightly out of breath, Agent Redding removed his ID and handed it to them.

Federal Bureau of Investigation. It looked legit to Henry. "They're okay."

Janet holstered her weapon.

Agent Redding shot his colleague a look. "Smooth move, Dupree," his voice dripped with sarcasm. He glanced round to see a host of rubberneckers gawking at them from the parking lot and sidewalk. "That didn't go well. I apologize, Detectives. This wasn't supposed to go down like this. I just wanted to talk. Do you have a few minutes?"

A more affable Henry said, "Sure."

The FBI man looked longingly across the street. "How about that bakery over there. I abandoned an excellent banana cream pie. Dupree, wait here."

The blond agent, massaging his neck, nodded.

As the trio crossed the street, Henry addressed Special Agent Redding, "For the record, there was no asking. Dupree went all J. Edgar Hoover on us. Didn't show his ID. Ordered us around."

A long suffering sigh. "Sorry about that. Dupree's new. He should know better. I'll talk to him."

Inside the bakery, Redding guided them to a booth by a large window that looked upon the street; a cup of coffee and a half-eaten slice of pie remained on the table. "I said I'd be back," he waved to a chubby waitress wiping the adjoining table.

She flashed a smile. "I believed you, hon. Didn't clear the dishes."

Redding slid onto the bench seat. The detectives sat opposite him. Janet settled in, pulling her dark silken hair away from her face. Henry noticed Redding pausing a moment to admire that face before he took up his fork.

"I didn't know how long you'd be at the machine shop, so I left Agent Dupree to wait for you while I grabbed a bite. No breakfast this morning. Or lunch. I was starving. It was supposed to be routine. Dupree was supposed to ask you nicely to talk with us. By the way, the pie here's fantastic. Want a slice? Maybe coffee?" Redding lifted a forkful of banana cream to his mouth.

Henry sat poker-faced, trying not to betray his curiosity in what interest the FBI had in them. It didn't take long to get his answer. Special Agent Redding set down his fork after a second bite, wiped his mouth with a paper napkin, then gave them his undivided attention.

"The two of you have been investigating the murder of Roger Beckman," he said. "I want to assure you the FBI has no interest in either Beckman or the artifact. Our interest is in Leland Hatcher."

Henry stared back. "Hatcher?"

"Mr. Hatcher's been our target for half a year," Redding spoke in a conspiratorial tone. "What I'm about to tell you is in strict confidence. The public knows Lee Hatcher has a millionaire businessman who does a lot of charity work. Well, that's mainly true. Problem is somewhere along the way, Hatcher's ambition outpaced his resources, and for years his business expansion survived on an elaborate Ponzi scheme. For years his businesses were on shaky ground. It's amazing he managed to stay afloat.

"In later years, he purchased distressed name brand businesses, gutted them, sucked the cash out and sold them off. Surprisingly, a few of these acquisitions actually became profitable. That allowed him to siphon off cash from these businesses to pay off early investors. A Ponzi scheme dies hard. Hatcher's been trying to wipe the slate clean for years, but the mess is too big to easily get rid of."

Fascinating as this was, Henry wondered, "And you know this how?"

"One of Hatcher's inner circle came to us eight months ago, the chief financial officer. She'd had enough. She knew her boss was a con man. Even though he was trying to go legit, Hatcher still had a long string of cheated investors and dodgy enterprises in multiple states." Special Agent Redding gazed at the last morsel of banana cream longingly, then, unable to resist, yielded to temptation. "That was tasty," he said, dabbing the corner of his mouth with the napkin. "Our team has been collecting evidence on Hatcher for five months, building our case slowly, digging through past transactions, and looking for falsified records. We're close to making an arrest."

Henry nodded. An arrest of this magnitude would set off a media firestorm.

Redding took a long drink from his coffee mug. "Our agents have stayed in the background, trying not to raise Hatcher's suspicions. Then you two showed up. At first, I wasn't concerned. Your interest was for an unrelated murder. No problem. We kept out of the way. Then the Chinese minister showed up, and Hatcher started acting funny."

"Shen Jiang-Li," Henry supplied.

"Right. It freaked Hatcher out when she told him the Chinese government wanted the dragon figure back."

Curious, Henry wondered, how Redding seemed to know Lee Hatcher's inner thoughts as if he had access to private conversations. Henry stared down the special agent. "You've bugged Hatcher's office."

"That we have. And his home. We have wiretaps on all his phones. The man can't talk to God without us overhearing it."

Janet inched forward. "You had us followed."

"Dupree," Redding admitted. "Minister Shen rattled Hatcher big time. The reprisal threats from the Chinese government unnerved him. I wasn't sure what he'd do next."

The waitress appeared with a pot of coffee. "A refill, hon?"

"Please." The FBI man slid over the mug.

"The bottom line," he said after she'd left, "is we're at a delicate juncture. I decided it was time I brought you in, so we don't spook Hatcher prematurely." Redding smiled. "Seriously, he freaked out after you emailed him today about a breakthrough on some goons.

The minute that happened, he got on the line to his buddy in Duluth, Frank Kajmac. Hatcher and Kajmac go way back. Grew up together. Back then, Hatcher was a street punk, an ambitious teenager trying to make his fortune. The two of them worked at the same consumer electronics store. That's where Hatcher cultivated and refined his smooth façade. He was naturally charming. Everybody liked him, and Hatcher took advantage of that. Lee Hatcher was the brains and had finesse; his old buddy Kajmac was the muscle. We suspect Kajmac's responsible for an arson that burned down one of Hatcher's failing companies in Milwaukee. He collected a bundle on the insurance."

Henry wasn't sure where Redding was going with this. "Bottom line, you're saying Lee Hatcher is a crook."

"Yes."

"And so we're clear, you're asking Janet and me to back off talking to Hatcher until you've charged him?"

"That would be helpful. As incentive, I can help you solve your murder."

Henry and Janet swapped looks.

"You can?" they both said.

Special Agent Redding looked pointedly at him. "Detective Lau, remember the night you rescued Roger Beckman from those three muggers, the ones in the back alley?"

He nodded.

"They were Kajmac's hired goons."

"Excuse me?" Henry leaned forward, eyes widening. "You're saying Hatcher got his buddy to send thugs to attack Beckman? It all makes sense now." He glanced excitedly toward Janet, who looked back with the same surprise. He turned back to Redding. "Let me see if I got this straight. Hatcher's business empire is collapsing. He desperately needs a fresh infusion of cash to plug financial holes. Then he learns one of his new art pieces may be worth a fortune, gets contacted by a cultural minister from China—or so he thinks—who demands he return the artifact to the Peoples Republic or face unpleasant consequences. That puts Hatcher in a tight spot. The Chinese are threatening to drag him into a messy court battle. So what does he do? He arranges for the relic to get 'stolen.' Kajmac's men will rough up Beckman and take the dragon head. How's that?"

The FBI man nodded. "You got it. The plan was for Hatcher to report the relic as stolen, tell the Chinese he no longer had it to return to them, and, on the sly, sell the piece on the black market."

Henry sat back and smiled. This was the same accusation the counterfeit Chinese minister had made. *How did she know? Or was she just guessing to throw suspicion at Hatcher, not knowing she was actually on the mark?*

An excited Janet broke in. "But that's not how it went down." She faced Henry. "You stopped those alley thugs from getting the artifact or any info about it."

"Right."

"So they tried again later, tracking Beckman to his home where they tortured and killed him."

"Making Lee Hatcher an accessory to murder. And he still ended up not recovering the dragon piece."

"Because Beckman was good at what he did. He hid it someplace and refused to talk, even when tortured."

"It's still missing." Henry looked at Redding. "You've got Hatcher bugged. Did he recover it? Has he said anything?"

The FBI agent shook his head. "Not that we're aware of. My guess is no. In a call yesterday Hatcher made to Kajmac, he sounded frustrated that Kajmac's men 'still hadn't delivered the goods.' That last bit is a direct quote. Coded language, but we can guess what he's talking about." Scraping the last crumbs of pie off his plate, Redding licked the fork clean, set aside the utensil and plate to settle into the padded bench seat.

A confused Janet tilted her head. "Am I missing something? Why bring us into the loop now?"

"As I said before, it was your partner's email to Hatcher this morning that forced our hand. He said something about finding some goons. That rattled Hatcher. He had a shit fit that he was about to be found out. So did we. We thought one of Kajmac's hired guns might work at Precision Machine Company, and you were going to confront him about Beckman."

"Funny thing about that," Janet smirked. "Both you and Lee Hatcher got it wrong."

Agent Redding's brow furrowed. "Got it wrong? How?"

"Henry's email to Hatcher. The goons he talked about weren't the guys who beat up Beckman in the alley. These guys jumped Henry the other day. Totally different bad guys."

"Well, it spooked the hell out of Hatcher; he thought you were closing in on him."

"Right," she said. "So what happens now that we're in your loop?"

Special Agent Redding's light brown eyes glanced between them as his voice softly entreated, "Your partner said it, Detective. I'd like you to back off on Lee Hatcher until we've made the arrest. We're literally within days of doing it."

CHAPTER 26

Janet had been thinking stir fry for dinner. That changed after the meeting with Special Agent Redding. No longer in the mood to cook, she decided to eat out. Feeling Italian, she went to her neighborhood bistro that served a sumptuous Capellini Al Pomodoro. She sat alone at a table for two. As she finished the last of her pasta and sipped her wine, she took out the little spiral notebook that belonged to Roger Beckman. She thumbed through it, looking for insight. Any insight.

Redding's briefing had been an eye-opener, made her understand how she and Henry had been conned by Hatcher. The slick entrepreneur had played them. It was Hatcher, via his rough and tumble buddy, Kajmac, who had unleashed the thugs after Beckman to reclaim the dragon head by whatever means necessary. When the alley attempt failed, they tried again at the professor's house, this time with deadly results. Or so Redding believed. Henry had doubts, and Janet was willing to go along with him. The killers seemed to be a different bunch, though they could have been replacements hired by Kajmac.

All loose ends to the Beckman murder. With luck, she hoped to find answers to some written on the pages of the late professor's notebook. Janet turned through the pages. Read all the entries. Found nothing new. What she noticed was how the writing style and entries changed for the last page. The handwriting was hasty and fragmented, not written in Beckman's careful hand as if he were under stress and too agitated to make meticulous notes. The source of that stress became more apparent as she read further. Her eyes hovered over the last three lines:

Not sure about L.H.

What to do about Shen?

Must decide! Go or no go?

Janet's lips pressed together as her wine glass levitated untasted. The excitement of the beginning notes was replaced by doubt. He no longer trusted Lee Hatcher and had concerns about the female cultural minister.

What to do about Shen?

That could mean a couple of things. Shen was putting a lot of pressure on Hatcher to hand over the artifact. Was Beckman anxious that she'd attempt to seize the artifact by strong-arm methods? Or did he suspect she was an imposter? And what was it he had to decide? From an aerial view, it seemed this could be Beckman assessing his own plan to hide the artifact. Hidden, it would be out of reach for both Hatcher and the Chinese minister. Was go or no go him being indecisive?

"More wine?"

Janet looked over. She hadn't seen the waiter poised by her with a bottle at the ready. She smiled thinly. "I'm good. Thanks. I'm ready for the check."

She fixed keen eyes back on the little college-ruled notebook and the three sentences which suggested an ethical dilemma days before the murder. Doubt. Indecision. Anxiety. Enough anxiety that Beckman didn't feel it was even safe to confide his complete thoughts in his private notebook.

Flipping by the empty pages, she hoped for an entry Henry might have missed earlier. She saw none. Only blank pages until she got to the end where the doodle on the inside back cover confronted her.

A house and a bumblebee.

She narrowed her eyes on it.

Did it mean something? Or was it just an aimless doodle, the kind you did while waiting on hold on the phone? Henry had been right:

the doodles were nowhere else in the notebook. Only a few hasty drawings of the dragon head. Drawings, not doodles. Doodlers were often consistent with the things they scribbled: lines, geometric shapes, words, or drawings.

She stared at the sketch as if willing it to reveal itself to her.

This had to mean something.

If the drawing was a message, it was meant only for Beckman, so naturally, he'd use something easy for him to decode but obscure to anyone else. Which meant she should not get too frustrated if she couldn't crack it. But frustrated she was. Coming up with the answer would be a nice feather in her hat for her first murder case. She really wanted to prove her promotion was deserved.

Relax, you're too hard on yourself.

Janet sighed. Pay attention to your inner voice, she chided herself. It was sensible. And usually right. The problem was her inner voice often took a back seat to her desire. She was hungry to prove what she was capable of yet insecure enough to think she had to do it all at once. She knew better. In her late teens, an unreciprocated crush on Tommy Johnson had taught her that you can't always force things to go your way. The letterman was too popular with too many other, more flirtatious, girls to notice her.

 Some things happen in their own good time.

If they happen at all.

The ferocity of her stare did nothing to intimidate the scratchy artwork. The doodle sat there in defiance at being deciphered. She kept at it, though, shuttering out the world. The clatter of dishes and glasses faded into the background; the idle table chatter morphed into an indistinguishable drone as she was pulled down, down into the drawing.

"Hello."

The intrusion yanked her out of her thoughts.

She looked up. A man was standing by her table. Not her waiter. He had a goofy smirk on his face. Thirtyish, tall, active-looking, confident. Someone who spent a fair amount of time grooming himself. Too much time.

"Yes?" she said through a polite smile.

"I'm sorry to interrupt. I was sitting over there and saw you and couldn't help thinking you looked familiar. Do we know each other?"

Janet ran his face through her memory. She would've remembered this guy. "I don't think so."

"You remind me of someone I knew in high school."

"Where did you go?"

"Edina High."

"Wasn't me."

She didn't volunteer where she'd gone to school. Volunteered no personal information. A woman couldn't be too careful.

The man looked disappointed. "Oh well, I must've been mistaken."

But he didn't go away. Just stood there. Now that the ice had been broken between them, he seemed to feel it enabled him to continue to blather on. "You looked so engrossed a minute ago. Deep in thought. I wasn't sure I should interrupt you."

"It's okay."

"If you don't mind my saying, it seems a shame for a pretty woman like you to be dealing with something so serious." He gestured at the notebook.

Ugh, what a line! Janet's smile went out like a burnt light bulb. The man had come over to hit on her and wouldn't give up. The high school jock come-on merely a ploy to get her talking. In another setting, in another mood, she might've been more receptive to chat with a good-looking stranger. Not now. Not this guy. He was a little too smooth. *And that comment about her not dealing with something serious because of her looks!* Where was a barf bag when she needed one?

She met his gaze, said politely, "If you don't mind, I'm working. Can't talk right now."

He didn't take the hint. Didn't go away. Annoying her further.

Instead, he plied his charm. "Looks to me like you need a break. Let me buy you a drink."

She raised her glass. "Already have one."

"Well, perhaps take a minute or two to enjoy it in pleasant conversation."

He wasn't getting it. Time to drop the hammer.

"Thanks for the offer, but I'm not interested."

"You sure, pretty lady?"

Janet tossed him a hard look and slid her badge wallet over with the shield prominently displayed. She watched his enthusiasm wilt like a slice of cheddar on a hot hamburger. Without another word, he swung about and returned to his table. Peace at last, she thought. Sometimes being a cop had its perks.

CHAPTER 27

Henry Lau emerged from his morning shower, refreshed after his workout. His lower back was a bit stiff, and his abs were still sore from getting walloped by a steel toe boot at Omar's. He looked forward to his upcoming chiropractic adjustment. Although his body had healed from the accident that nearly killed him six months earlier, there were lingering issues. There would always be lingering issues. He dealt with them.

He replaced the Band-Aid on his forearm; the wound was healing nicely. Partially dressed, he ran a comb through his dark shag, then lathered up his face and shaved. Halfway into it, he touched a sensitive spot on his chest he had largely ignored. He could see it in the bathroom mirror now, a slight discoloration the size of a poker chip. He stepped closer to the glass, curious at the faint pattern of the incipient bruise: three narrow rectangles like stripes on a chevron. A leftover from his recent visit to Silk Road Imports and the thrust kick to his chest. Henry squinted. Probably a shoe imprint.

Why was this familiar?

Only later, while on his way to work, did it come to him: he'd seen the same three-striped pattern in the death photos of Roger Beckman. The same bruising.

At the station, he found a message waiting from the St. Paul Police regarding his query about Mr. Tong's license plate. Turned out the owner of the vehicle was the subject of a current police investigation, as in an *active crime scene*. Henry made a few quick calls, left a message for Janet, then went to his car.

It didn't take long to get to the Frogtown St. Paul neighborhood. The stucco fourplex with the leaning pine tree was on Dale Avenue, just off Interstate 94. Easy to find. He just had to look for the police cruisers and crime scene trucks parked outside.

After identifying himself to an officer, he waited curbside for Sergeant Baker from the Homicide Unit. Minutes later, a barrel-chested man with a flattop haircut, pug nose, and square jaw tramped down the front steps like a human snowplow.

"Henry Lau," Baker said, as if confirming a rumor, "it is you. You're still alive. I heard about the accident."

They shook hands. Henry smiled. He and Fred Baker had met three years earlier during a martial arts defense seminar Henry held for Twin Cities law enforcement. Baker had been an attendee, a vocal one who wasn't initially friendly. Henry had good reason to remember the burly sergeant. Baker wasn't an easy man to impress. Henry learned that the hard way. He'd barely started his presentation when Baker interrupted him in front of thirty participants.

"Excuse me. The seminar description says you've got over twenty years experience in kung fu, but it doesn't list your belt ranking. You must be some kind of black belt, right?"

Henry paused. *Great, one of these guys.* Collecting himself, he patiently explained, "I have no belt ranking. The system I study under doesn't believe in them. Many traditional Chinese martial arts systems don't." His voice was authoritative yet nonthreatening. "Belts are an arbitrary signpost of achievement. The truth is a high belt ranking doesn't necessarily mean you're good in a real fight. Some schools use belt rankings as a marketing tool. Or a way to organize students. What matters is what you can do with what you know."

"Okay, sure." Baker didn't sound satisfied. "How many tournaments have you won?"

"I don't do tournaments for the same reason. Don't get me wrong, they can be fun, can test your skill, but they aren't a real fight. Too many rules."

"You been in real fights?"

"I have. And won. Many of them against black belts," he added with a sly smile which brought chuckles from the attendees.

Doubt still clouded Baker's face, so Henry waved him forward. A demonstration against the biggest, baddest guy in the group did wonders to convince skeptics. Sergeant Baker boasted he was a state champion wrestler in high school, a boxer and a former Marine, a fourth dan in karate. He may not have been the biggest guy in the group, but he'd do. Henry knocked him on his butt twice, both times within four seconds. Only then did Fred Baker appreciate the depth of Henry's skill and began to respect him. Then and only then could Henry move on to demonstrate non-violent restraining holds without further challenges from the skeptic.

Henry put the memory aside, glad he could now count on Baker as a friend. "Thanks for seeing me, Fred." He stepped aside for a crime scene technician toting an evidence bag.

"Glad to help." Baker shoved his hands in his trouser pockets and looked back with friendly deep-set eyes. "Funny how your DMV search coincided with my homicide."

"Small world," Henry nodded, looking to assure him. "I'm not here to get in your way, but if your vic is the guy I think he is, it might help us both."

"Great. Can't let you go inside. CSI is finishing up. But I can show you something. Hey, Joe, this way!" Baker motioned to three people clad in protective coveralls. One of them, balding with a short gray beard and pleasant Mediterranean features, turned and walked over.

Baker made quick introductions. "Joe, Detective Lau would like to see photos of the vic."

The forensic photographer turned over his high-resolution digital camera. A bright image lit up the small display screen. He rushed by shots of the crime scene until he got to the body: an Asian man in a white muscle shirt and blue jogging pants. Joe advanced to close-ups of the head.

"Yeah," Henry nodded, "that's my guy."

Baker said, "Name's John Lee. Lived here alone."

"I knew him as Mr. Tong. Any idea on how he died?"

"Looks like a beating, a bad one."

"Really? Show me."

The photographer advanced to a few other shots of the body. Discoloration in the face, chest, and arms.

"Hold on. Can you zoom in on that one?"

It was a large bruise on Lee's chest, one of many, this one partly obscured by the muscle shirt's neckline. The bruise had three short narrow stripes.

Henry grunted. "I know this pattern. It's a shoe print."

Sergeant Baker looked over with interest. "Well, well. Maybe our cases *are* connected."

Henry pointed at the photo. "Whoever killed my professor also likely killed Lee. I saw Lee yesterday. We had a scuffle. He and his friend got away. There was a third person at the scene I didn't know about. That's how I got my bruise."

Baker clucked his tongue. "So we're looking for a fighter. A kicker. Any thoughts?"

"No, I'm working on it." Henry gave Baker a short recap of the Beckman case and how John Lee, a.k.a. Mr. Tong, fit into it, omitting any mention of Leland Hatcher.

Baker made an uneasy noise. "Sounds messy.

The photographer looked between the two men. "Need me for anything else? I should be getting back."

Henry shook his head. "I'm good."

"Thanks, Joe," Baker said, sending him off.

"Find anything interesting at the scene?" Henry asked.

"Not much. There was a 9 mm handgun in his closet. Found a cell phone charger but no phone."

"It had contact info and recent calls. Probably the killer's number."

"Right. Lee's desk drawer was rifled. Looks like some folders were taken. Not sure what. Could be stuff that linked him to the killer." Baker shrugged.

The two men spoke for another minute until a thin elderly woman with stark white hair walked up. Dangling from her wrist was a large plastic shopping bag. "What's going on?" She glanced round anxiously at the police.

Baker explained, "One of your neighbors was killed."

She gave a fretful sigh. "This used to be such a quiet neighborhood. Can I get to my apartment?"

"Certainly, ma'am," Baker said.

Henry trotted up the steps to the front door. Held it open for her.

"Thank you, young man," she said. He closed the door after her and waited as she inserted the brass key in one of the rows of flat aluminum mailboxes, retrieved the contents, then shuffled to the lower level. Henry was struck by a thought, entered the apartment lobby, and scanned the mailboxes until he saw "J.Lee" listed above one. Paper was visible through the narrow slot. He motioned Baker over.

He pointed to the mailbox. "Lee has mail."

Enlightenment came to Sergeant Baker. In no time he found the building manager who opened John Lee's mailbox. Inside were four pieces of mail.

"Look at this," Baker said, his rough face breaking into a triumphant smile. He held up a Verizon bill. "This sucker gives us an account number. Now we can find out who John Lee's been talking to."

"You'll send me a copy of the numbers called?"

"Be happy to. And you'll keep me in the loop if you find out anything?"

Henry nodded. "Of course."

CHAPTER 28

A day later the message came from Fred Baker. With it was a list of John Lee's phone activity for the past two months. One number jumped out as the number most often called.

"Charlie Fong."

Janet licked the last spoonful of peach yogurt as she tossed Henry a quizzical look. "Who's Charlie Fong?"

"The guy who John Lee called a lot."

She stepped away from her desk to stand behind Henry's chair. She leaned in toward his monitor. "Yes, he did."

"There are six numbers Lee called most often. Charlie Fong's is *numero uno*. And there's this." Henry closed the attachment and pointed to Baker's email, plastered large on-screen.

Janet's eyes narrowed. "Our friend John Lee, aka Mr. Tong, is no stranger to trouble: convictions for burglary, assault, car theft. So what's the plan?"

Henry pivoted his chair so that he could look at her. "Visit the most called people and see what that gets us. Starting with Mr. Fong."

From a few cubicles away came the clickety-clack of someone typing furiously on a keyboard. Chief Bowman stood by the Keurig coffee maker, mug in hand, listening to two uniformed officers tell a fishing story. Janet leaned in and spoke with caution. "How far are we going with this? Special Agent Redding wanted us to lie low in the weeds until he makes his arrest."

"Yes, he does."

"But we're forging ahead?"

"On silent cat paws. We're exploring a line of inquiry. We still have a murderer to catch." Henry tapped his chest where he'd been kicked. "My bruise matches the ones on Beckman and Lee. John Lee wasn't one of the men in the alley."

"Lee could still be one of Kajmac's men."

"Possibly, but I don't think so. There's another group involved. Let's look at what we know. Lee Hatcher was totally taken in by the counterfeit Chinese minister. That sure wasn't part of his plan."

"True."

"And Charlie Fong's driver's license photo matches the guy I saw with Lee at Silk Road Imports. We're dealing with different players. Someone other than Lee Hatcher is trying to get their mitts on the dragon head. I'm thinking they're behind the murder."

Janet nodded thoughtfully. "Speaking of our bogus cultural minister, did you ever hear back from her?"

"Nope. She hasn't returned my calls. I left another message."

"She knows the jig is up. She's not stupid."

"Which is why we need to track down John Lee's associates. Lee's our only link to Shen Jiang-Li and whoever is pulling their strings. The small fish will lead us to a big fish."

She understood why Henry wanted to follow up on Charlie Fong, but she had reservations. By nature, she wasn't pushy. Diplomacy and tact were her strong suits, sometimes to her detriment. Her concern was that Special Agent Redding had asked them to cool it on Hatcher. "What if we dig up something that alerts Hatcher and messes up Redding's bust?"

"It may not happen. If it does, I'll take the heat."

That mollified her a little, although she didn't want Henry to get stuck with the blame either. "Isn't that kind of risky? We could be stirring up trouble."

Henry rocked back in his chair. "We're so close to figuring this out. Our deal with Redding was to leave Hatcher alone, not to stop our investigation. John Lee's murder is a lost opportunity to question him. Charlie Fong could go next. Time may not be on our side."

She took his point. In the long run, her duty was to do her job. Smoothing back her hair, Janet drew in a deep breath and said, "Let's do it."

"Good. So let's review where we are."

Janet grabbed her chair and rolled it beside his.

Clearing his throat, he went through his summary. "Remember when we met Lee Hatcher? He suggested Beckman had gone rogue, stealing the dragon head for himself, making Hatcher look like the victim. According to Beckman's ex-wife, Roger was notoriously ethical. There's no love lost between them. Why would Mary Jo Beckman say that unless she believed it? Maureen Levy said the same thing."

"But he did take it."

"He did, though not to sell but to keep it safe. He no longer trusted Hatcher to do the right thing."

"Did that matter? Beckman was paid to do a job, authenticate a piece of art. That should've been his only concern."

"Agreed, except Beckman was also a scholar with a strong moral code. He believed the dragon head was a stolen, lost relic and should be returned to its rightful owners. Enforcing that belief is a representative of the Chinese government, or so he thinks. Over time Beckman suspects his client is about to do something shady. I think this set up an ethical conflict."

"Do you really think Beckman would've given the artifact to the Chinese? Doing so would have ruined his reputation."

Henry shrugged. "Who knows? He had a difficult choice, one with unpleasant consequences no matter what he did."

A thought came to Janet, one she liked. "There's a turnabout for you. From a certain point of view, Beckman wasn't the bad guy; he was the hero. He put himself in danger to protect the relic."

"Right. Thing is we still don't know if he was able to authenticate the bronze piece. Is it genuine or a copy?"

The point was not lost on her. "I think he did authenticate it. Otherwise, why risk his reputation and endure getting beaten to death to protect a potential fake?"

Henry frowned thoughtfully. "Yeah, makes no sense. You're probably right. All answers lead back to the artifact. Our best lead right now is to look at the names on John Lee's call list, starting with Charlie Fong."

"Sounds like a plan."

"That means an early start tomorrow, before sun up. We'll stake out Fong's residence and tail him. See where he goes and who he talks to."

No early bird, Janet steeled herself for a long day.

The first hour into the stakeout wasn't bad. A new day with new possibilities loomed in front of her. She could do this. Ninety minutes in, just being stationary in the car seat was starting to get to her. She was antsy. At the two-hour mark, she was delighted to see a man exit the stucco building. Janet peered through the windshield to verify.

"That's him."

Down the cement steps bounced a short, lean, baby-faced man clad in a navy pea coat and olive camo jogger pants.

Janet asked, "Do we grab him now?"

"Let's see where Mr. Fong goes. We're in no rush."

"My butt would disagree. It's fallen asleep."

"At our next stop, you can get out and stretch."

Fong's next stop was breakfast at a local diner. That was followed by quick trips to the gas station, the post office, and a drive to St. Louis Park. Fong's dented pickup came to rest in the narrow parking lot in an industrial business complex on Oxford Street behind Methodist Hospital. Fong leisurely walked across the lot to enter a bland cream-colored one-story structure that you'd easily drive past without a second glance.

"KO Incentives," Janet read the sign above the door. "Can't find anything on the net," she added a minute later, eyes on her smartphone. "Next door is a commercial printer and a metal shop. Does he work here?"

"No. As far as I can tell, Fong has no steady employment."

She adjusted the visor to block the morning sun. Twenty minutes later, after Charlie Fong had yet to exit, she asked. "Seems like we're not getting anywhere with Fong. Do we sit and wait or bail and take him in?"

"Give him another twenty minutes. Then we go in."

Time ticked by at a sloth's pace. At the twenty-minute mark, Fong still had not returned to his car.

Now Henry finally stirred. "Time's up. We've got other things to do besides babysitting this character. We'll grab Fong and take him to the station for questioning."

The lobby of KO Incentives was tiled in patterned sheet vinyl. Roomy, with a large open lobby. A long customer counter ran along the far wall behind which stood a chubby man, perhaps forty, clad in a light blue shirt with KO Incentives stitched on the breast pocket. He leaned forward slightly, studying a diagram on the counter. Opposite him on the customer side, her back toward them, stood a trim young woman in a white fitted blouse and brown wide-leg cropped pants and brown loafers. She was pointing out something on the printed diagram. Along the side wall was a row of six plastic chairs. Seated in one was Charlie Fong, flipping through a magazine as if he had nothing else to do in the world.

Fong looked up as the detectives entered and his eyes grew as large as saucers.

"Shit!"

The man behind the counter looked to see what was going on. So did the woman, who turned round. She was Asian. Pretty. Slender. Well-defined eyebrows arched over startled mascaraed eyes. More than startled now. Alarmed. It was the face of Shen Jiang-Li. With more makeup, her hair parted in the center, dressed in casual business clothes, but undoubtedly the woman who'd passed herself off as a Chinese cultural minister.

Henry's mouth stretched back with delight. "Well, hello."

CHAPTER 29

The lady was not amused. She whirled accusingly at the nervous man in the chair. "Idiot. You led them here!"

Interesting! Henry noticed her words were spoken in perfect Middle American English without a trace of an overseas accent. He pulled back his jacket to show the Glock holstered on his belt. "Mr. Fong and Ms. Shen—or whatever your real name is—you're both persons of interest in a murder investigation. We need you to come with us to the station for questioning."

Charlie Fong protested, "I didn't kill nobody!"

"We don't know that yet, do we?" Henry smiled back politely.

Fong's shoulders slumped in defeat.

Not so the erstwhile Shen Jiang-Li, whose sultry dark eyes smoldered a challenge. "Are we under arrest?"

"No."

"Then you're not taking us anywhere. We have nothing to say."

"Let me explain," Henry advised as if he were a professor correcting an errant student. "I witnessed your friend here in a potential robbery at Silk Road Imports. He fled the scene with the man you introduced to us as Mr. Tong, who, by the way, was murdered last night. I can arrest Fong on suspicion of robbery and murder. And because of your connection to John Lee—aka Mr. Tong—I could haul you in on a related charge. If you don't like that, there's always impersonating a Chinese minister and fraud charges. *Federal charges*," he emphasized to enlighten her on the extra special fun she had to look forward to. "We know an FBI agent who's already familiar with your scam. If I have to arrest you, I'll take you to the station in handcuffs. Your choice. For the moment, neither of you are being charged with anything. But I do expect you to cooperate. Right now, we're just looking to get your statements."

Her eyes blazed. She stood tall, shoulders back, a sizzling stick of dynamite.

From the corner of his eye, Henry saw Janet approach the counter and move behind it. He looked curiously at the counterfeit Chinese minister. "By the way, who *are* you?"

Dark eyes glowered back in silence.

"Her name's Stacey Chow," Janet answered, reading a name off a driver's license she'd pulled from a tan leather purse from behind the counter.

A funny look came over Henry. "Stacey Chow?" He scoured his brain, trying to remember why that name seemed familiar. He laughed when it came to him. "Your mother is Darlene Chow, the owner of Silk Road Imports!"

Stacey Chow neither confirmed nor denied the statement, remaining beautifully petulant in her silence. Then a 1,000-watt floodlight snapped on in Henry's head. Eyes on Stacey, he said to Janet, "Stacey's mother is the mastermind behind all this."

An incredulous Janet stared back.

"I'm serious," Henry continued. "Charlie and his pal John Lee weren't at the import shop to rob or harass the owner; they were working *with* her. That's why Lee had to die."

"I don't follow."

"After Lee and Fong ran off, I told Darlene Chow I'd be able to track Lee down from his car license plate, which I'd taken a photo of. She knew once I tracked down Lee, he'd lead me back to her and her involvement, as well as her daughter's. Oh, yes, we definitely need to bring the two of you in for questioning."

Moving swiftly around the counter, Janet kept a watch on Stacey while Henry frisked Charlie Fong. Afterward, he guided his charge closer to the door and waited for Janet.

"Face the wall," she instructed the athletic brunette. "Spread your arms and legs. Hands on the counter." Janet patted her down.

There was something in Stacey's body language that reminded Henry of a cornered animal. Her weight shifted from one leg to the other and back. Her shoulders tensed. One foot planted firmly on the vinyl flooring.

Her foot.

Those brown shoes.

Why did they look familiar?

And then it came to him. The image of a shoe, a woman's shoe hurling at his chest. Of course! Stacey had been the third person in the back room at Silk Road Imports. She was the one who'd pushed the tower of cardboard boxes on him. She was the kicker.

The kicker—

Henry inhaled sharply. "Janet, watch out. She—"

The warning came too late.

Janet was stepping back from the pat-down as Stacey jumped sideways and whirled round with a savage roundhouse kick that clipped Janet's head, snapping it sideways. She dropped hard to the floor.

Stacey wheeled about to face Henry. His hand flew to his service weapon. His eye caught movement to his left. Fong charged in with a body slam that Henry barely managed to sidestep. Fong stumbled to the floor, but Henry had absorbed enough of the glancing blow to mess up his timing. His arm came up too late with the Glock. With alarming quickness, Stacey Chow leaped toward him with a spinning back kick to his gun arm. The Glock flew out of his grasp. Not finished, she kept whirling at him like a cyclone. Each kick whooshed by his face, just missing as he side-stepped them. Unfazed, she changed to a double roundhouse that he easily deflected, much to her annoyance. She switched to a high vertical axe kick intended to crush his face. It glanced harmlessly off Henry's *biu jee* elbows. He raced in with a double butterfly palm abdominal strike that sent her flying backward fifteen feet to violently crash into the counter.

He straightened, catching his breath. *Man, she was good!* One of the best kickers he'd ever seen: fierce, flexible, relentless. He needed to be careful with this one. He ignored the dull throb in his right arm where her foot had struck him.

With a painful grimace, she climbed to her feet, rubbing her abs, eyes fixed on Henry with mixed apprehension and rage. He tossed a glance toward Janet, who was on her knees, hands to face. She was in trouble.

"AIEEEEEE!"

The war cry came from behind. Charlie Fong was running at him with a chair over his head. Henry pivoted out of the way as his arms shot up in a crossed *biu sau* to protect his head, his front kick catching Fong's leading leg shin bone. Henry yanked the chair out of his hands and threw it aside. Then launched rapid punches to Fong's face. His punching hand slid behind his neck and yanked the startled face into a wicked elbow strike. Fong grabbed his bloody nose and staggered off in a painful whimper.

Henry let him go, sensing danger. Taking his eyes off Stacey Chow was risky. He spun on his heel just as a leg thrust rocketed toward his kidney. He pivoted and dropped the elbow that had just made mush of Charlie Fong's face, deflecting Stacey's foot. He immediately ducked to avoid the follow-up head kick while shooting out his free leg in a low sweeping arc that Stacey hopped over to avoid.

At his full height again, Henry saw her face contort with frustration. She sucked down a quick breath and flew at him with punches that he easily deflected, angering her further. With a cry of exasperation, she closed the gap in a hop step knee strike to his groin. His *gaun sau* downward palm shut it down. She recovered instantly by dropping her leg behind his front shin.

For a heartbeat, they stood leg against leg. Henry's eyes were still locked on hers, but decades of close contact sensitivity training had made him realize what was about to happen: she intended to buckle his knee from behind and steal his balance. Before she could react, he pivoted his knee two inches which altered his body structure and robbed her leverage. The thigh she pressed against now was as immovable as a tree trunk. This all happened at the speed of thought. Confusion flashed in Stacey's face as if this had never happened to her before. For an instant her attention was distracted. Henry felt the easing of her leg pressure. He seized the advantage, slammed into her with a savage shoulder strike. She bounced off him with a grunt. Before she could react, he charged into her with a volley of chain punches to her stomach. Followed that by a thrust kick to her midsection that sent her reeling backward into the counter once more. She yelped in pain and pulled herself upright. Startled, wary eyes sized up Henry. With an enraged scream, she snatched a nearby stapler and hurled it at him. It missed. Her hand grabbed the next closest thing, a ceramic coffee mug. Henry ducked as the mug harmlessly sailed by and crashed behind him.

Propelled by pure adrenaline, Stacey launched three spinning back kicks at him with startling speed and ferocity. When they missed, she switched to jab kicks to his head. Henry shifted out of harm's way, backpedaled to keep his distance, reading her movements, waiting for the right moment to attack. She was incredibly fast. Scary fast. He'd rarely seen a kicker that fluid and quick with that much stamina. How was she still standing? Did her blind fury keep her from feeling his strikes? The woman was dangerous! He'd treated her as such but now saw the need to ratchet things up. He needed to end this.

Now.

A hook kick just grazed his shoulder. He shuffled back to avoid her long flying legs, angling to the side to deliver a devastating kidney strike that would drop her stone-cold when—

His back foot shot out from under him.

The floor was wet.

The spilled coffee, he realized too late.

His balance broken, Henry struggled to get his back leg under him, a leg whose thigh muscle was already compromised. A precious second was lost, and Stacey Chow was too quick. With a jump, she whirled a flying side kick into his chest like a battering ram. He toppled back to the floor, landing on something painfully hard. His eyes jammed shut. He rolled off the object and labored to his feet as his lower back locked up. His heart pounded as he braced for the next attack.

It didn't come.

He didn't understand.

Then he saw why. The hard thing he'd landed on was his Glock. She was diving for it. No time to stop her, he realized. A heartbeat later, she had rolled to her feet and stood in a braced stance, aiming his sidearm at him. Her pain-ridden face gasped in heavy breaths, her arms trembled. She was exhausted. Hurt. Barely able to stand. Yet somehow, she was able to draw a bead on him. There was no mercy in those eyes as she brought up the weapon to fire—

"No!"

The anguished cry came from behind.

"Drop it! Now!"

Janet was on her knees, her weapon extended.

Stacey Chow either didn't hear the warning or didn't care. She was ready to shoot. Moved her trigger finger—

"Drop the—"

The air was punctuated by a gunshot.

Stacey's eyes widened in shock. Her body shuddered, yet she didn't give up, once again bringing up the Glock to fire.

A second shot dropped her. The rage of adrenaline that had kept her going had finally run out.

Henry hobbled over and retrieved his sidearm, then spun about. Janet, still on her knees, shakily kept her service weapon trained on the inert Stacey Chow. Only after she was convinced the woman no longer posed a threat did Janet lower her sidearm and slump against the counter.

"You okay?" Henry called, worried.

A thin voice came back. "My head hurts."

"You probably have a concussion. Don't move."

"No problem." she muttered as if through a fog. "Is she dead?"

"She's still breathing." Henry inspected the wounds, glancing at the frightened man behind the counter. "Call an ambulance. Tell them there's been a cop-involved shooting."

The other nodded and reached for the phone. Meanwhile, Henry's eyes raked the room for other threats. Charlie Fong was a lump on the floor, back against the wall, nose tilted up, a crimson-stained tissue jammed against it. No threat there.

With a groan, Henry got back on his feet, his lower spine complaining at the abuse. He moved like an old man. Falling on the Glock had shoved a disc out of alignment. His chiropractor would be annoyed that her hard work had been undone.

"You," Henry said again to the clerk after he'd made the call to 911, "any towels here?"

The befuddled clerk looked like he'd witnessed a car wreck, glancing at the injured around him. He blinked when he realized he was being spoken to. "Towels? Uh, we have some cloth towels in the back."

"Get some and press them against Stacey's wounds until the paramedics get here."

The clerk nodded obediently and disappeared for thirty seconds, returning with a handful of towels. Henry didn't like surprises. He did a quick pat-down of the clerk before directing him where to apply pressure on Stacey's wound.

Only then did he move to Janet's side and stroked the back of her head, the way he used to when she was little.

"You did good," he said softly in her ear.

Through the haze of a throbbing head, she managed a weak, contented smile.

CHAPTER 30

Several days had passed since the excitement at KO Incentives. Janet Lau sat on a foldable stool across from the beach at Lake Harriet, capturing—or trying to—the shimmering calm water and majestic bandshell in watercolor. The background was a wash of red, yellow, and orange leaves against skeletal trees.

Halloween was a little more than a week away.

Gray clouds started gathering from the west. Thunderstorms threatened that evening. Janet hoped the forecast materialized. She could use a good gully washer. She loved the rain. Found comfort in the soothing patter of bouncing drops, the cool air, and the clean-scrubbed earthy smell left afterward.

That was tonight. For now, she needed to focus on what was in front of her: her watercolor. She tried to rally her thoughts. The lingering, slowly dissipating mental fog made that a challenge. Trembling fingers tried to capture the bold lake water. Not too well. She chewed her lower lip and set aside the red sable brush in frustration, eyeing the canvas mounted on the travel easel. Well, it wasn't awful, she decided. More Impressionistic than she'd planned. The shaky swirls of cerulean blue and cobalt had an emotional undercurrent. Like her feelings. Messy yet textured.

She liked the effect, if not the entire watercolor.

It would do for now.

The tension eased from her shoulders. Enough painting for today. She closed tired eyes and tried to bask in the tranquil normality around her. People strolled along the path. Gulls swirled in the distance. There was even a bald eagle earlier that had skimmed the lake surface for fish. It had been an intensely challenging week, and she was relieved it was over. She needed quiet time away from it and from her own conflicted feelings.

Be in the moment. That was how it was done, right? Don't worry about tomorrow. Work on now.

Her eyes flew open at the sound of approaching footsteps. On guard. Turning to the side, she was relieved when she saw it was Henry.

"Well, hello," he said. "You look like you're taking it easy."

"Working hard on taking it easy," she came back with more enthusiasm than she'd first felt. He gave off such an agreeable vibe she couldn't help but reflect some of it.

He nodded toward her sweatshirt and baggy sweatpants. "Warm enough?"

"No problem. It's forty-eight degrees," she replied with the confidence of a seasoned Minnesotan who survived sub-zero winters every year. Forty-eight above was practically summer temps. "Besides, I've got this." She hoisted up a steaming paper cup.

"Coffee?"

"Pumpkin spice latte."

He made a face. Yes, it was that time of year.

She looked aggrieved. "Hey, cut me some slack. It's October, and you need to be nice to me. I'm recovering from a serious injury." She took a long slug and smacked her lips.

"You win. How's the head?"

"You were right. I was diagnosed with a mild concussion."

"That kick in the head was pretty hard."

"Yeah."

Concussion protocols were one reason for her being on paid administrative leave. The other was for having discharged her firearm, standard practice.

Henry laughed. "Concussion. Got it. No hard questions."

She loved him for not treating her like some broken flower he needed to be dainty around. He joked with her like he would any other colleague. Didn't make a fuss. Nevertheless, she was on medical leave for a reason, and that reason caused her enthusiasm to fade as she remembered. "Did Stacey Chow make it?"

"She did. Her injuries were non-life-threatening. Besides the bullet holes you put in her, she has two cracked ribs and multiple contusions, thanks to me. A full recovery is expected."

"Good."

That was a relief. Janet had never shot anyone before. Wasn't sure how she'd react if she had caused the death of another human being. Firing her service weapon at another person was still new territory. Part of the job she had to get used to. *If* she could get used to it. She hoped never to be forced into a situation like that again.

Just thinking about this stuff ripped apart emotional curtains she'd been struggling to keep closed. She had made a near-fatal mistake at KO Incentives. Let Stacey get the drop on her. Her confidence in her abilities, already wobbly, dwindled even more. With downcast eyes and a contrite voice, she murmured, "Sorry I messed up with Stacey."

"Don't dwell on it."

"I let you down."

"No, you didn't."

Her eyes challenged him. "I almost got us both killed."

Henry's voice softened. "Stacey surprised you. It happens. It could happen to anyone. But I know next time you pat down a suspect you'll be on guard."

"Damn straight!"

"See? You learned something."

"Yeah but—"

"No," he cut her off. "Don't let this drag you down. We all make mistakes. Believe me. I've been there."

So he had. She was familiar enough with his past to learn from it.

Henry held her gaze and spoke from the heart. "Life is messy. Life knocks you down. Sometimes so much you can hardly get up again. But you have to move on. You can't let your mistakes cripple you. That doesn't mean you ever forget them; you learn from them."

She said nothing, averting her gaze. Gave a reluctant nod.

"Janet," he said in a tone that made her look at him, "remember one important thing: *you saved my life*. When it really mattered you came through. You fought back."

She felt a rush of gratitude, in desperate need of hearing that, if only to know she hadn't been a complete fuck up. Her eyes welled with tears. "Thank you."

"You proved you deserve this job. I said as much to Bowman."

Janet lowered her head, overcome by a sense of validation she hadn't expected. She'd almost jumped to her feet to give him a hug but remained seated. Sudden vertical movements still made her dizzy. Collecting herself, she said, "So what have I missed?"

Henry's hands buried into his jacket pockets. Opening his mouth to speak, he waited for a dog walker on the sidewalk behind them to pass. He cleared his throat. "Stacey Chow is in the hospital, recovering from her wounds. She'll be arraigned and jailed after her release. Charlie Fong broke his nose in the fight and was arrested as an accessory to murder. He folded like a cheap paper bag. Told all he knew about Ms. Chow. He's afraid of her."

"Why am I not surprised?"

"From what Fong said, Stacey is as ruthless as they come. And vindictive. And a highly skilled martial artist. We saw that. She uses her skill to keep her people in line."

Janet's eyes flashed wide. "She was fierce."

"That she was. Agile, strong, relentless." Henry snorted as a memory elbowed him. "Oh, Larry Bates at the station is calling our altercation at KO Incentives 'the kung fu fight at the KO corral.'"

"For real?"

"Yeah."

"Geez…although, I kinda like it."

"And get this: two days ago I learned that KO Incentives is a wholly-owned subsidiary of Silk Road Imports."

Janet clapped her hands together. "Ha! A direct link to Stacey's mother."

"Right. More evidence that Darlene Chow is the mastermind behind the con on Lee Hatcher. With some digging, I learned that apart from her legitimate import business, Madam Chow also dabbles in the black market. After Roger Beckman told her about the dragon head relic, she managed to figure out his client was Lee Hatcher. She then got her daughter to try to force Hatcher to surrender it to her or face messy sanctions against his Chinese business interests."

Janet admitted begrudgingly, "Yeah, that was a brilliant bit of blackmail." Which was as far as she would go to compliment Stacey Chow. She took a long sip of her pumpkin spice latte.

With an ironic chuckle, Henry added, "What the Chows didn't factor in was that Leland Hatcher was as crooked as they are. Boxed in a corner, the easy way out for him was to arrange for the dragon head to 'get stolen' so he could tell the Chinese minister that he no longer had the thing to return."

"That's almost funny." Janet enjoyed the irony of crooks double-crossing each other. "And Beckman ruined Hatcher's plan by taking the relic to an unknown appraiser."

"Or so he claimed."

"Oh, right. Instead, he stashed it somewhere for safekeeping."

This much they'd gone over before. Now the rest seemed clear. "It was Stacey who killed Beckman, not the alley goons Hatcher sent after him. She's the one who went to his house at the crack of dawn the next morning. Right?"

"Stacey and her helpers: Lee and Fong."

"The three of them beat up Beckman, tried to get him to talk."

"No, that was all Stacey."

"Really?"

"Yes, Fong told me. Stacey is the enforcer. She tortured Beckman to tell her where he'd stashed the dragon artifact."

"But he didn't talk."

"He died keeping the secret."

Janet returned with a nod. "I remember his injuries. Ugly. Excessive. Stacey really did all of that herself?"

"Ms. Chow is one sadistic badass. She enjoys inflicting pain. Fong had stories."

"No need to share." Janet shrank back, her own personal recollections still a little too fresh. "The thing is, Stacey didn't get the dragon head, did she? That's why she took Beckman's smartphone, computers, and papers. She was hoping he'd recorded where he'd left the artifact."

"Beckman was too cagey for her," Henry said. "He kept all of that in his notebook, a notebook he'd locked away when he realized he could no longer trust the players he was dealing with."

Janet looked away at a quacking noise. A flotilla of Mallards was swimming close to shore. Duck butts reared up as they foraged the bottom. Draining the last of her coffee, she set the cup aside.

"Not everything's in the notebook," she reminded Henry. "Beckman's comments get sketchier at the end. He stopped recording his thoughts. I think he was stressing out. You can tell by how the writing changes. Weird thing is the notebook is the one place you'd expect him to've recorded where he hid the dragon head, but it's not there."

"I wouldn't say that."

"*Wait.* Are you saying he did and I missed it?"

"We'll circle back to that. I can't stop thinking how ruthless Stacey Chow was. John Lee was one of her crew, and she killed him the moment he became a liability. That's cold."

"*Damn* cold, if you ask me. It was all an act—the cultured, foreign politeness. Truth is Chow's as hard core as they come. But, I will say, she was consistent in the way she dealt with people. That's what did her in."

Janet felt a sense of relief, even pride at the results they'd made on the homicide. She allowed herself to enjoy the moment. To let go of not getting all the loose ends tied up. Life is messy and can't always be herded into a corral.

After a quiet minute passed between them, Henry said, "What about you? What's up next?"

Her eyes swung back toward him. "More prescribed time off. I'm thinking of driving up to Split Rock Lighthouse to do a watercolor. It's been too long since I went to the North Shore. I can also visit my grandmother." She sighed. "What I really want is to get back to work."

"I know the feeling."

"Yes, you do!"

He offered a crooked smile of encouragement. "It's only been a few days since you were hurt. You need time to heal. It won't be long. You'll be back soon enough."

Of course he was right. She'd need a clear head to do her job properly.

A cold wind rushed by from the lake water, which caused a light rain of yellow leaves from the nearby aspen. Janet rolled down the sleeves of her sweatshirt. "Anything else going on?"

He straightened, eyes brimming with amusement. "Did you catch the local news yesterday?

"No, I haven't seen the news for the past two days."

"Special Agent Redding made his move yesterday. The FBI arrested Leland Hatcher."

Janet couldn't help herself, laughing with delight. She loved it when cocky sons of bitches got the rug pulled out from under them. It made the world seem right. The moment didn't last. Her face dimmed as she recalled the sour note that diminished their celebration.

"Too bad we couldn't wrap everything up in a nice bow."

"What do you mean?"

"We caught Beckman's killer, but we didn't recover the dragon head. That's disappointing." Then she remembered. "Hey, you were going to circle back to the notebook."

"Right." He returned a self-satisfied smile that alerted her.

Her eyes bored into him. "Wait. Hold on. So Beckman *did* record where he put the artifact?"

"I think so."

"Where? I've looked at—oh! The doodle?"

A slow nod came in reply. "The house and the bumblebee."

From his jacket, Henry pulled out the little spiral notebook and opened it to the inside back cover. Handed it to Janet, who inspected the scratchy drawing once more.

She looked up again, excited. "You deciphered this? Tell me!"

"We had it wrong. That first sketch isn't a house. Look again. It has no windows. It also has a gambrel roof, and the door is too wide."

She brought the notebook closer to her face and squinted at the page. "Beckman was a crappy artist, but...you're right, that's not a house. A shed, maybe?"

"Close, try a barn."

"Sure, I see it now. He hid the artifact in a barn?"

"Too literal. Tell me what you see on the page."

"A barn...and a bumblebee."

"Lose the bumble."

"A barn and a bee."

"Say it again."

"A barn and a bee."

"Omit the coordinating conjunction."

"A barn. A bee."

She still didn't get it.

He put her out of her misery. *"Barnaby."*

"Barnaby? Why do I know that name?"

"Your eyewitness, remember?"

Her jaw dropped. "Ohh!"

"It's my next stop."

Two hours later, Henry strode up the sidewalk toward a terra-cotta stucco bungalow trimmed in blinding yellow and adorned with purple shutters. Before he reached the door, he heard the muffled barking of a small dog on the other side.

The door opened a crack.

"Oh, it's you, Detective Lau. Come in. Barnaby! Quiet. Bad dog. You know Detective Lau."

Mrs. Stademeyer pulled open the door to let Henry pass. She was wrapped in a floral smock and tangerine capri pants. The little sheltie took a hesitant sniff of the visitor and instantly shifted attitude from house guardian to official greeter. His fluffy tail swished back and forth across the floor.

Henry stooped to pet the excited dog, who snuffled its snout against his arm. "Hi, Barnaby. Are you a good dog?"

Yes, he was! Judging by the shine in his eye and adoring smile.

"Thank you for seeing me." Henry glanced over his shoulder as his hostess closed the door.

"No, thank *you* for calling. I was wondering what I was going to do. You just made it easy." Her thin, dry voice was relieved and appreciative.

Henry stood up with effort, his body still achy from his encounter with Stacey Chow. "Can you take me to it?"

"Yes! It's in the basement." Wobbly legs propelled her toward the kitchen at a measured pace. He followed, the little sheltie trotting by his side.

Henry's heart thudded with anticipation. This had been a long shot, but after deciphering Beckman's drawing—or hoping he had, the lead was too good not to pursue. From his previous visit to Beckman's neighbor lady, Henry knew that, on occasion, Roger looked after her house and dog when she went away. Knowing that, he'd wondered if perhaps she did the same for him. He'd called to ask her if Roger had left a package for her to look after.

He had.

Mrs. Stademeyer descended the creaky wooden basement stairs, steadying herself on the handrail. "The night before Roger died, he brought over a cardboard box. Asked me to keep it for him. He said not to tell anyone about it."

"Which is why you didn't mention it to us earlier."

"Right. Sorry. Well, he also said if anything happened to him that I should wait two weeks and let the police know."

"Why two weeks?"

"He didn't say. Maybe he thought something would happen by then. But since you asked about it, I figured I should tell you." Her bony shoulders shrugged.

The basement was half-finished. Shuffling toward the unfinished area, she stopped by a work table against the cinder block walls and flipped on a light switch. A bank of fluorescent lights blinked on. Her wizened face looked in the corner where boxes and odds and ends were stacked chest high. At the top was a new box the size of a small ottoman. "That one," she said with a note of trepidation.

Henry lifted the box, finding it lighter than he expected. He set it down on the basement floor. Kneeling, he pulled back the cardboard flaps to find a mass of bubble wrap. He paused, preparing himself for either a thrill or disappointment. There was no in-between. With that thought in mind, he peeled back the packaging with the caution of a heart surgeon performing an aortic valve repair.

When he saw what was inside, he let out a deep exhale.

Mrs. Stademeyer couldn't help herself. She edged closer and peered over Henry's shoulder into the open box. Staring back were the bronze eyes of a beast.

Henry plunged his hands deep into the box and lifted out the contents. Sat it down on the concrete floor. The object was larger than a soccer ball with a long, whiskered snout, side head fins, and piercing eyes.

"What is that?" wondered the elderly woman.

"A dragon head."

"Oh."

"It's a Chinese art relic Roger was holding for someone."

"I'm so glad you called when you did. I wouldn't know who to contact. You're a policeman. You'll return it to the owner, won't you?"

"I will."

That might prove tricky if any kind of legal challenge was made on the piece. For now, it appeared that Leland Hatcher was the rightful owner of the artifact, and Henry was obliged to return it to him. Others could wrangle over ownership if they wanted. That wasn't his concern.

He smiled at the implacable metallic face, satisfied he and Janet had brought a measure of justice to Roger Beckman. He also felt a swell of pride at how well his niece, his partner, had handled herself under pressure. She had much to learn but had shown herself capable. He'd make sure he gave her the skills to succeed. And while Janet might have lingering doubts about herself as a detective, he didn't. There would always be good days and bad days in law enforcement. The bad days could be brutal. Today, which had seen the last loose end of the case tied up, had been a good day.

A very good day.

And those days, Henry knew, were rare enough that they had to be held onto.

CPSIA information can be obtained
at www.ICGtesting.com
Printed in the USA
JSHW050137130522
25811JS00001B/30